Suddey
and gave a terrible cry, whether of pain or anger, Talon couldn't tell. The doctor grabbed his balding head with his right hand and pointed his left at Lofwyr, forefinger extended in accusation.

"Monster! Defiler!" he shouted. "You will not break me! I am a true servant of the gods! Death!" he cried. "Death to all tyrants!"

As Goronay spoke, the rosy crystal on the floor in front of Lofwyr began to glow brightly. Talon looked quickly from the crystal to the golden dragon looming overhead.

"Lowfyr . . ." he started to call out. Then, an arc of pinkish lightning exploded from the crystal. . . .

"Talon, look out!" Boom yelled. He grabbed Talon and pulled him back and down as the dragon slammed his tail into one of the macroglass windows. . . .

Goronay was laughing like a madman, practically gibbering. "Yes! Yes!" he shouted. "Now you will pay!"

Stephen Kenson

A ROC BOOK

ROC
Published by New American Library, a division of
Penguin Putnam Inc., 375 Hudson Street,
New York, New York 10014, U.S.A.
Penguin Books Ltd, 27 Wrights Lane,
London W8 5TZ, England
Penguin Books Australia Ltd, Ringwood,
Victoria, Australia
Penguin Books Canada Ltd, 10 Alcorn Avenue,
Toronto, Ontario, Canada M4V 3B2
Penguin Books (N.Z.) Ltd, 182–190 Wairau Road,
Auckland 10, New Zealand

Penguin Books Ltd, Registered Offices:
Harmondsworth, Middlesex, England

First published by Roc, an imprint of New American Library,
a division of Penguin Putnam Inc.

First Printing, February 2000
10 9 8 7 6 5 4 3 2 1

Copyright © FASA Corporation, 2000
All rights reserved

Series Editor: Donna Ippolito
Cover Art: Royo

 REGISTERED TRADEMARK—MARCA REGISTRADA

SHADOWRUN, FASA, and the distinctive SHADOWRUN and FASA logos
are registered trademarks of the FASA Corporation, 1100 W. Cermak, Suite
B305, Chicago, IL 60608

Printed in the United States of America

Without limiting the rights under copyright reserved above, no part of this
publication may be reproduced, stored in or introduced into a retrieval
system, or transmitted, in any form, or by any means (electronic, mechanical,
photocopying, recording, or otherwise), without the prior written permission of both the copyright owner and the above publisher of this book.

PUBLISHER'S NOTE
This is a work of fiction. Names, characters, places, and incidents either are
the product of the author's imagination or are used fictitiously, and any
resemblance to actual persons, living or dead, events, business establishments, or locales is entirely coincidental.

BOOKS ARE AVAILABLE AT QUANTITY DISCOUNTS WHEN USED TO PROMOTE PRODUCTS OR SERVICES. FOR INFORMATION PLEASE WRITE TO PREMIUM MARKETING DIVISION, PENGUIN PUTNAM INC., 375 HUDSON STREET, NEW YORK, NEW YORK 10014.

If you purchased this book without a cover you should be aware that this
book is stolen property. It was reported as "unsold and destroyed" to the
publisher and neither the author nor the publisher has received any payment for this "stripped book."

To Christopher, for everything.

Just like shadowrunning, this book was a team effort. Thanks go to Shadowrun developer Mike Mulvihill for his thoughts about just how devious dragons can be; to Donna Ippolito for editing under pressure; to Rob Boyle for his input and suggestions; and to my friends: Jan Campbell, Andy Frades, Lyle Hinckley, Sean Johnson, Bill Michie, and Rich Tomasso, for making Shadowrun as much fun as it has been. Thanks, chummers.

NORTH

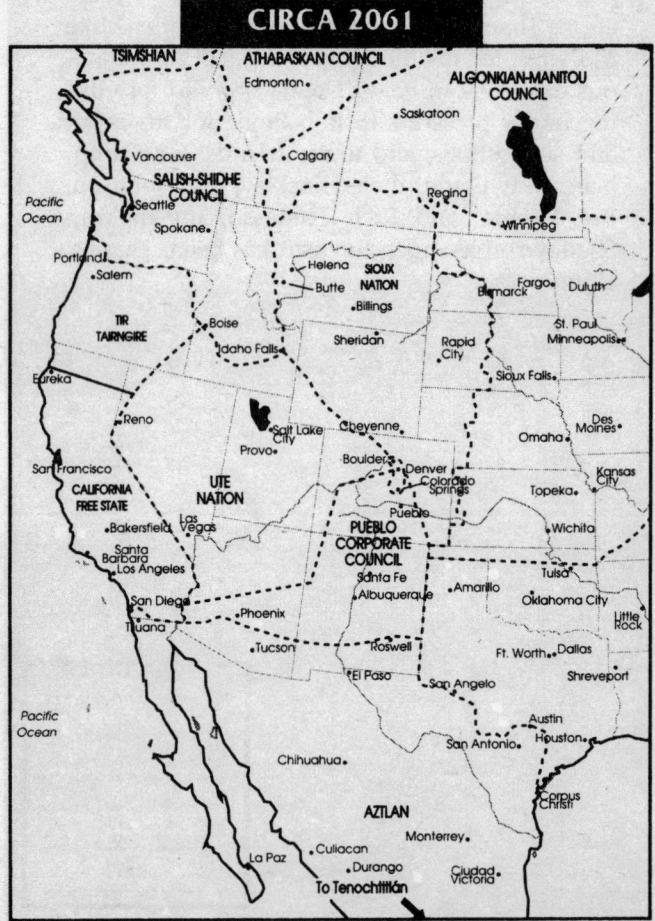

CIRCA 2061

AMERICA

Prologue

The gods have sent the rain as a sign of their displeasure, Dr. Alexi Goronay thought glumly as he picked his way around the shallow, muddy puddles filling the deep pockmarks dug into the earth by machine treads, shovels, picks, and work boots. The rich clay soil was rapidly turning into a sticky mire that sucked at the feet with greedy fingers, slowing everyone to a labored trudge through the muck. Combined with the cold and the high winds of the past few days, it was easy to believe that this small area of the Ukraine had somehow earned the displeasure of some divine force.

It could have been worse, the good doctor supposed as he struggled up a gentle slope to his waiting trailer, cursing to himself as the ground shifted and slid under his every step. This region should be getting buried under snow this late in the year, but weather patterns had been strange and it was unseasonably warm for early December. Not warm enough for the rain to be anything other than ice water, with snow unlikely.

Reaching the trailer, the doctor stepped carefully over the cinder-block steps set just under the metal one leading up into the corrugated steel trailer. He didn't want to push the blocks any further into the mud than they already were. Using the door handle to pull himself up onto the step, he pushed the door open and stepped inside, tugging the slightly protesting door shut behind him. He paused for a moment to enjoy the relative quiet and warmth. Still, the glow of the small camp heater in the trailer could not chase the chill from his bones or from the depths of his spirit.

It wasn't the rain that bothered him. Goronay couldn't count the times he'd encountered worse. He'd been all over the world and obliged to work under conditions ranging from blistering heat to bitter cold. His main concern was what the unseasonable weather would do to the dig site, only now in the early stages of being unearthed. The mess the weather was making of the ground, turning whole tracts into sloppy, sucking mires, was slowing the work of excavation almost to a halt. Some of his students were working a few areas under the protection of bright surplus tarpaulins and rain ponchos, but they could move at only the slowest pace. Already one near mishap had almost sent a bundle of artifact fragments scattering down a muddy hillside. Goronay had nearly canceled the dig on account of it.

But he did not. He could not. For one thing, his patron would be quite upset if the dig were canceled. The Saeder-Krupp Corporation funded his research through a substantial grant to the University, with the strong implication that they expected results. If he canceled the dig now, the project might lose its funding entirely.

There was something else that told him to go on, despite all the problems and despite his own better judgment, which said perhaps it would be wiser to simply cover things over and wait until conditions were more favorable. Some of his crew were already grumbling about finishing this thing before Christmas. It wasn't as if the dig site was allocated to anyone other than his department at the University, nor did it seem truly likely Saeder-Krupp would withdraw its support from the project, despite their threats. The funding was little more than pocket change to the world's largest and wealthiest megacorporation. Goronay also suspected that a famous archeological find would make for valuable propaganda in the international press.

The doctor was a man of science and he did not believe in anything that he could not dig up out of the earth and examine with his own two eyes. Failing though they might be, he thought, as he wiped off his glasses on a not much dryer cloth. And yet, something told him that now was the only time for this dig, a sense of urgency he could not explain, but that he felt with every fiber of his being. If they abandoned the dig now, they would not likely be able to get back here before spring, but even that wasn't it. No, there was a sense that something momentous was about to happen and that time was running out. If only the blasted weather would cooperate!

The doctor hung up his coat and hat to dry on the stand next to the small space heater and made his way over to the counter. While he waited for the water on the portable hot plate to boil, he glanced over the dig site information spread out on the table nearby. The site was not an overly remarkable one. The story was, in fact, fairly typical. Miners searching for new veins of ore to support Eastern Europe's hungry and hopeful industry had come across some unusual rock formations and done a little more digging, no doubt in hopes of finding some lost treasure that everyone seemed to think lay buried as part and parcel of every archeological find. All they discovered were some unusual stone and metal fragments, fragments that found their way to the archeology department and Dr. Goronay's desk by way of Saeder-Krupp, the mining company's parent corporation. The doctor had never seen artifacts of such a type from anywhere in the area. They appeared to be remnants of tools, or possibly weapons, but they were far too fragmentary and old to attempt to piece together what civilization or era they might have come from.

The most interesting thing about the fragments, the one thing that continued to make Dr. Goronay think there was something to be found at this dig, was that they appeared to be extremely old. Many thousands of years old, in fact. If so, then the metal fragments were of extreme interest. There were bits of iron, copper, silver, and gold, too pure not to have been refined, and yet refined metals such as these were completely unknown in the Ukraine region so long ago.

Just as the doctor sat down with a steaming cup of coffee to contemplate the selfsame fragments that lay spread out on the table along with the many papers, photographs, and topographical maps of the dig site, there came a loud knocking on the metal door of the trailer compartment that sounded like an amplification of the drumming rain outside. He opened the door to admit the sopping and panting form of Gregor, one of his students. The young man was drenched to the skin through his Soviet military-surplus rain poncho and winded from running and stumbling through the rain and mud to the doctor's trailer, but his face and eyes were wild with excitement.

"Gregor," Dr. Goronay said as his assistant tried to catch his breath, "what in God's name is going on?" Young Gregor could be a bit excitable at times, but Goronay had never seen him in such a state.

"Doctor, you must come and see!" Gregor paused for breath as the words seemed to stumble over each other in a rush to get out of his mouth. "In the east quadrant . . . we . . . we found something!"

Oh, hell, the doctor thought, *I didn't really need to dry off anyway.* He grabbed his coat and hat and followed Gregor back out into the pouring rain. He had to admit that the boy's enthusiasm was contagious. He could feel something stirring inside him, something that said, "This is it. This is what I've been waiting for."

Anya, another of Dr. Goronay's students, knelt under the tarpaulin tent near the find almost reverently, hovering over it like a guardian against anyone who might come near. A bright smile lit up her rain- and mud-spattered face as the doctor approached. He ducked under the tent and knelt down near where the find had been carefully laid out on some dry towels, though God only knew where they had managed to find any at that point. Gregor crouched impatiently on his haunches, bouncing a bit as he waited to see what would happen next.

"All right then," the doctor said with a grunt as he lowered himself to his knees, "let's see what we have here." Anya started to speak, but Goronay shushed her with a "tut, tut" and a wave of his hand. He preferred to examine a new find for himself before he heard a report from his juniors. He took his damp glasses from a coat pocket and slipped them on to get a better look.

The find was a squarish clay tablet, roughly a meter across and perhaps ten centimeters thick. It was surprisingly well preserved, with only some minor deterioration around the edges. If this find was anywhere near the age of the other artifacts, it was an archeological miracle that it was in such good shape.

The flat surface of the tablet was carved with graceful, angular glyphs laid out in a very precise spiral that wound its way from the outer edge and spiraled in toward the center, the glyphs growing progressively smaller until they reached a symbol carved in the very center of the tablet. The halogen lighting of the dig site and the dampness of the clay seemed to make the symbols stand out in dark relief against the pale surface of the tablet. Goronay took his time studying the symbols, with only a quiet "hmmm" escaping his lips as he gently wiped mud off parts of the find to examine them more closely. Finally he sat back, and a smile showed through his damp gray beard.

"Amazing. Simply amazing. I have never seen writing such as this. It shows vague similarities to some runic alphabets, but it seems to represent a completely unknown style and composition." He turned to Anya. "Where was this found?"

"Down at the eighth layer," she replied. "And doctor, when we lifted it out of the pit, it was very heavy. We believe that there might be something *inside* the clay. Maybe stone or even metal!" *Fascinating*, Goronay thought. What a discovery! If there was something covered over by the tablet, then it should be remarkably well preserved, given the state of the clay itself.

"And, Doctor," Anya said, with a shy pause, "I think it may be *magical*."

"Indeed?" The doctor replied. He was an old man and still not entirely used to the fact that magic had returned to the world. Anya's specialty, however, was psychometric archeology, and she used her extrasensory gifts to both track down archeological finds and to learn something of their history by reading their auras or some such thing. Dr. Goronay really didn't understand how it all worked, but he'd seen archaeological sensitives in action enough times to believe that they did.

"Magical in what way?" he asked.

Anya shrugged and shook her head. "I'm not sure," she said. "There are definite traces of . . . something around it, but like nothing I've ever seen before. I get the impression of great age. Whatever is associated with the magic might be inside the tablet."

"Well, then, we should get a look inside. Anya, get a crew together and arrange to have our find transported to the University as soon as possible. We'll need our special equipment to x-ray it and perform other tests to see what there is to see." The doctor smiled and clapped Gregor on the shoulder. "Gregor, help me carry it back to my trailer for safekeeping. It seems that Father Christmas has brought us a present a week early, my friends."

Dr. Goronay and Gregor carefully wrapped the tablet in plastic sheeting and covered it with towels before each taking an end of the parcel and lifting it. Anya was right, the tablet was heavier than it should have been, though Goronay was so energized, he felt as if he could lift ten times its weight off the ground all by himself. He and Gregor walked gingerly through the muck to the doctor's trailer, while another student ran ahead to open the door for them. Once, Gregor nearly slipped in the mud, but managed to regain his balance before sending their burden tumbling to the ground. He sheepishly grinned at the doctor, then returned his concentration to their task.

Once they'd set the tablet on the workbench inside his trailer, Dr. Goronay ignored his sodden clothing and his now cold cup of coffee. He began unwrapping the find, to examine it better under the light and to clean it off somewhat. He sent Gregor off to get some imaging equipment to take holopics of the tablet.

As Goronay brushed the moist dirt off the tablet, he happened to glance at the briefcase sitting next to the small desk. It triggered a sort of recognition in him, like he'd just remembered something. As if in a trance, he found himself moving over to the briefcase, setting it on the desk top, and opening it to reveal a flat object resembling a large, thick frisbee molded from dark plastic. He picked up his pocket secretary, inserted a data chip into the port, and keyed the memo mode. Holding it near his lips, he spoke into the receiver.

"Target acquired. Will meet at the pre-planned coordinates. Request instructions." He removed the chip and opened a small port on top of the plastic discus. He snapped the chip inside and closed the flap. Then he picked the thing up and carried it to the window. The rain still fell, cold and dark as he slid the window open. He pressed a hidden activation stud on the underside of the plastic disk, set it down on the sill, and backed away as it began to hum to life.

There was a faint "pop" as the disk deposited something on the window sill. Then it whirred, and a powerful fan lifted it into the air, like a little flying saucer. It hovered for a moment, then oriented on the open window. The whirring increased, and the plastic drone zipped out the window and disappeared into the night. The message was on its way.

Goronay ignored the departure of the drone. His attention was completely focused on what it left behind, the small plastic chip sitting on the window sill. He licked his dry lips, feeling like a parched man just discovering an oasis in the desert. He reverently lifted the chip in trembling hands and fitted it into the small socket located just behind his left ear. The chip slid home with a satisfying click. Goronay shuddered as it made contact, an involuntary moan escaping his lips.

The rush of power was orgasmic in its intensity. He could feel it filling his limbs, surging through him. He was like a hero of legend, like a god. There was nothing he could not do, nothing that could stand in his way. He dimly remembered the first time he'd felt this way, shortly after first seeing the artifacts from this dig site, when the strange men came to visit him in the dead of the night and showed him the power and glory that could be his. The power erased all doubts, all fears. He knew what he needed to do.

Goronay picked up a hammer lying on the countertop and swung it at the tablet with all his might. The hard clay cracked and splintered under the force of his blow, sending fragments flying everywhere. Goronay struck again, and again, and dark fissures ran through the whole object, the delicate glyphs and traceries obliterated by the force of his blows. Deep inside some of those cracks, something gleamed and glimmered.

Goronay began to brush the shards of clay aside to get a better look at it. Just then the door of the trailer opened and young Gregor backed in, carrying the holo-imaging camera. He closed the door, turned toward Dr. Goronay and froze, a look of shock and horror on his face as he saw his mentor, standing over the broken remains of their find, hammer in hand.

"Doctor . . . Dr. Goronay!" he stammered. "What are you doing!" He took a step back from the intense look in the doctor's eyes, knocking over a stack of printouts behind him and sending them fluttering across the floor.

Goronay smiled fiercely, the power singing and surging in his veins. He stepped forward, and Gregor tried to stumble back again, tripping over the papers and falling to the floor in a heap. He raised his hands in a feeble gesture to ward off what was coming.

"Doctor, please! No, don't! Please don't . . . !"

Gregor's pleas were like music to Goronay's ears. The doctor stepped forward and raised the hammer, bringing it down again and again on Gregor's skull until his cries were silenced and the white papers scattered over the floor were red with blood. Suddenly, the feeling of power faded and Goronay was himself again. He stood there for what seemed like an eternity, looking down in horror at the body of the young man who'd been so excited and enthusiastic about archeology, who often burst into his office with some new idea or discovery he wanted to discuss. Gregor would never become the scientist he'd dreamed of being. The bloody hammer dropped from Goronay's nerveless fingers, hitting the floor with a thud.

"Gregor," he whispered. "Dear God, dear God, what have I done?"

Goronay wrenched his gaze away from Gregor's body and turned back to the broken ruin of the clay tablet, and what lay gleaming within it. He knew what had happened. He could feel the chip, useless and burnt out, nestled into the jack implanted into the skin behind his ear. Already he hungered for another taste of what it contained. His masters would be waiting for him, the strange, dark men who came to him in the night. They would be waiting for him to do their bidding and they would reward him with power and glory once again.

Part of Goronay was sickened by what he'd done. He wanted to find some way to wake Gregor up, to fix what had gone wrong. But it was too late for that. He returned to the tablet and brushed away fragments to reveal its contents, then wrapped it in plastic and cloth to protect it. The doctor placed his precious bundle inside his briefcase, then pulled his hat down over his eyes and went to the trailer door. For the first time, he was grateful for the rain and the darkness.

As he opened the door and slipped out into the night, he realized that the gods had not sent the rain as a sign of their displeasure. They had sent it as a sign of their favor, to help their new servant fulfill his task. It was time, time for Ragnarok to come.

1

"We're a go, Talon. They're moving out."

The voice sounded from the subdermal induction speakers implanted in Talon's inner ear. He subvocalized through implanted pickups.

"Roger that," he said. "Here we go, team. Get ready."

Talon sat in a darkened alleyway astride a sleek red, black, and silver Yamaha Rapier, its engine humming quietly, the lights off. He wore a dark motorcycle helmet with a visor that concealed his face. The visor was equipped with electronics that lit up the alleyway as bright as twilight. A close-fitting leather jacket would protect him in a spill, and the ballistic cloth lining would do the same against small-caliber rounds. He also wore wrist-length black gloves and battered-looking jeans over black biker boots. All that kept him from looking like any other street biker were the ornate dagger at his hip, the sheath tied down to his left thigh, and the design on the side of the Rapier. Not the familiar Yamaha logo, but a complex Celtic knot in chrome next to the name "Aracos" written in graceful lettering.

Talon twisted the accelerator, and the engine revved with a whine.

"Would you please stop doing that?" said another voice in his head. This one didn't come through his headware speakers. It spoke directly into his mind.

"It relaxes me," Talon thought in reply. *"We've got to be ready to go as soon as they get here."*

"Well, it's annoying me," the voice said tartly, *"and it's completely unnecessary, anyway."*

Talon smiled and patted the side of the motorcycle's gas tank, releasing his grip on the accelerator.

"Okay, okay," he said quietly, out loud. "Have it your way."

"Thank you, I will," the voice said with a note of smug satisfaction. *"Isn't it nearly time?"*

Talon nodded and focused on extending his mystical senses outward, through the brick and concrete walls, through all the physical obstacles in his way, allowing him to see the nearby intersection as if he were hovering a short distance above it, with a clear view of all the approaching traffic. Even this late at night, there were a fair number of vehicles on the road. Cambridge was part of the Greater Boston metroplex, and Boston was a city that rarely slept. Most of the cars were electric models following the city's GridGuide system, which provided them with power and kept them moving along at a safe, sedate speed. The car Talon was looking for was one of the rarer internal-combustion models, a sign of conspicuous consumption on the part of the owner, but no more than he expected from a man like Nicholas Grace.

He spotted it about a block from the intersection. A black Phaeton limousine with polarized windows, cutting its way through the traffic like a moving shadow. Only the bluish-halogen headlights gave it any color or depth whatsoever. It matched the image Trouble had forwarded to Talon's headware memory. That was the target, all right.

Talon mentally keyed open Channel One of his headcom system.

"Target sighted," he said. "I'm on it."

As the limo turned the corner, Talon dropped his clairvoyance spell and gripped the handlebars of the Rapier. A few seconds later, the Phaeton cruised past the alleyway. Talon pulled smoothly out onto the street and began to follow.

As he wove through the late-night traffic, he recalled planning for this run and Hammer asking him why he didn't just make himself invisible to follow their target. Talon reminded the ork mercenary how hard it was to drive in Boston even under normal conditions, to say nothing of dealing with traffic that couldn't even see you. No, when it came to running a tail, sometimes the old-fashioned methods worked best. Not that Talon's magic wouldn't come in handy on this caper. On the contrary, Talon was counting on it—just not yet.

As he followed the limo, he glanced up into the night sky. The streetlights and the background neon glow of the city lights made it difficult to make out much of anything, even with the digital-enhancers in his helmet. But he knew that somewhere up there hovered a small surveillance drone, providing a real-time video feed of the area, including the limo and Talon not far behind. Val and Trouble were monitoring the feed, each deep into her respective virtual world. Valkyrie was jacked in to remotely control the drones needed for this operation, while Trouble navigated cyberspace to handle the informational side of things, keeping everyone coordinated.

Using his headcom system, he called up a window in his field of vision. It was projected onto the retinas of his eyes by tiny lasers, using data fed to his headware by Val's drone. The head's up display showed a graphic overview of the streets and the traffic, with the target limo and Talon highlighted in red. The locations of the rest of the team also glowed on the display. Everyone was in place.

He keyed open another comm channel with a thought. "Boom ol' buddy," he subvocalized through the link, "we ready to go?"

"All set," came a Cockney-accented rumble. "Val's got our bird at less than a kilometer from rendezvous. Let's just hope Gracie doesn't decide to pull out the major mojo."

"I can handle him," Talon said. "Not to worry."

"Who, me?" Boom replied. "Worry? Not at all. The day you can't take some academic magic-geek is the day we should give up this business. The only concern I've got is what he might have going for him that we don't know about. I mean, we've never had a shadowrun not go down exactly as planned, right?"

Talon ignored the sarcasm; it was just pre-run nerves. He had them, too, even after all his years as a shadowrunner. Their plan was good, but plenty of things could still go wrong. Talon understood Boom's concern, but there wasn't anything he could do about it now.

The limo was headed for the airport, where Dr. Nicholas Grace, professor of applied thaumaturgy, would be boarding a UCASAir commuter flight to

Washington D.C., the home town of Grace's associates, the Illuminates of the New Dawn. The IOND was a big-league magical association, a kind of "mages union" that included plenty of famed academics and corporate magicians from all over the world. Grace was a senior member of the organization, on his way home from a very important meeting with IOND members in the Boston area. Talon and the rest of his team were being paid to ensure that Dr. Grace's trip didn't go entirely as planned.

As they made their way toward the city, Talon could see the flashing yellow lights in the street ahead. Orange- and white-striped plastic sawhorses stretched across the road, and a hulking troll wearing a black jacket and pants with reflective white stripes along the sleeves and legs stood, directing traffic. The Knight Errant corporate logo gleamed on his shoulder and chest. Cars were already starting to back up, even at this late hour, as the big troll officer slowly waved them through, one by one.

The limo pulled up to the roadblock, and the troll raised one massive hand. The car slowed to a stop and the officer made his way over to the driver's side window, tapping on it with one blunt finger. Talon pulled in close behind the car as the troll leaned over and exchanged words with the driver, gesturing toward the side of the road. The driver said something Talon couldn't quite make out, and the troll gestured toward the side of the road again, this time more forcefully. The limo slowly pulled over as Talon glanced back over his shoulder to see an ork dressed in overalls and a hard hat pull a "ROAD CLOSED" sign across the end of the road about two hundred meters back, blocking off any more incoming traffic, and making sure there wouldn't be any witnesses for the next few minutes.

Talon smiled and pulled his bike up behind the limo.

"Keep an eye out for any astral trouble, Aracos," he thought.

"Don't I always?" the voice in his mind responded, with a touch of reproach. Talon patted the motorcycle as he dismounted behind the car, drawing a gun made of flat black plastic from under his jacket. The troll officer removed a massive pistol from under his jacket and leveled it at the driver's side of the car.

"Don't move," he said flatly. The driver's side window was still down, and Talon could see the limo driver put his hands on the steering wheel, keeping them in sight. He was hired muscle. According to the profile Trouble had put together, he was pretty good, too, and smart enough not to try anything stupid. Not until he got some sort of opportunity.

The passenger in the back of the limo nearly gave it to him. The car's windows were tinted and nearly impossible to see into, but it was quite possible to see out. That was all Dr. Grace needed to try and use magic against the troll leveling a gun at his driver.

Talon felt more than saw a surge of magical power as Grace cast a spell intended to reduce Boom's brain to slag. Fortunately, although Talon couldn't see Grace, he could see Boom, and he'd already extended his own magical shielding to protect the big troll. Grace's manabolt splattered against the shield like water striking a dam. Boom barely felt a thing.

As Boom moved to secure the driver, Talon was

already in action. He stepped around to the rear door of the limo and drew a blade from under his jacket. Not the golden, rune-etched dagger at his hip, but a modern combat knife, edged with a monofilament cord. The blade sliced right through the lock on the door, sending small parts scattering to the pavement. Talon felt another surge of mystic power gathering in the air above the limo.

"*Aracos!*" he called out.

"*I'm on it, boss!*" came the response. Suddenly, Talon's motorcycle dissolved like mist, replaced by a shimmering falcon with golden feathers that soared above the limousine as a misty shape materialized there. It looked like a dark thundercloud with faintly humanoid features and glowing pits of electric blue light for eyes. An air elemental, and a fairly powerful one at that.

The falcon tore into it with a piercing shriek, razor talons rending the misty form as the elemental buffeted the bird with its powerful winds. The falcon flapped its wings and remained steady against the onslaught.

Talon yanked open the back door of the limo. There was a bang and something struck him squarely in the chest. His jacket's ballistic armor lining protected him, but the impact nearly knocked him down. It was like getting hit in the chest by a baseball bat. Nicholas Grace sat huddled in the back of the limo, leveling a slim pistol at Talon. It looked almost comical in the hands of the small, bookish mage, with his gold-rimmed glasses and his immaculate charcoal gray suit. Talon was prepared for some additional magical assault, but he hadn't been expecting someone like Grace to use a gun.

Talon leveled his own gun at Grace and fired. The dart struck an invisible wall a few centimeters away from the mage, deflecting harmlessly. Damn! Talon thought. A barrier spell. He should have expected it.

The doctor held the gun in his right hand and pointed his left at Talon, rolling out harsh words in what sounded like ancient Hebrew to Talon's trained ear. A crackling bluish bolt of lightning shot out and Talon held out one hand to deflect it, his magical shields barely holding against the force of the spell. He concentrated his own effort on breaking down Grace's barrier, throwing the force of his will against the enchantment to dispel it. Fortunately the barrier was hastily cast. It broke quickly under the force of Talon's magic and vanished. Before Grace could reassemble it or cast another spell, Talon brought up his Narcoject pistol and fired again.

There was a chuff of compressed air, and the small dart caught the mage just below the clavicle, easily penetrating the cloth of his suit. Grace slumped back against the other door as the fast-acting neurostun started to work its way into his system. In seconds, he would be paralyzed, then unconscious. Talon kept him covered for a few seconds, to be sure the drug did its work, while Boom covered the driver. Grace's eyes quickly glazed over and rolled back in his head as the golden raptor slashed through the hovering air elemental one final time. The spirit dissolved like smoke on the wind, and the falcon settled onto the roof of the limo with a caw of pride. Good thing, Talon thought. With Grace out of commission, the elemental was free from his control. The elemental might have gone berserk if Aracos hadn't dealt with it.

"Talon, what's going on?" came a concerned voice over his commlink.

"Our target put up a bit of a fight," Talon replied, "but it's under control. How are we doing?"

"Smooth as silk," Trouble's voice came back. "The driver tried to radio in a message when he saw the road block, like we figured, but Val's got the airwaves over you jammed up good. No reaction from Knight Errant dispatch or the traffic grid yet, but you haven't got too much longer before the GridGuide system starts to notice the hold-up or some irate motorist decides to put a call in to traffic control. I'll keep things busy as long as I can."

"Roger that, we're almost done," Talon responded. All that remained was to get what they came for and clear out.

He opened up his senses to the astral plane, his vision expanding beyond the mundane to take in the glowing auras around himself, Boom, and the others present. He could see the dormant glimmering of magical items on Dr. Grace's person, and he carefully examined them for any signs of booby traps or magical fail-safes. He also checked the car to make sure there weren't any dangerous spells or enchantments, but he detected none. The car was a rental, and it was unlikely that Grace would expend the time or effort to place any dangerous spells on it, but it paid to be careful.

On the floor of the back seat was Dr. Grace's briefcase. Talon pulled it out and checked it over, then neatly sliced open the locks with his monoblade. Inside was a small, wooden box that glimmered with magical power. It was protected with a spell of some kind.

Talon set the briefcase down on the car's trunk without touching the box, then held his hands out over it. The golden falcon dropped from the roof of the car to settle on his shoulder as he worked.

"What do you think?" Talon asked his familiar.

"Looks pretty tricky," the spirit responded, "but I think we can take care of it."

"All right then, let's do it."

Talon focused his will on the glowing aura around the box and felt Aracos do the same. Together they pulled at the pattern of the spell around the box, unraveling its structure, breaking down the energies that bound it together, until the spell began to dissolve and the glow slowly faded into nothing. Talon was sweating a bit from the effort when they were done, and he could tell Aracos felt it, too. The spell was tough.

Without the protective spell, the box's lock was easily dealt with by mundane means. Talon opened it up and looked inside. On a cushion of wine-dark velvet there rested an old-fashioned key, made of a rich golden metal that gleamed faintly in the street lights. The aura that glowed around it was almost painfully bright, filled with barely restrained power. Talon snapped the lid of the box shut and stood up, turning toward Boom and opening his commlink as he did so.

"This is it, let's go," he said to Boom and the rest of the team. He moved up to where the troll was covering the limo driver and raised his Narcoject pistol. In one easy motion, he shot the driver in the neck, quickly sending him into dreamland. He closed the back door of the limo as a dark panel van came down the street towards them and stopped. Boom slid the back door open and started tossing the sawhorses in the back. In moments, all traces of the roadblock were gone. Talon and the troll climbed into the back of the van and the golden falcon on Talon's shoulder took wing, then vanished into thin air, returning to his home in the astral plane. Talon could feel the spirit's smug sense of satisfaction lingering like a faint perfume. Although he would never admit it, Aracos loved being a shadowrunner just as much as his master.

In the front seat of the van sat two figures. Valkyrie, the team's rigger, was in the passenger seat, for a change. She was jacked into the remote control deck in her lap, its cables trailing up to the jack behind her left ear. Her head lolled to the side; her mind was far away, her attention focused on controlling the surveillance drone hovering overhead that kept watch on the entire operation.

In the driver's seat sat Harlan Hammarand, or Hammer, as he was generally known. The burly ork mercenary looked over his shoulder to offer a tusky grin to Talon and Boom. Hammer had seen action in some of the roughest spots in the world, but nobody was happier than him when things went smoothly.

"All set?" he asked.

Talon nodded. "We've got the goods. Let's get out of here and set up delivery to Mr. Johnson."

"Fine by me," Hammer said. He pulled the van back out and headed for the city.

2

Mr. Brackhaus set the meeting for two hours later, in front of the Dunkelzahn Institute. Talon wasn't crazy about the location, but his employer was insistent, so he agreed, reluctantly. A few hours before dawn, Talon found himself waiting in the cold outside the Institute's headquarters in Cambridge, feeling more than a little bit exposed.

With his leather jacket, short haircut, silver earring, and backpack, someone could almost mistake Talon for a graduate student from nearby MIT&T or Harvard. If not for the extremely early hour, he could probably get away with it. The identification he carried would support it. Talon looked younger than his thirty-one years—even without the help of twenty-first-century cosmetic surgery or body-sculpting techniques. Magicians tended to avoid such procedures, since changes in the body's delicate balance could often affect their ability to use magic. Talon had gone in for a few body modifications—most people did sooner or later—but all his extras were inside: cellular headlink, crypto-circuit, and data storage. The only one visible, however, was the gleam of a datajack port behind his right ear, common enough in this day and age.

Talon glanced around the darkened street for about the hundredth time and wished Brackhaus had chosen someplace less public for the meet. There wasn't much traffic, but such a public place offered too many unknowns.

Part of his unease came from the open design of the plaza in front of the Institute's main building. Brick-lined walkways cut through the grounds, which were arranged in contemporary elven style, with perfectly trimmed bushes and flower-beds, most of them dead or dormant in the depths of Boston's winter. The paths were brushed clear of snow, and snow banks lined the sides of the road, with much taller mounds forming a high wall around the parking area. It didn't take long for the metroplex to run out of places to heap the plowed snow.

The Institute building was a simple two-story affair, its red brick facade blanketed with deep green ivy. The building itself was only a few years old, and Talon was sure all that ivy was the result of a major dose of magic. He also knew that the interior was as modern as anything in the Boston area, since the Dunkelzahn Institute for Magical Research engaged in some of the most cutting-edge experiments in theoretical and applied magic. He could think of plenty of people involved with the DIMR who would love to get their hands on the wooden box hidden in the backpack he wore, and what it contained. In fact, from what Trouble had dug up on the key, Grace had arranged to have it "liberated" from somewhere in Tir Tairngire a few years previously, and Ehran, one of the Tir's Council of Princes, sat on the board of the DIMR. A little too close for Talon's comfort.

Another part of his discomfort stemmed from what the Institute itself represented. The DIMR was a memorial to the great dragon Dunkelzahn, founded with money from his estate. Dunkelzahn had been a champion of the rights of the Awakened and metahumanity in the Sixth World, a new age of magic, where myths and legends came to life. Unlike other dragons, who tended to shun "lesser" beings like humans, Dunkelzahn seemed a true friend of humans and metahumans alike. He had appeared on the trideo in the early years of the Sixth World, helping to calm hysteria and providing information about the nature of magic and magical beings during those first interviews with a stunned new media. The ratings were so good the dragon eventually got his own talk show. To people of the twentieth century the idea of a dragon hosting a talk show would have seemed preposterous. Even Talon, a child of the twenty-first century, found it amazing sometimes.

Dunkelzahn's popularity was so great he eventually took the unthinkable a step further. He decided to run for president of the United Canadian-American States in 2057. The presidential race that year was a whirlwind of political maneuvering and public relations, but the dragon managed to win in the end, becoming the first non-human president ever.

Unfortunately, Dunkelzahn's term of office was cut tragically short. After leaving a victory party at the Watergate Hotel on Inauguration Night, Dunkelzahn climbed into the presidential limousine—in human form, thanks to dragon magic. A short distance from the hotel, a massive explosion destroyed the limo and everyone in it. They never found a body, but it was clear that nothing could have survived the blast.

The assassination of President Dunkelzahn sent shock waves through the nation, but it was nothing compared to the aftermath of his death. Dunkelzahn left an extensive will detailing the disposition of his estate and his last wishes. The dragon's resources turned out to be more vast than anyone ever dreamed, and the money and other bequests from Dunkelzahn's estate reshaped the political and economic landscape, both in the UCAS and abroad. One of the many institutions originally funded by Dunkelzahn's will was the DIMR, a foundation for pure research into the mysteries of magic, to allow humanity to better understand the nature of the world in which they now lived. Another was the Draco Foundation, also part of the dragon's legacy.

The Draco Foundation administered Dunkelzahn's remaining estate and saw that the dragon's final wishes were carried out. Some of the instructions Dunkelzahn left behind required less than logical—and often less than legal—action, which in the twenty-first century meant shadowrunners. The Draco Foundation had enough money to hire the very best, and one of the people they had hired was Talon. He'd worked with Assets, Inc., the DF's own shadow team, for a few years following Dunkelzahn's death. In that time, he traveled all over the world and saw some amazing things.

Eventually, he decided he couldn't go any further within Assets. Until then, Talon had always been a runner in a team, had never really operated one on his own. When circumstances drew him back to Boston last year, he decided to form his own crew with the runners he met on that caper, with the help of his old friend, Boom. His little band of shadowrunners were really starting to make a name for themselves in the Boston sprawl, but Talon still couldn't quite shake the feeling that his departure from Assets, Inc., although amicable enough, constituted some sort of betrayal on his part, a desertion of the dragon's legacy. He felt Dunkelzahn's presence strongly here on the Institute grounds, even though he hadn't known the great dragon in life.

Talon was just grateful that the Institute's board of directors had rejected the proposal to erect a statue of Dunkelzahn in the center of the plaza. He wasn't sure he could handle having the dragon staring down at him right then. The abstract bronze sculpture, shaped like an ancient astrolabe, was considerably more friendly.

"Heads up, boss," came a voice in his head. He had Aracos keeping watch.

Talon yanked his thoughts back to the present as a dark four-door Eurocar came prowling down the street. It pulled up to the snow-covered curb and the rear door opened. Talon walked calmly toward the car, all his senses alert for any signs of trouble. He didn't think it was likely that Nicholas Grace or any of his cronies from the Illuminates of the New Dawn could have found him or the key in only a few short hours, but it paid to be at least a little paranoid in the shadow business. It had saved Talon's life more than once. He'd already arranged to have one of Val's drones nearby to keep an electronic eye on the meeting, and he could feel Aracos hovering close by in astral space, invisible, silent, and intangible to the physical world, but able to materialize in an instant, if needed.

"Ready?" he thought to his spirit ally.

"I'll keep watch," Aracos said. *"Don't worry."* With that Talon climbed into the back of the car and closed the door behind him.

The Eurocar slid away from the curb smoothly. There was still very little traffic, and the driver took his time. The car's windows were tinted, so it was almost impossible to see in from the outside. The driver kept his eyes on the road and pretended not to notice anything going on behind him. It was like nobody else was in the car with him. Perhaps he really didn't notice anything. Talon thought he might be fitted with data filters to keep him from consciously remembering anything potentially sensitive while on "duty" like this.

Next to Talon in the back seat was his employer for this run, his "Mr. Johnson." Hans Brackhaus—Talon was fairly sure that wasn't his real name—was an unimposing man. He was of average height and build and indeterminate age, somewhere in that vague range between late thirties and early fifties that corporate execs maintained through the use of modern medicine and cosmetic work. His hair was dark with just a touch of gray to give him a distinguished, reliable look. His eyes were light blue. He wore a dark, finely tailored suit, pale blue shirt, and a jewel-toned tie. If Talon had to create the image of the perfect, archetypal corporate suit, it would look a lot like Hans Brackhaus, which, he suspected, was the idea. The only unusual element of Brackhaus' appearance was the ornate walking stick resting against the seat near the door on his side. It was black lacquered wood with a golden handle in the shape of a dragon's head.

"Talon," the older man said by way of a greeting.

"Mr. Brackhaus."

"You have the item then?" Brackhaus had a slight German accent, noticeable only in certain elements of his grammar and the pronunciation of certain words. Otherwise, his English was flawless.

Talon had slipped off the backpack when he got into the car. He unzipped it and removed the wooden box, which he placed in Brackhaus' hands. Brackhaus opened the box and looked inside, a tight smile crossing his otherwise stony expression.

"*Ser gut*," he said quietly. "Very good. I assume there were no . . . complications?"

"None other than the ones you requested," Talon replied. "I still would have preferred to lift the key *before* Grace left town and leave him with a substitute, so the Illuminates wouldn't be sure when and where the real key went missing. Taking it from him en route to the airport and giving him a chance to see us was something of a risk."

"Yes," Brackhaus said, closing the wooden box and resting it on one knee, "but that is what I am paying you for, Herr Talon. My employer wanted to send a certain message to the Illuminates, among others, and this"—he tapped the box with one finger—"is merely a means to an end. The risk you took was not unnecessary, believe me."

Brackhaus' employer was none other than Saeder-Krupp, the world's largest megacorporation, with interests in industries worldwide. Saeder-Krupp was owned by another dragon, the great dragon Lofwyr, as different in many ways from the nearly sainted Dunkelzahn as night from day. Talon had no idea if Brackhaus was high up enough to deal personally with the dragon, but Lofwyr was known for his complex schemes, so it came as no surprise that the run had unusual risks for no apparent reason.

Talon shrugged. "Doesn't matter to me either way. You get what you pay for. Speaking of which . . . ?"

"Ah, yes. Of course." Brackhaus reached into the inside breast pocket of his jacket and withdrew a slim, plastic wand, about ten centimeters in length, and handed it over to Talon. "This contains the remainder of the fee we agreed upon, in certified credit kept in a numbered offshore account. Is that acceptable?"

"Very," Talon replied, turning the credstick over in his fingers once before making it disappear into one of the many pockets in his jacket. "I believe that concludes our business."

"Not quite," Brackhaus said, and Talon tensed for a moment. Did the Johnson have some kind of double-cross in mind? It was not unknown for employers to dispose of shadowrunners to eliminate loose ends that could be traced back to them. Normally, runners were too valuable an asset to waste in that manner, but shadowrunning was a dangerous business, and the megacorporations weighed their decisions based on how things affected their bottom line. Sometimes a shadowrunner was more of a liability than an asset.

"There's no need for concern," Brackhaus said, as

if he could read Talon's mind. "Quite the opposite. You and your associates did quite well on this job and I have another that might be of interest to you."

Talon settled back into the cushions of the Eurocar. More work was always a good thing, even with the big nuyen they'd just made.

"I'm listening," he said. *"Aracos?"*

"Dunno, boss," the spirit replied in his mind. *"His aura doesn't show anything except calm and confidence. He's like a stone, totally unreadable."* Talon couldn't say that surprised him.

"Just say the word and I'll frag him."

"Hang on," Talon thought. *"Let's see what he's got. Just keep an eye out for trouble."*

Brackhaus reached into his jacket once again and withdrew a flat plastic case. He flipped open the screen of the pocket secretary and touched the control pad. The screen lit up with a digital picture of an older man, human, with gray hair and a somewhat bushy beard and mustache.

"This is Dr. Alexi Goronay, of the University of Kiev, where he is a professor of archeology. Two weeks ago, Dr. Goronay and a team of students from the University were excavating an archeological site in the mountains of the Ukraine. They discovered an unusual artifact during the dig, a clay tablet carved with symbols, which Goronay brought to his trailer on the site. Less than an hour later, Goronay disappeared and one of his students was found murdered in the trailer, beaten to death with a hammer. The tablet was smashed into fragments."

Talon looked up from the display and met Brackhaus' eyes. Aracos was right; there was no emotion displayed there, only a calm, businesslike demeanor, as if they were discussing the weather rather than a brutal murder.

"What's your employer's interest in this?" Talon asked.

"Dr. Goronay's research was funded by grants from my corporation."

"Hmmm, I didn't know Saeder-Krupp sponsored so many educational programs," Talon said dryly. The sarcasm seemed lost on Brackhaus, or he chose to ignore it. "So what do you want us to do?"

"The fragments of the tablet left behind in the trailer indicate that it was hollow, as was suspected by one of Goronay's students, who helped unearth it. Whatever was inside disappeared along with the doctor." Brackhaus reached down and touched the control pad of the pocket secretary again. "This was taken yesterday in Essen, in the Rhine-Ruhr megaplex." The screen showed a grainy, digitally-enhanced holopic of a street, with people moving along the sidewalks. One figure was circled in red. Talon looked closely at it.

"Dr. Goronay," he said.

"Yes."

"Who's the guy he's talking to?"

"We don't know as yet. We've tentatively identified him as a member of a policlub called Alt Welt."

"I'd heard they were out of business," Talon mused aloud. "What would a professor of archeology want with a member of a radical policlub?"

"We believe Goronay stole whatever was hidden inside the artifact unearthed in the Ukraine and now plans to sell it."

"Why would he do something like that?" Talon asked. "And why would a lame-duck policlub like Alt Welt be interested in buying an archeological artifact? What good is it to them?"

"We don't know," Brackhaus said. Talon seriously doubted that, but did not say it.

"That's why my employer wishes to engage your services," Brackhaus went on. "We want your team to locate Dr. Goronay and recover both him and the stolen artifact. We're prepared to pay you one hundred thousand nuyen in certified credit and we will handle any other expenses involved in the recovery."

Talon had a number of questions clamoring for attention in the back of his mind as he studied the blurred image of Dr. Goronay on the tiny video screen. He ignored them for the time being. Brackhaus wouldn't answer them anyway, and there was no need to give the Johnson any further reason to lie to him. There was clearly a lot about this job that Brackhaus wasn't telling. Still, a hundred thousand nuyen was a lot of money, enough to keep him and his team set for a good while.

"I'll have to speak to the rest of my team," Talon said.

"Of course." Brackhaus flipped the pocket secretary shut and slipped it back into his jacket pocket. "You can reach me at the same number you used for the last job if you decide to take this one. However, I'll need a decision in the next twenty-four hours or I will be forced to inquire elsewhere. After that time, the number will become inactive. Notify me as soon as possible. Time is of the essence."

Talon nodded. "I'll call you as soon as I have an answer, one way or another."

"Excellent." Brackhaus gave him a slight smile. The Eurocar slowed and pulled to the side of the road and Brackhaus extended a hand to Talon. Talon shook it firmly as he reached for the door.

"A pleasure doing business with you," Brackhaus said. "I hope we can continue to work together in the future."

"Thank you, Mr. Brackhaus." Talon climbed out of the car and closed the door behind him. They had brought him back to the Dunkelzahn Institute, to the same spot where they'd picked him up. The dark Eurocar pulled quietly away from the curb, its tires crunching over the snow. It soon turned a corner and disappeared from sight. Talon stood and watched it go, thinking about the job and the money Brackhaus offered. But there were an awful lot of unanswered questions . . .

"Too many, if you ask me," Aracos said in Talon's head.

"Actually, I didn't," Talon thought. *"Haven't I told you not to eavesdrop?"*

"Hey, it's not my fault. You were thinking too loud," the spirit said in a mock hurt tone. Although Aracos was as good a familiar and ally as Talon could ask for, sometimes he found their mental connection to each other a little too effective. He lapsed into silence again for a few moments.

"So," the spirit asked, *"are you going to take it?"*

Talon shrugged. *"I don't know yet. I still have to talk to the others . . ."*

"Yeah," Aracos said, almost to himself, *"you're gonna take it. We going back to the club?"*

Talon raised an eyebrow. There were definitely times when his ally was a little *too* insightful.

"Yeah," he said. "Let's go."

The air near the curb shimmered as the spirit's sleek motorcycle form appeared, engine already humming. Talon was particularly proud of that element of Aracos' design. It had taken some doing, figuring out how a spirit could manifest in the form of something as complex as a motorcycle, but familiar spirits already assumed shapes as complex as animals and peoples, why not machines? It guaranteed that Talon was never without transportation and never had to find a parking space. Aracos didn't need gas or tune-ups either.

"Well," the spirit said, *"hurry up. The sooner we get there, the sooner I can get a drink. And no more revving the engine, okay?"*

Of course, regular motorcycles didn't complain, or require Long Island Iced Teas to keep them happy, so maybe it evened out. Talon sighed and hopped on, and the two of them roared off into the night.

3

Speren Silverblade enjoyed watching sunsets, so he didn't mind waiting. Especially since the balcony of the palace on Royal Hill, facing away from the city of Portland and the Sunset Gate, afforded a spectacular view. Below the hill stretched kilometers of virgin forest and rolling hillsides cut by the meandering blue waters of the river. Only the evergreens retained their leaves at this late season, the rest of the trees having shed theirs in a riot of autumn colors. Now the forest giants waited, silent and sleeping, for the coming of spring.

Speren also looked forward to spring, with all the festivals and celebrations that occupied his homeland of Tir Tairngire during the re-awakening of the Earth. The elves were in tune with the cycle of nature, unlike the humans and others who still raped and polluted her on a regular basis. It did Speren good to know that places like Royal Hill still existed, where the beauty of nature could be appreciated and protected.

Of course, there were always concessions. If Silverblade had been standing on the eastern side of the palace, toward the Sunrise Gate, he would see the city of Portland, Tir Tairngire's gateway to the outside world, sprawling before him in its riot of concrete and steel, surrounded by high walls as much for its protection as to contain the city and its inhabitants, to keep them from contaminating the purity and simplicity of the rest of the Land of Promise.

Portland was a microcosm where the elven nation could receive shipments from outside its borders, allow tourists to come and see what they had built, and generally keep the outside world away from the rest of Tir Tairngire. Speren found Portland pleasant compared to most cities he'd visited, but it was still a city. Nothing to compare with the beauty and serenity of the deep forest. He hoped this time it wouldn't be too long before he returned home.

"Sir?" A voice interrupted his reverie. "Sir, the Prince is ready to see you now."

Speren turned to the young woman, who was dressed in the official clothing of the Winter Court: pale tones of gray, blue, and cream. By comparison, Silverblade's own garb seemed archaic: a long, hooded cloak of wool to keep off the late winter chill, dyed a deep indigo, the color of the night sky. His tunic was a simple one of soft gray cloth, his trousers a blue several shades lighter than the cloak and tucked into polished black leather boots. A wide leather belt worked with complex knot designs fastened his tunic and held a silver-chastened sword in a scabbard at his left. With his shoulder-length hair, its golden color turned into molten fire by the last rays of the sunset, and his bewitching green eyes, Speren Silverblade looked like an elven hero out of a trideo drama or fantasy tale. It was something he was proud of, something he used to his own advantage from time to time.

With a nod of acknowledgment to the young woman, Speren followed her through the corridors of the palace, glancing at the artworks displayed along the walls, in glass cases, and on pedestals placed strategically along their route. He'd seen them many times before, but they never failed to impress him.

He often wondered why so many human works were shown in the palace. Perhaps it was because elves had only lived in the Sixth World for fifty years, ever since the birth of the first elven children around the time of the Awakening. Although they'd achieved more in that short time than any other race—building a nation of their own and resurrecting much of their ancient culture—elves still had a great deal left to accomplish. Perhaps the work of human hands reminded the Princes how much there was yet to be done. Or perhaps it reminded them that humans should not be underestimated. Speren couldn't say, and speculating on the motives of the Princes of Tir Tairngire wasn't generally a healthy pastime.

The Prince's aide led Speren not to the Prince's office or apartments, but to the Palace exercise room. The space was large, with a high ceiling and polished hardwood floors overlaid with padded exercise mats. It was actually a ballroom, one of several, turned over to the Princes and their families for use in exercising. Various pieces of equipment were placed around the room, but a good half of it had been cleared for the open mats, surrounded by mirrored walls sporting a ballet bar, since the exercise room was used quite often for dance training. At the moment, a dance of a different kind was going on.

Two elves, a man and a woman, faced off against each other on the exercise mats. The man was tall, with raven-dark hair worn long in the same popular style Speren affected, but pulled back into a pony tail secured with a green ribbon. He moved with the ease and grace of a dancer, circling his opponent. She was small and slight by comparison, her flaming red hair drawn back with a golden clip. Both of them wore loose-fitting pants and shirts of pale green silk and soft slippers that whispered on the surface of the mats as they circled in a strange sort of dance.

Suddenly, the man exploded into motion, pivoting on one leg and lashing out at the woman. She reacted instantly, turning gracefully to the side to allow the strike to pass her by, then reaching out and seizing the proffered arm. With a twist of her torso, she sent the man flying past her to slam unceremoniously onto his back on the mat. She turned and placed one small foot on his chest, her arms held in a defensive pose.

"Hah!" the man laughed from where he lay. "Defeated again! You're learning well, my Prince."

The woman smiled and took a step back, offering one hand to help the man to his feet.

Speren took the opportunity to step forward. "Yes, quite well, I'd say," he remarked.

The woman glanced over at him as if noticing him for the first time, and a smile lit up her face. "High praise indeed coming from so skilled a warrior," she said to Speren, who nodded in acknowledgment of the praise.

"Speren, I believe you know my instructor, Galen Moonsinger."

The elven warriors bowed slightly to each other.

"Mr. Moonsinger's reputation precedes him," Speren said.

"I could say the same for you, Silverblade," Galen returned, with an ironic smile.

"Thank you, Galen," the Prince said. "You may go, I need to speak with Speren." The instructor bowed to Silverblade, then more deeply to his Prince, and left the room.

Jenna Ni'Ferra, a Prince of Tir Tairngire and member of the Council of Princes, went over to the barre and picked up a towel to mop at her brow before draping the cloth over her shoulders. Speren stood and waited for the Prince to speak, as courtesy demanded.

"You have studied carromeleg, have you not, Speren?"

Speren knew that the Prince surely knew the answer to that question already. Speren Silverblade was a paladin of Tir Tairngire. More importantly, he was a member of the most exalted company of that exalted order, the legendary Ghosts. Paladins were all trained in the elven martial arts, and Ghosts were required to be masters of several.

"I recall my training well," he said. "I took my share of bumps and bruises."

"I think it is a good lesson to learn," she said. "Many people learn carromeleg for its spiritual qualities, for health and centering. While there certainly is value to that, I sometimes think it is more important to learn that anything worthwhile in life comes with its share of bruises and falls, don't you agree?"

"Absolutely, Highness."

Jenna took the ends of the towel in her hands, suddenly all business. Her green eyes, the color of summer leaves, fixed on Speren's.

"I have a mission for you," she said.

Speren bowed with a courtly wave of his hand. "I am yours to command."

"This is a matter of some . . . delicacy," she went on. That meant that this mission did not come from the Council of Princes as such, but from Jenna directly. That was not unusual; the Princes each had their own liege-men to command, but it warned Speren that there might be additional complications. He did not allow any curiosity or concern to show on his face.

"As you know," Jenna said, "it is one of the goals of the Council to help restore our ancient culture. Already we have revived our people's language and many of our arts." She gestured to take in the palace and her own carromeleg uniform. "Still, there remain an untold number of things from the distant past that lie hidden, waiting to be found, and we are not the only ones searching.

"An archeological dig in the Ukraine recently unearthed such an artifact, a piece of our cultural heritage. The dig was sponsored by monies from Saeder-Krupp."

"Lofwyr," Speren said.

Jenna nodded. "Lofwyr."

The great dragon was himself a member of Tir Tairngire's Council of Princes, a Prince in his own right. Inclusion of the dragon on the Council had been the idea of High Prince Lugh Surehand, an idea bitterly opposed by many of the other Princes. Surehand had forced it through, gaining support from Lofwyr in the bargain. Still, there were many in Tir Tairngire who neither liked nor trusted the great dragon, and Jenna Ni'Ferra was one of them. Although she preferred the title of "Prince" to the weaker one of "Princess," Jenna was a staunch supporter of traditional elven values and beliefs. One of those was a deep-seated mistrust of the motives of dragons.

"Fortunately," she said, "something happened at the dig site. The professor in charge apparently suffered some sort of breakdown, killed one of his own students, and stole the artifact. We believe he plans to sell it, or that he may be working for someone else with an interest."

"The Danaan Families, perhaps?" Speren offered. "Or another of the dragons?"

"Perhaps," Jenna said. "We cannot be sure."

"Then I am to retrieve this artifact?" he said.

Jenna offered him one of her radiant smiles. "Quite so. Our intelligence reports that the professor has likely made contact with the underworld in Germany, in the Rhine-Ruhr megaplex."

"Right in the midst of Lofwyr's domain."

"Yes, so you can see why this matter could not be put to the Council, and why discretion is required. You will leave for Germany at once and secure the artifact. When you have done so, you will return it to me. I've had all the necessary files and information prepared for you. You can review them on the way to the German Alliance. The travel arrangements are already made."

Nothing further needed to be said. Speren crossed his right arm over his chest and executed a precise bow.

"I will go at once, my Prince, and I will return when I am successful." He turned on his heel and walked to the door.

Jenna's voice called after him. "Speren?"

"Yes, my Prince?"

"Be careful."

"I am always careful, my Prince."

When he came out into the corridor again, he found Jenna's assistant waiting to give him the mission briefing and other information. Speren wondered about Lofwyr's interest in this lost piece of elven history. Anything that drew the attention of a great dragon had to be far more than a mere historical curiosity. Speren knew the legends and tales of elven might and power in ages past as well as anyone. Whatever this artifact was, it was enough to draw the attention of the most powerful being on Earth.

4

It was early evening when Talon pulled up in front of the Avalon on Landsdown Street. The street was only starting to get busy, and the place wasn't open for business yet. The restaurants were filling up for dinner, and soon the clubs would be full too. He pulled around to the side of the building complex and dismounted, Aracos' motorcycle form fading as the spirit returned to his intangible astral form.

Talon took the concrete steps up to the side door two at a time and went inside. The bouncers and other employees recognized him and gave him no more than a passing glance as he continued on past, up the stairs to the second-floor office. As he came to the landing, Aracos spoke in his mind.

"All clear, boss. Everyone's waiting," the spirit said.

Talon was glad to hear it, but felt a slight twinge at having Aracos check up on his chummers. It wasn't that he didn't trust them, but shadowrunning was a dangerous business, and Talon hadn't lived this long by not being careful. He went to the office door and knocked twice.

"It's me," he said, opening the door.

"About bloody time," Boom grumbled in his deep bass.

Inside the office sat the rest of his team: Boom, Trouble, Val, and Hammer. They looked up expectantly as he entered.

"So what's up, Tal?" Boom asked. "Everything go all right with the Johnson?" The troll was wearing an amazingly loud Hawai'ian shirt that barely covered his huge frame. He sat behind a wide desk that looked like a child's compared to Boom's nearly three meters in height. Boom owned the Avalon, one of the hottest nightclubs in Boston, thanks to a bequest from Dunkelzahn's will. He was also one of the most skilled fixers in the plex and an old friend of Talon's. Ever since Talon had returned to Boston, Boom had become active as a shadowrunner again, in addition to handling the team's financial affairs.

"Everything went fine," Talon said. He took the credstick from his jacket pocket and tossed it onto the desk. "As a matter of fact, Mr. Brackhaus was so impressed with our work that he offered us another job. And this one pays a hundred grand."

Boom let out a low whistle and picked up the credstick, slotting it into a hand-held reader to check the balance.

"A hundred thousand?" Trouble said. "That's not bad. Who does he want killed?" She was a decker, the team's Matrix specialist, a ghost in the machine, able to work wonders with computers and communications.

"Nobody," Talon said. "That's the good part. All he wants is to get back some artifact from an archeological dig."

"If that's the good part, what's the bad part?" Hammer asked. The ork had been to a lot of places and gotten himself out of a lot of close scrapes. He tended to look on the bad side of things, a habit that had saved his hide more than once.

Talon took a seat next to Trouble on a leather couch. Boom was seated behind his desk, while Val and Hammer occupied the two chairs to either side.

"The bad parts are: One, the target who has the artifact is in the German Alliance, somewhere in the Rhine-Ruhr plex, one of the biggest sprawls in the world. Two, he's a professor of archeology at the University of Kiev in Russia, who apparently beat one of his own students to death with a hammer before he absconded with said artifact. And, three, the dig he was working on was sponsored by Brackhaus' boss, Saeder-Krupp."

"That means Lofwyr's involved," Boom said, setting the credstick aside for the moment.

Talon shrugged. "There's not a whole lot going on with S-K that Lofwyr's *not* involved with, chummer."

"Still," Trouble said, "that leaves a whole lot of unanswered questions about the run."

Talon nodded. "I know. I've been thinking about those for a while. The main ones I can see are: why do Brackhaus and Saeder-Krupp want to hire out-of-town talent for this run when there are plenty of shadowrunners in Germany who'd gladly take it on, and what is it about this artifact that it's such a big deal for Saeder-Krupp to get it back? They sure as hell aren't worried about its historical value or putting it in some museum."

"Look at the last one first," Boom said. "What is this 'artifact' Brackhaus is talking about?"

"That's just it, he doesn't know, or at least he claims not to know. The artifact they dug up was some kind of clay tablet. Apparently, Dr. Goronay smashed it and took something that was hidden inside. Since the only other guy who saw what was inside is dead, nobody knows what Goronay found."

"Hmmm, that makes things more difficult," Boom said, rubbing his chin. "Could it be magical?"

"Maybe. I've run into drek people have dug up from gods know where that had some serious mojo to it. I ran into plenty of things like that working for the Draco Foundation, and even that key Brackhaus hired us to find is pretty old, not like a conventional magical item at all. Maybe Lofwyr's collecting a set of them or something."

"Going to be difficult to find something when we don't even know what it looks like," Boom muttered.

"We don't have to," Trouble said. "Sounds like we just have to find Goronay. Find him, and we find whatever he took."

"The question is: do we want to do it?" Talon looked around the room at the rest of the team.

"Not me," Val said, speaking for the first time since Talon entered the room. "I'm out." She stood up from her chair, snatched her leather jacket from the back, and headed out the door.

"Val, wait a—" Talon started as the door slammed shut behind her. He turned to Hammer. "What the hell was that about?" The ork had worked with Valkyrie longer than any of them, so he knew her best.

"Not sure," he said, "but Val's from Germany, you know."

"No," Talon said, "I didn't." But then, he knew very little about the team's mysterious rigger. Val was an expert in piloting or driving just about anything, but she kept pretty quiet about her past.

"Yeah," Hammer said, "I got the impression that she had some pretty bad drek happen there, that she was just glad to be out of it. I dunno what happened, though. She didn't offer, and I didn't ask. Want me to talk to her?"

"No," Talon said. "I'll do it." He was supposed to be in charge of this team, that made it his job. He nodded in Boom's direction. "Start talking about what we're going to need for this job so we can tell Brackhaus—assuming you chummers are still interested." Everyone in the room nodded as Talon headed out the door.

He found Val standing on a balcony overlooking one of the Avalon's dance floors. Employees were cleaning up, stocking the bar, and getting the place ready for the customers who would begin packing the joint in a few more hours. Her jacket was thrown over the railing on which she leaned as she looked down at the darkened floor below.

"Val—" Talon began, but she cut him off.

"How do you handle it, Talon?"

"What?" Talon was taken aback by the question.

"The magic. How do you handle it?"

"You mean doing magic or being a mage?"

"Both," she said.

Talon shrugged. "I dunno. I just do. I learned to deal with it a long time ago, and I learned to use magic from a very good teacher. After that, I learned stuff in college and on the streets."

"Did you always want it?" Val asked.

Talon took a couple steps closer and stood next to her at the railing.

"No," he said. "I mean, every kid at one time or another wants to be Awakened, I guess, to find out they have the Talent. But when mine first showed up, I thought I was going crazy. I was just a kid at the time, fifteen, sixteen. I'd spent most of my life in a Catholic-run orphanage and my head was full of weird ideas about what magic was. When I started seeing things, feeling things, I figured I was losing it, or maybe even that there was something really wrong with me."

"But you figured out how to deal with it," Val said, not looking at him. "You're a mage now."

"With some time, and a lot of help."

"I never figured out how to handle it," she said quietly.

"You . . . you have the Talent?" Talon asked, stunned. He'd never gotten any hint of magical ability from Val.

She shook her head. "Had, not have. I did have it, though, once." She took a shuddering breath and let it out slowly, leaning more heavily against the railing. "You were raised Catholic. Well, I can tell you, that's nothing compared to where I grew up. Ever heard of Westphalia?"

Talon nodded. "Theocracy, isn't it? In the German Alliance?"

"Right in one," Val said glumly. "Though most of the traditional religions managed to deal with the

Awakening sooner or later, the church in Westphalia became a refuge for all the true die-hards who were convinced that the Awakened were the spawn of Satan, that magic was evil. They broke off from the rest of Germany to protect themselves from the corruption they saw in the rest of the world. Total religious fanatics. I grew up there."

Talon kept his mouth shut and just let Val talk.

"When I was about fifteen, I started seeing things. Little things at first, then more and more. I could tell what people were feeling, just by looking at them, and I didn't always like what I saw. If I'd just kept my mouth shut . . . but I couldn't. I didn't know what was happening to me. I didn't know any better. I told my father and he took me to the parish priest, who told him that I had the devil in me, that I was possessed. They performed exorcisms, and prayed, and carried on, but they couldn't make the visions stop. I could sense how much they feared me, even my own family.

"I just couldn't take it. So I left. I ran away. I managed to get out of Westphalia and into the German Alliance. I went to the Rhine-Ruhr Megaplex and met up with some people there. Ever been?"

Talon shook his head. Val smiled slightly and looked down again at the dance floor, lost in memory.

"It's quite a place, one of the biggest cities there is. Makes Boston look like a town. You can get just about anything you want, provided you've got the cred and you can protect yourself from the other predators who might try to take it away from you.

"I wasn't so lucky," she said. "I ended up in some

bad scenes. You know: chips, hustling, doing whatever you've got to do to stay alive." Her slim fingers caressed the chrome-lipped jack behind her ear. "I don't remember a lot of it. Sometimes I had trouble telling what was real and what was just a sim I was jacking. I probably would have died if somebody hadn't helped me out, kind of like how Jase helped you, Talon.

"Her name was Estelle, and she was amazing. She was a witch. A lot of people went to her for advice, for card-readings, herbal remedies, drek like that. She saw that I had a touch of the Talent. She helped get me off the streets and off the chips. It was hard, really hard, kicking the chips. I was so afraid of dealing with reality, but she helped me through it. Eventually, I managed to get clean.

"Estelle had some friends, people who worked in the underground: neo-anarchists, shadowrunners, witches, that sort. They helped to smuggle food, medicine, and tech to different places in the Alliance, especially Berlin, past the government and corporate cordons. I started helping them out. Turned out I was really good working with the beat-up vehicles they had. I'd always had a knack for mechanical things, even as a kid, but my father didn't think little girls should get their hands dirty. I loved working on those old crates. They were held together with spit and bailing wire, but we kept them running.

"Along the way, 'Stelle tried to teach me some magic. I really gave her a hard time. I was still so freaked out about it. I mean, I saw Estelle and her friends do magic, and it wasn't that scary when they did it, but every time I tried to learn to do something, all I could think about was the priest yelling about how the devil had my soul and how my father looked at me like I was something . . . something disgusting to him." Tears ran down Val's cheeks, and Talon was tempted to reach out and brush them away, but he stayed where he was, listening to her story.

"I got more and more into the rigging side of things; learning to drive just about anything, working with the border runners to bring in supplies for the black market, dodging patrols and having a blast. I lived for the rush of it, and knowing I was doing some good. Eventually, I decided to use the cred and the contacts I'd built up to get the cyberware to rig for real. Estelle tried to convince me not to, said it would damage my Talent beyond repair. I didn't care. I didn't want it, I couldn't deal with it. We fought like cats and dogs about it. Finally, I left. I went to Berlin and got my brain re-wired, got a rigger link and some other cyber. There was plenty of demand in Europe for a good rigger who knew how to get past border patrols.

"It was almost like the chips," she said softly. "Jacking into a car or a chopper and feeling it like it was my own body. The rush I got from rigging was the best thing in the world. I noticed after a while that my visions went away altogether, but I didn't really care. I was kind of glad they were gone.

"After a while, I hooked up with a mage, Geist." Val smiled ruefully and snorted a laugh. "Funny, I always seem to end up running into mages who change my life." She glanced over at Talon.

"Anyway, Geist and I were hot and heavy for a

while, about two months. After that, we realized we were totally wrong for each other, but that we worked well together. We pulled some runs in the UCAS with Hammer and ended up in Boston. Hammer convinced us to stay, and things around here were just heating up, so we did. Geist bought it on a run against one of Villiers' companies a few years back when Fuchi came apart in '59. I stayed with the team. You pretty much know the rest."

Val folded her arms along the railing and leaned her head forward, as if all the talking had exhausted her. The tears were drying, and she seemed tired. "I haven't thought about Germany for years, or what I lost there. Lately, though, working with you, I wonder sometimes what might have been if I hadn't decided to throw away what I had. I'm a damn good rigger, and I love doing what I do, but sometimes I can't help but wonder about the magic . . ." She shrugged, as if to end the whole train of thought.

Talon took advantage of the moment to speak.

"Look, Val," he said. "If you don't want to take this run, I understand. You do what you've got to do, nobody's going to say otherwise. But we could really use someone who knows her way around Germany, and this job is going to take a lot of sophisticated surveillance if we're going to track down our target in any kind of reasonable time. So, if you know a good rigger . . ." He left the rest unsaid.

Val straightened up, looked Talon in the eye, and smiled a bit. "I don't know anyone better than me."

Talon smiled. "Neither do I. I'll settle for second best."

"You don't have to," Val said. "I'm in."

"You don't—"

"Yes I do," she said. "You need me for this one. Besides, it's been a long time since I've been back home."

Talon nodded. "All right then. Let's do this." He put his arm around Val's shoulders and they walked back to Boom's office, where the rest of the team was discussing how to spend their expense account for the run. Mr. Brackhaus had been quite generous on that score, which told Talon this run was serious business as far as Saeder-Krupp was concerned. He just hoped that, when all was said and done, none of them would regret taking on the job.

5

Talon wasn't overly fond of airports. They were too exposed, too open, and there were too many people. Not that he expected trouble at this one, quite the contrary. Modern airports like Logan International in Boston were sterling examples of modern twenty-first-century security measures. Since they were also a favorite target of terrorists of all stripes, government and corporate security was tightest at the various ports of entry and exit, especially international airports. That was what worried Talon.

Technically, he and his four "traveling companions" were "terrorists" by a lot of definitions. As much as corporations found them useful, shadowrunners were criminals. Not only non-persons, but the very "dangerous elements" that security forces watched out for. Even with a top-grade fake ID in his pocket, Talon always felt exposed whenever he walked into an airport. He sensed numerous eyes on him, checking him over from a distance, and he focused on using his training and experience to look like just another corporate suit heading out on a business trip.

"Is it me," Trouble said quietly, "or have they increased security around here lately?"

"Not you," Talon replied. "Ever since Novatech set up shop in Boston, things have gotten tighter. It's brought in a lot more corporate competition, and that attracts plenty of wackos."

"You mean, like us?" Trouble said with an impish smile.

"Exactly."

Talon and Trouble walked together through the terminal toward their flight. They looked like any other couple, or perhaps a corporate exec and an assistant (Talon wondered who people would think was which). He had a soft-sided nylon bag slung over his shoulder, while Trouble carried a hard-sided briefcase. Both wore conservative, corporate-style clothing. Talon was in a gray suit over a burgundy shirt with a Mandarin collar and no tie, as was fashionable among many younger corporate employees. Trouble looked sharp in a gray skirt, short jacket, and dark green blouse. With the chrome hints of datajacks on both of them, they presented the perfect image of corporate conformity.

Talon could hear Boom and Hammer somewhere behind them. The troll and the ork walked together, talking and joking loudly, drawing occasional stares from the people around them. It wasn't that trolls or orks were an unusual sight in a large airport, but the fact that Boom insisted on wearing the loudest shirt he could find and talking with Hammer in deep tones that carried considerably. For all the world, the two appeared to be two metahuman chummers gabbing about a wild vacation they were embarking on.

While Talon preferred to blend in, the big troll hid in plain sight. "When you look like me," Boom said, "subtlety isn't your best choice." Talon supposed that it worked. People would recall the outrageously clad, loud-mouthed troll, but they would be hard-pressed to remember any significant details. The whole thing would be out of their minds once Boom passed, leaving people shaking their heads and wondering about "those wacky metahumans."

Val walked by herself, nondescript in jeans and leather jacket, keeping quiet and blending with the crowd. Talon would have preferred for someone to accompany her, but Val wanted to be alone, and he respected that. He was just glad she'd decided to come along. Talon thought about the things Val had told him at the Avalon and wondered how well he might deal with returning to a place that carried such memories. It was only a year since Talon had returned to Boston to face demons from his own past, so he could imagine what this was like for Val. It was something she could only get through on her own.

Black-clad Knight Errant personnel handled general security for the airport, and the lines at the security checkpoint were moving fairly briskly. Talon moved up to the head of the line and presented his credstick to a bored-looking security guard standing next to the scanning archway and x-ray machinery. The guard slotted the stick into the small data-reader he carried, glancing at the information displayed on the screen, then up at Talon and back again. The information on the credstick identified Talon as Andrew Nolan, a wagemage working for Novatech. Owning up to his magical abilities made it easier for Talon to conceal their full extent from any magicians or guardian spirits that might be watching, without having to conceal them entirely.

"Do you have anything to declare, Mr. Nolan?" the guard asked.

"Indeed I do," Tal replied, hefting his shoulder bag.

The guard nodded. "Please place the bag on the moving belt and go on through," he said. Talon did as he was told. The scanning arch swept an invisible MRI scan through his body as he stepped through it. It would pick up the cyberware in his head: datajack, internal memory, cellular link, and so forth. There was nothing there out of the ordinary for a mid-level corporate employee, and all of it was registered in the identification he gave. There was probably some sort of astral scan as well, but Talon wasn't concerned about that. Having magical abilities wasn't illegal, and his ID showed him to be a registered and licensed magician. There was nothing incriminating for an astral observer to detect.

On the other side of the arch, another uniformed guard took Talon's shoulder bag off the belt.

"Could you open this please, sir?" she asked.

"Of course," Talon said. He unzipped the bag and presented it to the guard. Sitting on top of the folded clothes and other sundries was an ornate dagger with a jeweled, golden hilt in a sheath of tooled leather. The guard took a nylon pouch from under the counter and presented it to Talon.

"Please place your magical devices in here," she said, glancing at the dagger like it was a snake. Talon accepted the bag, picked up Talonclaw, and dropped it carefully inside. Several other small items followed the blade. Then he pulled off the adhesive strip and sealed it. The guard placed a bar code on the outside of the bag and had Talon sign a datapad before carefully placing the bag in a plastic bin behind her. Enchanted items, particularly weapons, were carefully controlled, especially after some unfortunate incidents years ago, when Awakened terrorists used magic to destroy or hijack flights. Talon knew his dagger would be carefully examined for any signs of dangerous spells or other enchantments. Andrew Nolan was registered to carry and use a weapon focus against magical threats, so again there was nothing incriminating about the blade for anyone to find. Still, Talon hated entrusting the weapon to the airport handlers. There was a good chance he would need Talonclaw's power before this run was over, so he sure wasn't about to leave it at home.

At least Aracos didn't have to go on the plane with them. Talon could just imagine his ally's complaints at the indignities of air travel, to say nothing of the food. No, Aracos returned to his home in the depths of the metaplanes before the team arrived at the airport. Only once they were safely in Germany would Talon summon him again. He sometimes wondered what it was that spirits like Aracos did when they were back "home," away from the physical world altogether. Aracos was remarkably unrevealing on that score. All he would say is "stuff," and Talon chose not to press his familiar for more detailed information.

Trouble likewise stopped to check in with the female security guard, yielding up her cyberdeck for examination and certifying that it contained no illegal or contraband data. Her identification said she was Mary O'Connel, corporate data-specialist, and licensed to carry a sophisticated cyberdeck. The Novatech casing on the deck made it look legit, and Trouble had installed enough baffles and masking programs to cover up the cyberdeck's expanded functions. Besides, the guards were far more interested in making sure it wasn't a bomb in disguise than in the possibilities of computer crime. The deck quickly passed inspection and they were on their way.

Talon grinned as he heard Boom behind them, loudly greeting the security guard who asked for his identification like they were long-lost friends.

The flight to the Rhine-Ruhr megaplex was a suborbital, so they were able to avail themselves of the first-class passenger lounge while they waited for the boarding call.

"I've gotta give the boss one thing," Talon said to Trouble as he picked up the German-import beer and poured it into the heavy glass mug left by the bartender. "He certainly doesn't skimp on the travel budget."

"Or on the accommodations," Trouble agreed. "We've got a corporate condo waiting for us, probably the nicest place we've ever stayed in." They were talking about Herr Brackhaus, of course, but kept any names or references to their real business out of it, just in case anyone was listening. Even the sparsely populated lounge was too public a place in which to discuss shadow-biz. Until they were safely inside a vehicle or other safe space in Germany, they had to stay in character.

Eventually, an attendant announced the boarding of their flight, and Talon&Co made their way to the umbilical tube connecting the terminal to the waiting suborbital. Crossing the transpex tube toward the passenger compartment, Talon was struck by the sheer size of the spaceplane. It measured easily the length of a football field, and was aerodynamically curved like a wave frozen in motion and cast in metal. The hull was sleek, with stubby wings and massive SCRAMjets that allowed the craft to fly at speeds in the neighborhood of Mach 20, at an altitude just shy of low-orbital distance. Most of the plane's bulk was taken up by the massive jets and the equally massive amounts of fuel they consumed.

Inside, the passenger compartment was much like any other aircraft except there were no windows. Instead, flat trideo screens occupied spaces on the walls and the backs of the seats, allowing passengers a view of the outside world from several different angles, as well as an expansive menu of entertainment and telecommunications options.

Everyone settled into their seats, and Talon was sure that Boom and Hammer were pleased to be traveling first class. The seats were large enough to accommodate even Boom's broad, bulky frame—a pleasant change, since public transportation wasn't always designed with larger or smaller metahumans in mind. The flight attendants advised the passengers on the suborbital's safety features, including a warning to Awakened passengers not to use magic during the flight, since it was prohibited by international aviation regulations. Then they proceeded to serve beverages and bland packages of snack foods as the spaceplane prepared for takeoff.

In short order, they were underway. Talon watched on the side viewscreen as the ground dropped away sharply, the Boston sprawl shrinking to become a toy model as the vast blue expanse of the Atlantic stretched before them. When the spaceplane achieved sufficient altitude, the pilot kicked in the SCRAMjets, and Talon recalled just what "steep" and "fast" meant.

The public address system beeped, and the captain's voice filled the cabin. "Ladies and gentlemen, we've reached our cruising altitude of 23,000 meters, proceeding at 29,000 kilometers per hour. At present speed we should reach our destination in the German Alliance at approximately 14:15, local time. Have a pleasant flight."

Talon called up the chronometer function of his headware, and the time appeared in cool blue numbers on the edge of his field of vision: 07:04:12. He sent a mental command to the chronometer to adjust to the European time zone, which changed the hour to 13:04:15. That left a flight time of just over an hour from Boston to Germany. Not bad.

Settling back into his seat, Talon turned to Trouble. "Do you have the datafiles on Germany?" he asked. "I'll check them over on the way."

"You could have read them last night, like everyone else," Trouble said with a smile. She took a datachip from one of the pockets in her briefcase and handed it to him. Talon slipped it into the slot next to the display screen on the back of the chair in front of him, then pulled out a length of cable from under the dataport and snapped one end into the jack behind his ear. Full hypertext data unfolded in front of him, allowing Talon to review the files Trouble had compiled on the German Alliance and the Rhine-Ruhr Megaplex. Talon had never been to Germany before, and it paid to be prepared. He downloaded the basic German language files into his headware memory, as the program recommended, then began scanning through the history files. As he expected, they were very complete.

The German Alliance was formed in 2045, out of the dozen or so nation-states left over from the breakup of the Republic of Germany. The first decade of the twenty-first century saw no end of trouble for Germany: economic collapse of the industrial Ruhr area, ecological disasters in the North Sea and other regions as poisonous chemicals from landfills and dumping grounds leeched into the soil and water. The unrest created by these disasters led to the formation of new political groups agitating for change in the German government. The numerous rival factions eventually managed to divide political control of the country among them in a fragile coalition that lasted only a few short years before collapsing into chaos, widespread strikes, and country-wide riots.

A military junta briefly seized control of the German government, before the first wave of Virally Induced Toxic Allergy Syndrome swept across Europe. The government clamped down on the riots that followed, and millions of people died from the deadly disease. It was followed closely by the coming of the Awakening in late 2011, when the power of magic returned to the world. Creatures out of myth and legend appeared in the wilderness and in desolate areas of the cities. Changeling children were born to human parents, the births initially blamed on the toxic contamination of soil and water. Most importantly, some individuals began to display "paranormal" abilities, the ability to use magic.

These events helped accelerate the decay of German society. The government, echoing an earlier era, was forced to build a wall around the city of Berlin and the surrounding area to contain the violence and increasing terrorist attacks on the nation's capitol. Eventually, the government was forced to abandon Berlin altogether, giving the city over to anarchy and moving the seat of government to Hanover, in the North German League. Decades later, Berlin was still a virtual anarchy, a haven for political dissidents, smugglers, and criminals, along with all the many inhabitants unable to escape the grip of the city's economic depression.

In 2031, the Russians attacked Europe, desperate for the resources necessary to shore up their failing economy. The EuroWars lasted for years, with the various German states managing to unite to fight off the Russian army, with aid from their few European allies. Eventually, the conflict drew in most of the nations of Europe, until the Russian advance was broken in 2033.

The EuroWars were the culmination of all the disasters Germany had suffered over the past three decades. The nation fragmented into numerous small nation-states, each with its own interests and agenda. Some of these states were dominated by new races of metahumans who emerged during the Awakening;

elves in the Duchy of Pomorya, trolls in the Kingdom of the Black Forest. Berlin remained a "free city," homeland of anarchy. It took many years for the battered remnants of the old Republic of Germany to pull themselves back together.

One of the driving forces of the reunification was Saeder-Krupp, the world's largest megacorporation, which grew from an alliance of powerful corporations in the early twenty-first century. Saeder-Krupp's headquarters was in the Northrhine-Ruhr region of Germany, in the city-sprawl of Essen. Saeder-Krupp was run by Lofwyr, the great dragon who first appeared shortly after the Awakening to stake a claim to power in Europe. Through a series of brilliant stock manipulations, aided by an astounding store of gold and silver, the dragon leveraged a buyout of several major European corporations, bringing them together to form the Saeder-Krupp corporate empire.

One of the corporation's stated goals was the restoration of a shattered Europe, particularly Germany. Aided by Saeder-Krupp's economic clout, the German states managed to pull together and form the Allianz Deutscher Länder, the Alliance of German States, to replace the old Federal Republic of Germany. Since then, the Alliance remained reasonably stable and devoted to Lofwyr's goal of European Restoration.

Of course, there were those who didn't agree with the goal of rebuilding Europe according to the designs of politicians, corporations, and the dragon who dominated them. Europe—Germany, in particular—was rife with policlubs that opposed the Restoration and supported a policy of Europa Dividus, which called for maintaining the independence and individual cultures of the various European nation-states. Many groups even opposed the German Alliance, preferring the independent anarchy of its member states. Some of the policlubs used terrorism to make their point, including Alt Welt, the "Old World." That was the policlub to which the man seen talking with Dr. Goronay was believed to belong. The data Trouble dug up on Alt Welt was a good seven years out of date. They were believed to be defunct, or nearly so, but apparently they weren't.

The Rhine-Ruhr Megaplex, home to the world headquarters of Saeder-Krupp, was a microcosm of Germany itself: a collection of independent cities, fused together by mutual need and circumstance. Home to some 25 million people, centering around the cities of Cologne, Düsseldorf, Dortmund, and Essen, the home of the massive Saeder-Krupp arcology. The megaplex dwarfed the sprawling metroplexes of North America, unless you subscribed to the theory that the entire east coast of the UCAS, from DeeCee to Boston, was really nothing more than a single city-sprawl, broken up into neighborhoods. Even the vast Seattle sprawl was tiny by comparison to the Rhine-Ruhr, having slightly more than a tenth its population. Finding one man in a giant city of 25 million wasn't going to be easy. Talon realized that Brackhaus was definitely going to get his money's worth.

The captain's voice caught Talon's attention as he finished going through his spiel.

"Ladies and gentlemen, we are about fifteen minutes from our destination at Düsseldorf's Lohausen Airport. We will be landing shortly. Thank you for choosing UCASAir. On behalf of your flight crew, we would like to welcome you to the German Alliance. Please enjoy your trip."

6

The view across the Baltic Sea was breathtaking from the balcony of Duke Jaromar's private residence in Königssthul, but Speren had no time to truly appreciate its beauty. He was on a mission for his Prince, and his duty took precedence over all other considerations. Still, the view was a pleasant one, and made the waiting he was forced to endure more bearable.

He'd made his way to Pomoryan, the small duchy in the northernmost reaches of the German Alliance, solely to speak with Jaromar. Although carefully neutral in political matters, the elven-controlled Duchy of Pomoryan had been known to trade favors with the Princes of Tir Tairngire in the past. Of course, they also forged political alliances with Tir na nÓg, Tir Tairngire's political rival across the Atlantic, in the nearby British Isles. Tir na nÓg was considerably closer to Pomoryan, but to date, the tiny Duchy had not attracted too much attention from either elven power, which seemed to be the duke's preference.

"Herr Silverblade, my apologies for keeping you waiting," came a voice from behind Speren. He turned to see the duke himself standing in the open doorway onto the balcony. Duke Jaromar Grief was tall, like most elves, with a thin, almost emaciated form. His dark hair was neatly combed back from a high forehead that spoke of intellect, and his small beard was neatly trimmed. He was dressed in clothing nearly as archaic as Speren's own: a deep blue frock coat over a blue waistcoat stamped with gold leaf designs. Foamy lace showed at his collar and cuffs. He wore tight-fitting pants tucked into polished black riding boots, which were spattered with mud. From that, and the riding crop he held in his hands, Speren concluded that the duke had been out on a morning ride.

Jaromar touched the fingers of his left hand to his chest and bowed slightly by way of greeting. Speren copied the gesture, bowing a bit deeper, as was fitting when greeting someone of the duke's stature. Jaromar was not as powerful as the Princes of Speren's homeland, but he was still the ruler of his own kingdom, and that made him worthy of respect.

"Please, Your Grace," Speren replied, "it is I who apologize for intruding on your household. However, I have come about a matter of some urgency."

"I am always pleased to assist my noble cousins of the Land of Promise," the duke replied smoothly. "Please, won't you come in and join me? I was about to have breakfast." Speren nodded and followed as the duke went back inside.

The manor of Königssthul was nowhere near as splendid as the Royal Palace in Tir Tairngire, nor even as lavish as the duke's official residence in the capitol city of Saßnitz, but it was still quite large, and charming in its own way. As they walked, the duke described to Speren how the manor house had been restored from an earlier existing structure not long after he had assumed the role of duke. The house was surrounded by acres of land along the shores of the Baltic Sea, and the duke kept a stable of horses, for he was an avid equestrian.

Jaromar led Speren into a dining room dominated by a long hardwood table, easily capable of seating two dozen. Crystal chandeliers hung from the plastered ceiling, and one wall was dominated by a tall tapestry hanging from a brass rod; on it was woven a rampant griffin in gold on a field of deepest blue. The curtains were drawn back from the high windows at the far end of the room, filling the chamber with light. Speren could already see that the table was set for two, with crisp white linens, fine china, and silverware.

A human servant wearing the duke's livery appeared with a bootjack to help remove Jaromar's muddied riding boots, exchanging them for a pair of soft house slippers. Speren had already surrendered his sword upon entering the manor. He now yielded up his cloak to the servant, who disappeared through one of the many doors surrounding the room as the duke settled himself at the head of the table and gestured toward the chair at his right.

"Please, join me," he said, and Speren sat down. Another servant brought covered platters and trays of food to the table and began serving as the duke leaned back in his chair and regarded Speren.

"So, then, what brings you to my humble home, Herr Silverblade?"

"You may call me Speren, Your Grace."

"Very well, and you may call me Jaromar. We are

all brothers here, after all." The duke dismissed the servant with a wave of his hand. "Do try the sausages," he said. "My cook prepares them specially."

Speren looked down at his plate. The slices of sausage, poached eggs covered in creamy sauce, and roasted potatoes were hardly the sort of food he was used to at home. He found it a wonder that Jaromar maintained his emaciated physique if this was his regular fare. Speren took up knife and fork and began neatly cutting up the food while he talked.

"Very well, Jaromar. My Prince, Jenna Ni'Ferra, has dispatched me on a matter of some . . . delicacy," he began. "Of late, word has reached her of the activities of a political organization in the German Alliance, an organization opposed to the interests of Tir Tairngire, a group known as Alt Welt."

The duke dabbed at his lip with a linen napkin. "Yes, yes, I know of them. Political agitators opposed to the Reconstruction, though hardly of any great concern. I find it surprising that Prince Jenna would consider them any threat to the Land of Promise."

"Hardly a threat," Speren said. "As you say, they are only a small group. But one of their political targets is Saeder-Krupp, and that is of concern to the Council of Princes."

"Because of the dragon," the duke said with a distinct note of distaste, putting aside his fork. "Why does Jenna Ni'Ferra send her liege man to investigate something connected with Lofwyr? Surely the dragon has servants and watchers enough to deal with a problem in his own back yard."

"I cannot say, Jaromar. I can tell you only what my Prince has commanded me to do. She requires more information about the organization, and I have been dispatched to gather it. I have been told that you have assisted us in the past, and I can assure you that she would be most appreciative of your help in this matter."

Jaromar sat back in his chair and considered. For a moment, Speren thought he'd given away too much. Certainly Jaromar was suspicious, but as yet he had nothing to put with his suspicions to come to a conclusion, and there was a great deal more to be gained from cooperation than there was from obstinacy. Additionally, although Speren had not said so, it was well known that Jenna was no supporter of Lofwyr, nor was Jaromar. If the Prince wanted information on political dissidents opposed to Lofwyr's plans for European Restoration, it could only be as a thorn in the dragon's side. Speren, of course, had no such designs, but let Jaromar think what he pleased, so long as it got him what he needed.

The duke's thin face split into an oily smile. "Of course, I would be delighted to assist the inquires of the Prince in any way I can," he said smoothly. "I have friends in other parts of the Alliance. I will contact them and see what I can learn that may assist you."

"My thanks," Speren said, inclining his head in a slight nod. "First I will need whatever information you can provide about the organization's history and its known members."

"Of course, of course," the duke said, with a wave of his hand. "I'll see that you're provided with whatever it is you require. Anything to assist Prince Jenna.

I hope the information I have will be useful in fulfilling your duties, paladin."

Speren speared a slice of sausage on his plate and raised it in salute of the duke.

"I'm sure it will be, Jaromar. I'm sure it will."

7

"Alt Welt," Trouble said. "German policlub, meaning 'Old World.' Supporters of a policy known as 'Europa Dividus,' keeping the nations of Europe separate and independent following the EuroWars. Fairly active on-line with information sites, various political tracts, and email lists to organize political protests, things like that."

The team was settled into the small condoplex in Düsseldorf, going over the data Trouble had gathered on their target. Trouble stood near the head of the table in the small dining room, the flexible viewscreen of her cyberdeck rolled out to display various images and datafiles as she talked. She directed the images through the slim fiber-optic cable slotted into the jack behind her ear.

Talon, Boom, and Hammer sat around the table, listening carefully to the report. Each of them had already reviewed the information at least once before leaving Boston or on the flight to Europe, but this was the first time they'd gone over it all as a group.

"And no indications Alt Welt has any ties to terrorist organizations?" Talon asked. That was part of the data that puzzled him.

"Nothing definite," Trouble said. "On the surface, they're just another policlub."

"Yeah, and the Universal Brotherhood was just another crackpot religion," Boom muttered to himself.

Trouble shrugged. "That's the thing. If Alt Welt does have terrorist ties, they're pretty well hidden. I did as much digging as I could in the Matrix, but the information there is limited. The German grid is a hopeless patchwork anyway. Finding useful data among all the government servers is like looking for a needle in a haystack. I might be able to dig up more now that we're here."

"So, we still don't know why a group like Alt Welt would be interested in whatever it is Professor Goronay's got to sell," Talon mused.

"Well, considering we don't even know what he's selling, that's not saying much," Hammer put in.

"True," Talon said. "Okay, put Alt Welt on hold for a while. What's the scan on Goronay?"

Trouble blinked for a second, her eyes refocusing, and a new image appeared on the cyberdeck's screen. It was a head-shot of an older man, his hair gone nearly white and thinning above a broad forehead. Bushy brows nearly met above clear, intelligent blue eyes framed by wire-rimmed glasses. He had a full beard, the same color as his hair, and a fairly prominent nose. His craggy features were weathered and ruddy from years spent in the outdoors, and Talon could almost see him with a pipe clenched between his teeth as he spoke or lectured.

"Alexi Goronay," Trouble said. "Professor of Archeology at the University of Kiev, Russia. Age sixty-one. Born in St. Petersburg, educated in Moscow and

Kiev. The picture is from the University records. Goronay has worked at different archeological sites all over the world, and is considered an expert in his field. Has, among other things, published papers postulating the existence of magic-using cultures before the Awakening."

"Interesting theory," Talon said.

"Are you saying Goronay thinks magic existed before the Awakening?" Hammer asked.

Trouble jumped in before Talon could say anything. "Lots of people do, apparently. Archeologists like Goronay believe that a lot of myths and legends about magic, along with all the magical lore that existed before the Awakening, is left over from some distant time in the past when magic worked. For some reason, the magic went away, and all we were left with were the myths, stories, and traditions handed down over the centuries until 2011, when the magic came back."

"You *have* been reading," Talon said with a grin.

"Naturally," Trouble replied. "You don't have to be Awakened to pick up on the theory. Even we mundanes can do it."

"Touché."

"So why'd the magic go away?" Boom asked. "And why did it come back?"

Trouble glanced at Talon, who just shrugged. "Who knows?" she said. "It's only a theory, and nobody can really explain it. But then, nobody can really explain why magic started working again in 2011, either."

"There's all sorts of theories," Talon said, "and most of them involve a lot of chaos mathematics and drek like that. Suffice to say that right now nobody really has a clue. It's just the way things are."

"Magic." Boom gave a slight shudder. "You just never know, where it's concerned."

Talon thought the comment strange coming from a being who would have been considered "magical" not so many years ago. Then he thought about what it must be like to be a troll or an ork. For them, magic might be more of a raw deal than it was for a magician like Talon, and not something they'd want to put their trust in.

"That's pretty much it," Trouble said, blanking the viewscreen and pulling the plug from her datajack. "You've all seen the rest of the file on Goronay and there's not much else to say. He was married, but his wife's been dead for eight years. They have no children, no other living relatives. He's not political, which is typical for most academics. His papers haven't stirred up any major controversies, except maybe among a few fellow academics. No shady past, no indications of any skeletons hidden in his closet."

"What about medical records?" Talon asked. "Anything that might suggest why he'd go crazy like that?"

Trouble shook her head and rolled the cyberdeck's viewscreen back into its case. "Nada. I managed to get hold of his medical files through the University's insurance provider. He's in good health, goes for regular checkups. Doesn't smoke, drinks moderately, and keeps in shape. No history of psychological problems of any kind, apart from the fact that apparently he's not terribly social. Nothing out of sorts for an elderly university professor."

"Damn," Talon said quietly. "That doesn't make things any—" The sound of the door opening carried into the room, and every member of the team was immediately on his or her feet, hands hovering close to their weapons.

"Its okay, guys, it's just Val," came the voice of Aracos from out of the air.

"I wish he wouldn't do that," Hammer muttered to Talon, who ignored the comment and silently told the spirit to do the same.

"Thanks, Aracos," he said aloud.

Val came into the room and glanced over at Talon. Her face was tightly controlled, not showing any sign of what she was feeling, and Talon resisted the urge to use his magical senses to read her aura to find out.

"Well?" he said.

"She'll see us," Val said. "I set up a meet for two hours from now."

"How many?"

"Just you and me. If it's more than that, she won't come."

Talon nodded. "All right then. You guys keep working on the other angles while Val and I talk to her . . . contact, okay?"

"Check in after the meet," Trouble said. "If we don't hear from you, we'll come looking."

Talon tapped the side of his head and grinned.

"No problem. I'll give you a buzz on the commlink when I've got something, and I'll bring Aracos along to keep an eye on things. He can always come back and let you chummers know if something happens."

"Like you could leave me behind," his ally spoke into Talon's mind.

"What's it called again?" Talon asked as Val drove them along the winding road out of Düsseldorf, toward the outskirts of the plex.

"Zombietown," Val said. "That's what most people call it."

"Sounds charming."

"Oh, it is," she said with an ironic smile. "But it's also pretty lawless, at least in the lower levels. There's not much chance of running into any unexpected problems with the local law down there."

"So it's something like the Ork Underground in Seattle?"

Val shrugged. "Couldn't say. I've never seen it."

"It's an interesting place," Talon said. "Remind me to tell you about it sometime."

Val took a moment before she spoke. "You know, we haven't really talked much since you got us together," she said.

It was Talon's turn to shrug. "My loss. It's just that you never seemed all that interested in talking, and I try to stay out of people's personal business. Force of habit."

"I understand," she said. "It's not a criticism. I just wanted to say . . . well, thank you for the talk we had at the Avalon, and for letting me come on this run."

"Null sheen," Talon said. "I appreciate your help."

"This will be a good thing," Val said, almost to herself. "It's something I've needed to do for a long time."

Talon wondered who she was trying to convince,

him or herself. There was a moment of uncomfortable silence in the car as Val guided it smoothly along at speeds that probably would have gotten them pulled over immediately in Boston (assuming such speeds were even possible on any of the city's congested roads).

"So, tell me more about this 'zombietown' place," Talon finally said.

"Its real name is Wuppertal, built up around the Wupper River. About forty years ago or so, the government decided to handle the area's overcrowding by simply building right over the whole river valley. The city covers the valley, and the river runs under it. Concrete pillars and support structures divide the undercity into four levels that descend down to the old riverbank. The lower levels have artificial light and ventilation systems to bring in clean air from above, but it still tends to stink down there.

"Because the undercity only has artificial light, it's attracted a lot of metahumans who can't take natural sunlight. They live down there, along with a lot of norms who come for the cheap rents and whatever work is available. The ones who don't find jobs get pushed down to the lower levels, where things are even cheaper. The lowest level has a lot of squatters and cast-offs, who probably don't have much chance of finding their way out again."

Talon shook his head sadly. "Like I said, sounds charming. And your friend is going to meet us there?"

Val nodded. "There are plenty of places to meet in Zombietown where we won't be overheard. Estelle prefers it that way."

"Do you really think she can help us?" Talon asked.

"I don't know if she will," Val said, "but if anyone knows the ins and outs of the Alliance and all the policlubs, it's 'Stelle. She's respected by a lot of people in the shadows."

There was a note of pain in her voice that made Talon want to ask if Val was all right with this, but he decided to leave it alone. Val would deal with things in her own way. If she wanted to talk about it, she would.

The Krystalnacht Club was near the lowest level of the underground city, reachable through a rat's maze of narrow corridors lit by flickering electrical lights, its stagnant air pushed slowly around by giant ventilation fans. The entrance led down several steps into the sunken club floor. A bar curved around one side of it like a coiled snake, while tables filled the rest of the establishment. There was a small stage where a pair of scantily clad elven dancers gyrated slowly, almost trancelike, and a few tables where various dice and card games were going on, to considerably more interest than the dancers.

The whole of it was lit by neon signs adorning the walls and by dim track lighting on the ceiling. Tall panels of glass glazed in a cracked, spider web pattern broke up the walls and refracted the colored light from behind them, casting strange shadows over everything.

Talon let Val lead the way into the club as he had through most of Wuppertal. The undercity was a maze, but Val navigated it as if she had lived there all her life. Talon wondered how much time she'd spent here before deciding to leave Germany, but she wasn't making any more small talk. Talon, too, preferred to keep alert for anything that might be lurking in the shadowy alleys and dark corners of the underground.

Val stopped at the top of the stairs leading down into the club and slowly scanned the room. Then she descended the steps, with Talon close behind. The pair of them drew curious glances from the various club-goers, who almost instantly turned back to their drinks, their games, and the gyrations of the dancers. Like anywhere else in the shadows, too much curiosity in a place like the Krystalnacht could be dangerous.

Val led Talon to a corner booth where a woman sat, alone. She looked human, with blond hair pulled back into a thick braid at the base of her skull. There were a few streaks of gray in it, worn like proud badges of a life hard-won. Her face was handsome rather than pretty, with solid features, a firm mouth, and blue eyes like the depths of a frozen lake. There were a few crow's feet around her eyes, some lines around her mouth, giving her an air of maturity. She wore a dark, heavy cloak of forest green, almost black in the dim light of the club. Underneath was a sturdy-looking tunic and leather vest. Both hands rested on the table in front of her, the fingers long and slender, the nails trimmed short. A gold ring carved in the shape of twining vines and leaves gleamed from her right hand.

"Estelle," Val said to the woman, "this is Talon." She spoke in German, which the language chip downloaded into Talon's headware translated for him. "Talon, this is Lady Estelle."

Talon nodded to the woman and felt the force of her gaze.

"She's definitely a mage, boss, and she's got some pretty serious mojo," Aracos said in Talon's mind. *"She either isn't bothering to hide it, or she's even tougher than she looks to me. She's also got some company close by. There's an air elemental hanging over the table. Looks pretty tough, too."*

"Could you take it out?" Talon thought.

"If I have to, but I'd rather not have to find out."

"Hopefully, it won't come to that."

"Your spirit is powerful," Estelle said by way of a greeting.

Talon wasn't sure whether she meant Aracos or his own spirit, so he simply nodded politely. "Thank you."

"Please sit," she said. Talon and then Val slid into the booth opposite Estelle. "Whatever you want must be quite important if it brings Val back here," she said, turning her attention to Val for the first time. "I recall you saying you never wanted to come back."

"I didn't," Val said. "But like you said, it's important. As I told you on the telecom, we need some information."

"What kind of information?"

Talon took a folded sheet of paper from inside his long coat, unfolded it, and held it out to Estelle.

"Information on either of these two men. The one on the right is Dr. Alexi Goronay. We've heard that the man on the left is a member of Alt Welt."

Estelle took the sheet of paper and looked at it for

a while. According to Val, the people Lady Estelle worked with weren't terribly fond of nationalist policlubs like Alt Welt, so Talon hoped she would be willing to tell them what she knew. If not for old times' sake where Val was concerned, then to frag off a rival policlub.

"You've been misled, then," Estelle said, dropping the paper on the table. "Alt Welt isn't a real power in Germany. It's little more than a sham, a front used by other policlubs to hide their activities and give the government and the authorities somewhere to focus their investigations. A few years ago, it was der Nachtmachen who were using it, now it looks like someone else is.

"This man," she said, pointing at the paper, "is a member of der Runenthing. Do you know of them?"

Talon shook his head.

"They're a sort of policlub," Val told him. "Actually, they're more of a magical lodge. They're devoted to worship of the Aesir, the old Norse-Teutonic gods, and to the preservation of ancient Aryan styles of magic, especially rune magic. They're also racist neo-Nazis who are against women, metahumans, foreigners, and pretty much anyone else who isn't a white Aryan male."

"Very good," Estelle said. "I'm surprised you remember so much."

"I've got a good memory," Val said.

"So I see. Must be all those computer chips you've had put into your brain."

Talon felt Val tense next to him and gently laid a hand on her knee. She relaxed slightly as he brought the talk back to the matter at hand.

"Do you know his name?" he asked, jerking his chin toward the printout.

"*Ja*," Estelle said. "I do. The question is, how much is that information worth to you?" She looked from Talon to Val and back again.

"Five hundred nuyen," Talon said quietly.

Estelle snorted in derision.

"Six hundred," Talon countered.

Eventually, they settled on an even thousand. Talon had been willing to go higher, but not much. After he took the money, in mylar hardcopy bills, from his coat and passed it quietly to Estelle, she counted it, then stashed it away under her cloak.

"His name is Heinrich Zoller. He is a *zauberer*, a mage, with der Runenthing. I know little else about him, apart form the fact that he is fairly wealthy and active politically in various neo-Nazi causes."

Talon nodded to Val, and the two of them slid out of the booth.

"Pleasure doing business with you," he said, and they began to walk away.

"Valkyrie," Estelle's voice called after them. "It was . . . nice to see you again."

Val didn't turn back as they continued to walk out of the Krystalnacht, but Talon could hear her muttering under her breath.

"Likewise, sister," she said.

8

"A mage, huh? That makes things more interesting."

Trouble slid onto the bed on the side opposite where Talon sat. She had just jacked herself out of her deck, where she'd been doing additional research on Runenthing and Heinrich Zoller.

"It always does," Talon mused aloud, keeping his eyes on the viewscreen folded out on the table in front of them.

Val sat in the middle, oblivious to the conversation going on around her. A slim optical cable ran from the jack behind her ear to the compact remote-control deck in her lap. Another cable ran across the floor to the small transmitter dish clipped to the windowsill. Val's eyes were closed, but open on the inside to the data being fed to her by her remote drone.

As they watched the screen, the drone was hovering over a neighborhood kilometers away, keeping watch on a residence registered to Heinrich Zoller. According to Trouble's Matrix research, Zoller used the apartment infrequently, but he'd been there recently. That made it the most likely place to start surveillance. The drone's video and audio pickups provided a clear picture of the whole area, capable of zooming in on any fine details as needed. It kept an internal high-resolution recording of everything it saw, beaming back a simsense signal to the control rig, which Val routed through the monitor so the others could watch the drone's progress. So far, things had been quiet.

"So, anything more on Zoller or the Runenthing?" Talon asked Trouble, leaning back on the bed. He thought surveillance and stakeouts were some of the worst parts of shadowruns, but they were necessary.

"More of a profile on the Runenthing," she said, "or the *Verband für Völkische Zauberel*, as they are officially called—the Association for National Sorcery, or something like that." Trouble stumbled over the pronunciation, but she wasn't currently using a language chip and didn't speak German. Talon had decided to shut his chip off for a while; the translations back and forth were starting to feel like having a linguistic tennis match going on in his head.

"Val's right, they're not nice folks. About the only good thing about them is that they recycle. They're strongly eco-conscious, big on protecting nature and things like that, but they also want to get back to the good old days when men carried swords and axes, women stayed at home and made babies, and the only trolls around came up out of the water to try and rip people's arms off and get slain by heroic warriors."

"Boom'll love that," Talon said. The troll and Hammer were currently out getting something to eat. Talon tried to picture his friend the cockney club owner as a mythological troll in some re-make of Beowulf. He couldn't imagine it without laughing.

"It gets better," Trouble said. "Like Val said, they're also into magic big time, but only a strictly Norse-Germanic brand of shamanism following the old Norse gods—no goddesses, of course—and they think every other spell-slinger on the planet is beneath them. Nice bunch of mages, according to the stuff on the German shadow nets."

"They're not mages," Talon said.

"Huh? Come again?"

"They're not mages," Talon repeated, propping himself up on his elbows. "You just said they were shamans. A shaman is a magician who follows a shamanic tradition of magic. A mage is a magician who follows a hermetic tradition, like me. If they're shamans, then they're not mages." It was a pet peeve of Talon's. Mundanes used the terms "mage" and "magician" like they were interchangeable.

"Okay, okay, whatever," Trouble said. "They still sound like trouble."

"Are they involved in anything shadowy?"

"Not that anyone can say for sure. In fact, they're pretty clean for a group of misogynist racists. There are rumors connecting them to some things, natch, but all anyone can say for sure is that the Runenthing really hates this other group, SIE, which is some feminist secret society based around witchcraft and goddess worship. Sort of the kinder, female version of these skags."

That certainly made sense. Talon suspected that Lady Estelle was a member of SIE, and that Val had been one too. But Val didn't offer any information either way, and Talon saw no reason to press her for it. She trusted Estelle's word, and that was good enough for him.

"What about Zoller himself?" Talon asked.

"There I've had a little more success." Trouble slid across the bed next to Talon and called up a file on her deck, unrolling the fold-out screen so he could see it.

"Zoller, Heinrich," she read. "Born August 29, 2023, in Frankfurt. Family involved in the Frankfurt Bank Association, which pretty much runs the city these days. Hennie was born with a silver wand in his mouth. His magical talents showed up as a teenager and he attended Heidelberg on the family money, doing very well as a hermetic studies student. See? He was a mage, so there." Trouble stuck out her tongue at Talon, and he rolled his eyes. Then she continued.

"However, it seems that Hennie got involved in some pretty radical causes while he was in college. Guess he wanted to rattle Mommy and Daddy's cages. That's when he started to get into the Runenthing-thing. He changed his major in his third year to study 'nature magic,' whatever that is, and did pretty well at that, too, although it's not considered nearly as prestigious as mage-stuff."

"Nature magic is what a lot of Europeans call shamanism," Talon said. "It's a combination of old paleo-pagan beliefs, modern shamanic techniques, and a healthy dose of 'nouveau witch' for good measure. Basically the stuff the Runenthing does."

"So they're like the spell-slingers up around Salem?" Trouble said, referring to the large active witch community near Boston.

"Close enough," Talon said. "Hmm, that means ol' Heinrich has been in Runenthing for something like, what, sixteen, seventeen years? That should put him pretty high up on the totem pole, so to speak."

Trouble smiled. "Ha. Mage jokes. Yeah, as a matter of fact, it does. Seems that Hennie is one of the group's top dogs. Kind of weird that Saeder-Krupp ID'd him as being with Alt Welt."

"Yeah, it is," Talon said. "That's one of the things that's bothering me. It isn't like S-K to slip up on something so basic."

"You think Brackhaus might be trying to pull something?"

"Could be. We won't know for sure until we . . . hello!"

Talon sat up and looked at the display screen on the table.

"There's our guy now," he said.

The screen showed a view of the apartment building. Zoller was walking up the front steps, wearing a long, dark overcoat cloaked over the shoulders of his nondescript dark business suit. He had sandy hair and a full beard, just like in the photo with Dr. Goronay.

"Val can you . . ." Talon began, but she was already zooming in on Zoller, whose image swelled to fill the entire vidscreen.

"Can you tell anything about him?" Trouble asked.

"From here?" Talon said. "No. And his place probably has too many magical wards for me to check it out astrally. We're going to have to make do with video surveillance for now."

Zoller entered the building, and Val shifted the

attention of the drone to one of the windows of the apartment they'd ID'd as Zoller's. The drone directed one low-power laser at the window pane and focused another on the iron grille-work outside. The vidscreen immediately began relaying the faint sounds of traffic and other activity outside the apartment. One by one, the sounds were masked out, until only a faint background hiss remained. The lasers read the vibrations in the window glass and the metal, translating it into sound. Val consciously blocked out the outside noises to focus on the sound inside the apartment.

They could hear the door open and close as Zoller entered. As expected, he made his way into the small office Val's drone had scoped out earlier. He tapped the telecom on and sat down in a padded desk chair, sipping something from a steaming mug.

Trouble got up from the bed and moved over to the small table with her cyberdeck. She sat down and jacked in to monitor Zoller's call. She had previously decked into the local telecommunications grid to tap Zoller's line.

"Heinrich," a voice from the telecom said, slightly distorted by the laser mike, "arrangements have been made for the sale of the item. Contact me about the particulars and we can conclude our business." Zoller reached out and hit another key on the telecom.

Suddenly, the vidscreen image from Val's drone turned to hard static. Val groaned and her spine stiffened for a moment, then she leaned over the side of the bed and started to retch.

Damn it! Talon thought. He jumped up from the

bed and scrambled over to Val's side. He held her head, keeping her from swallowing her own vomit, while fumbling for the cable plugged into her neural jack. He pulled it out as quickly as he dared, disconnecting Val from the remote deck and the signal from the drone. She coughed and nearly gagged as Talon turned her over, resting her head on his lap. He placed his hands against either side of her head and spoke the words of a healing spell, feeling the power pour through his aura and into hers like a gentle heat. The rolling chant was soothing, and Val's trembling and coughing began to ease.

Talon glanced over at Trouble in case there was some kind of two-pronged attack going on. Whatever had dumped Val had apparently not affected Trouble at all, however. She remained jacked into her deck, head resting on her chest, eyes rolled back in her head, focused solely on the virtual world of cyberspace. Her hands danced across the keyboard of the cyberdeck like a musician playing a familiar tune.

Val coughed again and opened her eyes, blinking a few times to adjust to the light of the room.

Talon shifted around so she wouldn't be looking at him upside down. "What happened?"

"Bughunter," she rasped out. "On one of the rooftops. I didn't see him until it was too late."

Talon grimaced. Bughunters were people with a paranoid obsession about drones, believing the drones were spying on them. They thought spydrones worked for the government, the corporations, the alien visitors from Sirius B, or whatever other crazy conspiracy theory was working its way through the sub-culture at the time. They did whatever they could to knock out any drones they could find. One of their favorite weapons were taser missiles called "bugzappers," which packed enough juice to fry a drone's onboard circuitry and to send a powerful feedback signal into the rigger who was operating it. The signal pulse from a bugzapper could induce an epileptic seizure and even be fatal if the rigger got hit really hard. Talon was glad he'd been able to unplug Val in time.

"The drone?" he said, knowing the answer.

"Skragged. I didn't get anything on the telecom call, and there's probably nothing to recover from the drone at this point." Whatever the bughunters didn't destroy, the urban scavengers would be quick to pick up.

A knock came at the door, and Talon reached for the Slivergun resting in his shoulder-holster.

"Room service!" came Boom's voice from outside, and Talon relaxed as the troll squeezed his massive frame through the door, followed closely by Hammer, each of them carrying paper sacks spotted with grease stains.

"Whew!" Boom said, wrinkling his broad nose. "What's that smell?" In a second he took in the sight of Val lying with her head in Talon's lap, looking pale, and the crackling static on the vidscreen, with Trouble tapping away on her cyberdeck in the background.

"What happened?" Hammer asked.

"We lost the recon drone," Talon said, helping Val up to a sitting position. She steadied herself by gripping his arm. "A bughunter came along unexpectedly, right in the middle of our boy making a telecom call."

"What about?" Boom said, closing the door behind him and then setting the food on a side table.

"Hopefully, we can still find out," Talon said, jerking his chin toward Trouble.

"Are you okay?" Hammer asked Val.

She nodded and swallowed hard. "Yeah, yeah, I'll be all right. The bugzapper packed a real jolt and I've still got a little dump shock from Talon pulling the plug. Still, it beats the alternative." She shuddered a bit in memory of it.

"Let's get you, and the floor, cleaned up," Talon said. "Maybe by the time we're ready to eat, Trouble will have figured out a way to pull something out of all this."

As it turned out, Trouble got more than Talon expected. Once she'd logged off and jacked out of the Matrix, the rest of the team brought her up to date on what happened to the recon drone and Val. They sat around the table eating slightly cold sausages with peppers and onions, along with some crusty rye bread. Val took one look at the food and turned a bit green, preferring to quietly sit and sip some water. As they ate, Trouble described what she'd been able to track down in the Matrix.

"Zoller's mysterious call was to one Rashid Hasur, a black-market dealer in 'rare antiquities' in Europe and Northern Africa. Apparently, Hasur is in Germany to help arrange an auction to sell an item Zoller and the Runenthing have: a rose-quartz crystal, carved in the shape of a heart and etched with some kind of runes. Dr. Goronay authenticates it as the artifact he helped unearth, and the Runenthing thinks its magical."

"So the Runenthing is only interested in the artifact to sell it," Talon said.

Trouble shrugged. "Seems like it. From the sound of what Hasur said to Zoller, it's likely to net some serious nuyen on the black market. They're setting up the auction for two days from now in Essen. All sorts of big noises with an interest in 'antiquities' are supposed to be there."

"Frag, then Brackhaus could just go there and buy it himself if he wants it so bad," Val said, setting her glass on the table.

"That's what he's paying us for," Talon told her. "And probably a lot less nuyen than he'd have to pay at an auction, especially considering that Saeder-Krupp already considers this little trinket theirs. Takes a lot of stones for Zoller and his bunch to think they can auction it off in Lofwyr's own back yard."

Trouble looked thoughtful. "Maybe they don't know where it really came from."

"Doesn't really matter," Talon said. "What matters is: can we get into wherever they're holding this auction, get the crystal and Goronay, and get out without any trouble?"

"Sounds like we're going to an auction, then," Boom said with a grin.

"Got it in one, chummer. Trouble, let's start looking at that info. We've got a shadowrun to plan."

9

Speren Silverblade had no trouble whatsoever fitting in at a gathering of some of Europe's wealthiest and most influential people and their various proxies and representatives. It hadn't taken long for Duke Jaromar's contacts to learn about the auction: the duke was well-known as a lover of elven history and culture, a collector of fine art, so the invitation would have come his way even had Speren not inquired. Jaromar was more than willing to pass over this particular opportunity as a favor to the Princes of Tir Tairngire, and gave his invitation to Speren, to attend as his representative.

Speren had traveled from Pomorya to Essen in the Rhine-Ruhr megaplex and could hardly imagine a contrast more jolting. The megaplex embodied all that was wrong with modern culture and society, as far as Speren was concerned. It was overcrowded, filthy, and stank of industrial chemicals, petrochemicals, and the huddled masses of humanity that lived in it. The buildings were ugly blocks of ferrocrete, glass, and steel, the roads choked with traffic, the streets jammed with people, and the shadows filled with scavengers, both human and otherwise.

After his visit to the pastoral and peaceful islands of Pomorya, Speren could hardly wait to complete his work and leave the teeming city behind. He found it hard to believe that Lofwyr, the unacknowledged lord of the megaplex, actually allowed it to exist in such a state. Still, who could really understand the motives of dragons, especially those as Machiavellian as the CEO of Saeder-Krupp?

Fortunately, the setting for the auction was considerably more civilized than most of the megaplex. Helsingen was one of the classiest sections of Essen, and the site of the auction was in the recently built Altstadt Hotel, which prided itself on maintaining the charm and elegance of a bygone era. The hotel was done in late nineteen-century German style, with elaborate scrollwork and floral patterns decorating the walls, fine Persian carpets, and liveried servants to attend to the needs of the guests. Behind the facade of pleasant civility was a formidable security presence. Speren spotted alert security guards among the other hotel employees, along with carefully concealed surveillance and security equipment and magical wards to ensure privacy and shield the hotel against hostile sorcery. The guests of the Altstadt could be assured of privacy and discretion, which was just what the current gathering called for.

Speren chose to dress accordingly for the occasion. Under his hooded cloak of midnight blue, with its lining of ballistic cloth capable of stopping small-caliber rounds, he wore a white silk shirt with ruffles at the throat and wrists. His blue vest matched the color of his cloak and was woven with a golden pattern of twining leaves. Black trousers and his black leather boots completed the ensemble. Speren wore his sword at his side, drawing no small number of looks from the hotel's security. Still, it was not an unusual affectation in the company of so much wealth, and Speren would not even consider leaving the sword behind when dealing with a matter of such importance.

He presented his invitation to the usher at the door and entered the ballroom where the auction would take place. Most of the invited guests were already in attendance, milling about and talking or waiting patiently in their seats for the auction to begin. There were various corporate executives, including a small group of Japanese who stayed close together and spoke in low tones. Speren spotted a few French aristocrats, clad outlandishly in puffy velvet doublets, hose, and floppy hats decorated with feather plumes. Members of some old-money European families were on hand as well, somber in formal evening wear. The air was electric, filled with tension as the guests milled about and exchanged pleasantries, waiting for things to get going. The illegality of the occasion only added to the excitement. For many, the sheer naughtiness of their activities was part of their entire reason for being there.

For his part, Speren had no intention of bidding on the item for sale. Although his mistress could certainly afford to pay whatever price was needed, her instructions had been clear. Speren was not only to recover the artifact, but to find out more about what became of Dr. Goronay, who was nowhere to be seen in the ballroom. He preferred not to involve himself in the bidding unless absolutely necessary.

Settling down in one of the chairs well away from anyone else, Speren rested his hands on his knees and calmed himself in meditation. He focused his thoughts and felt the material world slip away as he descended into a deep trance. His spirit slipped free from his physical body and into the astral plane.

As he expected, the ballroom was awash in emotions of expectation and greed. The dark, crude auras of most of the attendees were in stark contrast to their outward air of sophistication and nobility. Speren drifted up above his physical body, which remained sitting quietly in meditation below him, thinking how easy it was to recognize true nobility when one was possessed of the ability to look into others' hearts. A quick survey of the room turned up nothing of particular interest. A few of the auction attendees carried minor magical items on their persons, but certainly nothing of any concern.

Speren's astral form glided over the room, an invisible wraith, passing through curtains and walls like they were no more than smoke. His quarry was nearby; he could sense it. The hunt was drawing to a close. He stopped short of the hotel's outer wards, which protected the outside walls of the building from casual astral intrusion. His interest lay inside the Altstadt.

In the small conference room behind the main ballroom, Speren spotted two men talking. One was a dark-skinned Arab with neatly trimmed black hair, a small goatee, and dark eyes that gleamed with avarice. He wore a cream-colored suit with a red handkerchief tucked into the breast pocket, like a splash of blood on snow. His aura showed a touch of nervous tension almost blotted out by the overwhelming sense of greed. This was a man to whom profit and the pursuit of profit were everything, a true player in the shadowy world of buying and selling. Still, he was of little interest to Silverblade.

The other man, however, caught his attention at once. He was tall, with Nordic features, dark blond hair, and a full beard. His winged brows and sharp, hooked nose gave him the look of a bird of prey about to swoop down and attack. His aura was a bland mask of studied calm and disinterest, but Speren examined it carefully and saw the true fires lurking within. This man was more than he appeared. He was a powerful magician, as powerful as Speren himself, perhaps. The cane he carried lightly in his right hand held an enchantment, making it a focus for the magician's powers. This was one individual Speren would need to deal with carefully.

Fortunately, the magician was not using his own abilities to view the astral plane at the moment, so Speren remained invisible to both men as they spoke.

"Quite a turnout for such short notice," the magician said. "You've done well, Rashid. Very well."

The Arab accepted the compliment with a slight incline of his head and a flicker of pleasure through his aura. "My thanks, Herr Zoller. Of course, it is as much the bait as the skill of the fisherman that draws in the fish. The merchandise you are offering has drawn considerable interest."

"Yes," Zoller said slowly, tapping the head of his cane against his open left hand. "Hopefully not too much interest."

"No, no," Rashid said in soothing tones. "My associates and their clients are individuals of the utmost discretion. You can be assured that our business has not traveled beyond our circle. We will have no trouble."

Zoller's aura hardened like his stare. "We had best not, Rashid. We had best not." He held the smaller man's gaze for a few long seconds before turning away and resuming tapping his cane. "How long before we begin?"

Rashid glanced at the gold watch he wore on his left wrist. "Only a few more minutes. We should be nearly ready."

"Very well," Zoller said. "I will get the item."

Excellent, Speren thought, as Zoller moved toward the door.

"What about this professor who found it?" Rashid asked just as Zoller was reaching for the doorknob. Zoller stopped and turned back to the other man.

"I'll bring him as well. He can authenticate the piece and help to drive up the bidding."

"And afterward?" Rashid asked.

Zoller's aura darkened again. "That is not your concern," he said. "Keep your attention on the business at hand."

"Of course, Herr Zoller," the fixer replied with an oily bow. Zoller turned and left the room, and Speren's astral form followed close behind. With luck, Zoller would lead him directly to the hiding place of the artifact and Dr. Goronay. Then, while the two men were on their way to the auction room, Speren could return to his body and take the steps needed to secure both of them for his Prince.

Zoller made his way down the hall and out, over

to the wide bank of elevators of the main lobby of the hotel. The floor was done in white-veined black marble, the walls in dark green wallpaper that complemented the brass fittings and framework of the elevators, whose doors were covered with elaborate scrollwork. He tapped his cane impatiently while waiting for the elevator car to descend. Speren felt much the same. He wished he could move on ahead, but there was little point until he discovered where Zoller was going.

When the elevator car finally arrived, Zoller took a step forward to enter, then suddenly paused on the threshold with a strange look on his face. Speren noted a flicker in Zoller's aura as the man hesitated for an instant before turning away from the elevator and allowing the door to slide shut behind him. There was a look of concern on his face as he reached into his overcoat to produce a small cell phone.

Flipping the phone open, Zoller hit a single button and held it to his ear. Speren moved close to hear the hushed tones as he spoke in German.

"There's a disruption of the wards in my suite," he said. "See to it. I'm on my way now to investigate." He snapped the phone shut and pocketed it, striding toward the stairwell. At the foot of the stairs, he stopped, closed his eyes, and muttered a short phrase in German under his breath. His aura grew brighter and more solid as he extended his presence into the astral plane. Speren kept close to the entrance, behind Zoller, where he hoped he could not be seen.

Suddenly, the astral plane around him was lit up as a ghostly warrior appeared, dressed like a German soldier from the nineteenth century, complete with helmet, breastplate, and a filigreed fencing saber at his side. Zoller spoke to the spirit, which regarded him with deep, faintly glowing eyes.

"Go to my suite," Zoller said. "Find any intruders there and destroy them, but do not harm the crystal. This is my will."

The spirit bowed faintly. "As you command," it said in German, then took flight up the stairs at great speed, not giving Speren's astral form so much as a second look. Speren was pleased that spirits were often so literal-minded. The hearth spirit Zoller summoned had probably noticed Speren's astral form, but since its master hadn't bothered to include intruders outside his suite in his orders, the spirit simply ignored Speren altogether.

Speren wasn't about to waste such an opportunity, and he slipped up through the stairs to catch up with the spirit. It would lead him where he needed to go. He thought briefly about staying with Zoller, but his instincts told him that the magician would follow quickly enough. Speren had not gotten where he was without knowing when to take risks.

In moments, both spirits passed through a dozen floors to reach Zoller's hotel suite. As the magician said, a ward existed around the suite, a magical barrier to block the passage of astral forms, no doubt put there by Zoller himself. Already under Zoller's command, the hearth spirit was able to pass through the ward with no more difficulty than passing through the physical wall. Speren, however, was blocked by the shimmering barrier. He knew that any attack on the ward would alert Zoller, but there was no time to waste. Speren drew the astral double of Argentine, his magical sword, and swung it at the barrier with all the power of his will behind it.

Although Zoller's ward was skillfully built, it was no match for Speren's enchanted blade, which sliced through the barrier as if it were made of paper. In an instant, Speren was through the ward and into the suite, the gash he cut through the barrier closing behind him like a healing wound. Inside the main room of the suite were four intruders, three of them physical beings—a human, an ork, and a troll. The fourth was a spirit in the form of a golden-winged falcon. The human was just slipping a flat rosy crystal, cut in the shape of a heart, into a soft black bag. Silverblade was nearly blinded by the powerful radiance of the stone's aura before it was swallowed by the bag. It had to be the item he'd been sent to find. Slung over the troll's shoulder was an unconscious man with gray hair and a full beard, wearing a rumpled suit. Dr. Goronay himself.

Shadowrunners, Speren thought. They had beaten him to his target. Even as he considered his options, Zoller's hearth spirit assumed physical form, appearing as a fierce warrior clad in armor and wielding a razor-sharp sword.

"Hold, intruders!" it said. "Surrender or die!"

10

It had all been going so well, Talon thought as the uninvited spirit materialized inside the hotel suite. But most shadowruns did, at first. Breaking the ward protecting the crystal was a calculated risk. Now they were paying the price.

Both Hammer and the spirit moved with blinding speed, the spirit through the power of its magical nature, Hammer via the technology of superconducting nerves and spinal subprocessors. In this particular case, it appeared that technology won out over magic, as the ork mercenary raised his snub-nosed Ingram smartgun and fired off a three-round burst at the onrushing spirit.

Had it been only a being of flesh and blood, the impact of the 9mm rounds would have wounded or even killed the spirit, would at least have knocked some of the wind out of it. The spirit, however, was no mortal creature, but a being of the astral plane. Its body might look and feel solid, but it was not flesh and bone. Hammer's gunfire had no more effect on it than it would on stone, wind, or water.

The spirit's shining sword flashed out. Hammer

dropped his Ingram and fell back, cursing, bleeding from a deep gash along his forearm.

Boom didn't even bother trying to shoot at the spirit. He'd worked with Talon long enough to know that it wasn't worth the trouble. Instead, he jerked his right fist downward, and a curved blade of surgical steel slid from the concealed sheath inside his massive forearm, nearly as long as the saber the spirit wielded. Boom stepped forward and slashed at the soldier-spirit as it turned away from Hammer. He was rewarded for his effort with a slash along his shoulder from the spirit's own blade. Once again, had the spirit been merely mortal, Boom's great strength and longer reach would have made all the difference. But combat with spirits was more a matter of will than of physical strength, and Boom's willpower, while formidable for a troll, was no match for such a powerful spirit.

The best way to fight magic was with magic, Talon thought. He could try and use his own magic to banish the spirit back from where it came.

"Boss!" Aracos spoke in Talon's mind. *"There's another spirit in the room, a projecting magician."*

"Zoller?" Talon thought.

"No. He's an elf, and he's armed."

An elf? Talon had no idea who it could be. Certainly not one of Zoller's people, they were all human. This certainly complicated matters. Talon needed to be careful how he used magic if there was another magician present. There was little this stranger could do from the astral plane to interfere with Talon's efforts in the physical world, but he could immediately attack if Talon used his own astral abilities. If Talon focused all his concentration on banishing the spirit, it would leave him defenseless against any other attacks, and the astral magician might have other allies around. It was too much of a risk.

"You take the magician," Talon thought to Aracos. *"I'll handle the spirit."*

"You got it," Aracos said.

From across the room, Talon pointed at the spirit and gathered magical power to him. It seethed like a glowing ball of energy around his hand, visible from the astral plane, but unseen to mundane eyes, except perhaps as a faint shimmer, a kind of distortion in the air. In an instant, Talon gathered the power and spoke a sharp word, sending it flying at the spirit like a lightning bolt.

The spirit stiffened and jerked as the manabolt slammed into it, tearing away its very substance, striking where it was most vulnerable, on the spiritual level. The spirit was quite powerful, however, and the spell did not slay it, as it would any lesser being. It was injured, but Talon was afraid he'd only made it angry.

With a growl of anger, Hammer charged into the spirit and tackled it. The silvery saber flipped out of the spirit's grasp, vanishing like smoke, as Hammer bore it to the floor. Boom rushed to help, and Talon stepped forward, readying another spell.

"Boss! I've got real problems here!" Aracos screamed in his thoughts. *"He's got a mageblade."*

Damn! The astral magician was a more serious problem than Talon had thought. With a powerful enough magical weapon, he could cut Aracos to ribbons. Talon could use his own astral abilities to go to his ally's aid, but that would leave Hammer and Boom to fight the spirit, and he could already see it struggling against them. It would also leave Talon vulnerable to both the astral magician and the spirit, and he doubted he could fight off both as the same time.

"All right," Talon thought to Aracos. *"Get out of there. See if you can get that magician to follow you or something."* He felt the spirit's assent and turned his attention back toward the soldier-spirit the others were struggling to hold onto. Although smaller than either of the heavily muscled metahumans, the spirit was not limited by the constraints of its size. With a mighty surge, it threw both the ork and the troll off it and rose up, the sword reappearing in its hand as it did so.

Talon wasn't about to give it another chance to attack. Gathering power again, he flung it at the spirit with all his might. The spirit cried out in pain, the first sound it had made since calling for them to surrender. The physical form of the soldier wavered and rippled like a trideo image whose projector was out of whack. The power of Talon's spell shredded its life force, the core of its being. The physical manifestation followed suit and broke up, melting away like fog, its cry echoing faintly in the air.

"Talon, we've got problems." It was Trouble's voice sounding in his head, coming over his headcom. "Hotel security cams show three men heading up the stairs with Zoller and another three in the elevator on the way to your floor."

"Can you override the elevator?" Talon asked.

"I'm trying, but the hotel's system is on alert and I've got my hands full dodging some ice right at the moment. Even if I can override, I'll probably have to shut down the whole system. You guys better get out of there ASAP."

"Copy," Talon said. "Boom and Hammer are both hurt, but we've got the artifact. We're getting out of here, but we're going to need some cover."

"Roger that," Trouble replied. "I'll keep 'em busy for as long as I can."

Talon mentally keyed open a channel to Val.

"Val, did you copy that?"

"Roger," came the rigger's voice, muffled by the background noise of chuffing rotor blades.

"We're heading for the roof. Be ready to get us out of here."

"I'll be ready," she said. "Out."

Talon turned to the others, who were on their feet again.

"You two okay?"

Both nodded. "I'm okay," Boom said. "Mostly my pride, and I've been kicked there more times than I can count." Hammer also waved off any concern as he covered his Ingram.

"All right, then, let's buzz."

They headed for the door, Hammer first, Talon close behind, with Boom bringing up the rear, carrying Dr. Goronay, still unconscious from the effects of Talon's sleep spell. They held weapons at the ready, scanning for any signs of danger.

Talon reached his mind out toward his familiar. *"Aracos?"* he thought.

"Here," the spirit's thought-voice came. *"I'm outside*

the hotel. I took off, but the astral elf didn't try following me. He's probably still in the room with you. Do you want me to try and run interference?"

"No," Talon thought. *"Stay outside. We're headed for the roof. You can meet us there."*

"Got it," the spirit said. *"Be careful, boss."* Talon felt a surge of genuine concern before he closed the thought-link.

Frag, he thought as they cautiously emerged into the hallway. *Double-frag*. The other hotel guests, if they had heard any of the noise in Zoller's suite, were smart enough to stay in their rooms and call hotel security, rather than sticking their heads out to possibly get shot at. Thank the gods for small favors.

However, the presence of the astral magician dogging them continued to complicate things. Talon and Aracos could probably handle him together, but they were on the run, and Talon couldn't leave his physical body helpless while his astral form tried to deal with the magician. And if he tried to stay in his physical body and deal with him, his astral opponent gained an advantage in maneuverability. He couldn't even afford a glance into the astral plane to see what he was up to without opening himself up to an attack. He simply had to bide his time, and hope the magician didn't complicate things any further.

They headed for the stairs. Getting caught in an elevator was the last thing they needed. Hammer took point and pushed open the stairwell door, Ingram at the ready. He looked, then stepped aside and waved the others through.

Talon turned to Boom. "After you," he said. Still

carrying the unconscious Dr. Goronay, the troll grinned and stepped through the door.

"Thank you, kind sir," he replied.

Talon followed close behind. Almost as soon as Hammer hit the stairs and they were on their way up to the next floor, they heard a clamor coming from below as three burly humans dressed in security uniforms came thundering up the stairs, followed closely by Heinrich Zoller.

"Halt!" the lead man called in German.

"Keep going!" Hammer shouted. He spun and fired a burst from his Ingram down at the guards. The bullets sparked and ricocheted off the railing and the stairs, but the guards flattened themselves against the walls, seeking cover. The shadowrunners charged up the stairs to stay ahead of their pursuers. Hammer fired another burst behind them before following. Gunshots blew holes in the plasterboard of the walls as they ran.

Talon waved to Hammer to pass him. "Keep going," he said. He paused and raised his hand toward the way they came, focusing his will. He could hear the guards and Zoller catching up with them as he gathered mana from all around him and channeled it, whispering words of power under his breath.

There was a whooshing sound, and a crackling plane of magical energy sprang into being. It ran from wall to wall in the stairwell, capping off the landing entirely with a translucent ceiling of purple energy. Talon leaned for a moment against the wall, drained by the effort of calling the barrier into existence. He kept his concentration focused on maintaining the barrier as the security guards rushed up the stairs and nearly ran into it. Then he turned and headed up after the others as quickly as he could. It wouldn't take Zoller long to dispel the barrier he'd created, if he was any judge of the other magician's abilities, but it would buy them some time to reach the roof. Talon hoped Zoller would exhaust himself against the barrier spell, becoming less of a threat.

"Nice trick," Hammer called back as Talon started to catch up.

"Thanks," Talon panted. "Let's hope it works."

It was eight flights from Zoller's suite to the roof of the hotel. To Talon, it felt like fifty. He was gasping for air when they reached the doorway onto the roof. Boom pushed the door open and looked back at him with concern.

"You okay?"

Talon gulped air and nodded. "Yeah, I'll be fine. That last spell took a bit out of me. But it . . ." Talon's eyes shifted, like he was looking at something no one else could see.

"What?"

"They've broken through," he said. "Zoller must have dispelled the barrier. Let's get out of here."

On the roof was a landing pad used by influential guests of the hotel to fly in directly from the airport or from some corporate enclave via helicopter or tilt-rotor aircraft. Currently there was only one vehicle parked there, a Hughes Stallion helicopter; Herr Brackhaus had been most generous in providing it at Talon's request, with no questions asked. Val sat jacked into the control panel, keeping the rotors going at a constant slow start-up speed, ready for takeoff.

Boom loaded Dr. Goronay into the chopper like an adult handling a small child, before climbing in himself. He gave Talon a hand up, and Talon sank gratefully into the seat as Hammer swung himself up into the cabin and yelled to Val over the whine of the rotors.

"Take it up!"

The rotors began to whine as they accelerated, kicking up a powerful wind. Then the Stallion lifted smoothly off the helipad, so quickly Talon felt like he'd left his stomach behind.

As they angled away from the pad, the roof access door banged open and Zoller emerged with his guards. His overcoat flapping in the wind like dark wings, Zoller gestured angrily toward the chopper, and the guards opened fire. Hammer yanked the side door shut as several bullets bounced off the fuselage. Zoller was holding both hands out toward the helicopter, shouting something drowned out by the noise of the rotors and the gunfire.

"Talon . . ." Boom began.

"I see it," Talon said. He concentrated and extended magical shields over the helicopter and its occupants. A moment later, he felt the force of Zoller's spell slam into them. Barely visible arcane energies crackled around the helicopter like prismatic lightning for a moment as the spell tried to fight its way through Talon's shielding, but they held against the onslaught, and the Stallion continued to gain distance and altitude away from the hotel.

Boom gave him a thumbs up. "Good job, Tal."

"Thanks," Talon said. "But we're not out of this yet." He reached out with his mind, calling to his ally.

"Aracos, what's going out there in the astral? Is that elf magician still with us?"

"Looks like, boss," the ally spirit said. *"And that's not all. Zoller's working on calling up another spirit."*

Frag, doesn't he ever get tired? Talon thought. He'd definitely underestimated Zoller's power. Zoller should be at least somewhat fatigued from calling up the hearth spirit, taking down Talon's barrier, and trying to break through Talon's shields, but he just kept pushing.

"What's the elf doing?" Talon asked.

"Nothing right now," Aracos said. *"Just watching, as far as I can tell. He's not making trouble."*

"Are you hurt?"

"Not too bad, just a scratch. Still, I don't think I'd want to fight that guy, not with that sword he's got."

"Let's hope it won't come to that. You're going to have to deal with the spirit Zoller's whistling up. If I go astral, that'll leave the chopper defenseless if Zoller decides to toss another spell at us."

"I could always materialize," Arcos said.

"What?"

"I could materialize. Then I could fight the spirit and protect the chopper against any outside sorcery at the same time. That way you could go astral and help."

"Damn," Talon said aloud. It was obvious. He should have thought of it himself. *"I knew there was a good reason I kept you around, omae!"*

"Well, we all know who's the brains of this outfit," the spirit quipped.

"I'll pretend I didn't hear that. All right, let's do it."

"Talon!" Val called from the flight deck. "Zoller's got some kind of storm spirit, coming at us fast!"

"On it," Talon said, sinking back against the seat and automatically falling into a deep and complete trance. He loosed his astral form and slipped out of his physical body and outside the helicopter, where he immediately saw a large, dark cloud rushing toward the Stallion. In the heart of the cloud was a humanoid figure, a heavily muscled Nordic warrior, with bristling red hair. Lightning crackled around his body, and he rode in a kind of chariot, drawn by two goats whose hooves struck sparks as they charged across the sky.

Talon also saw as Aracos assumed the material form of a great, golden-winged falcon. Existing on both the physical and astral planes simultaneously, and capable of action on both, Aracos extended his magical power to protect the Stallion should Zoller decide to try casting another spell at it. Then he tucked in his wings with a mighty cry and dove at the storm spirit.

Talon glanced down and behind the onrushing spirit and saw another astral form there, watching the battle unfold. He was an elf, as Aracos said, wearing garments of light that looked like they came from some trideo fantasy epic, holding a slim-bladed sword unsheathed in one hand. He seemed content for the moment to watch, making no move to interfere on behalf of either side. Talon didn't have time to figure out who he was or what he wanted. He drew the astral form of Talonclaw from the sheath at his side and dove into the fray.

Aracos slashed at the storm spirit with claws and beak. The spirit struck back with a glowing hammer it held in its fist, sending Aracos reeling for a moment. Talon leapt in and slashed with his enchanted blade. The astral dagger bit into the spirit's form, releasing a gout of blue-white energy and eliciting a shout of pain and anger. The storm spirit turned on Talon, its eyes glowing pits of hellish electric light. It brought its hammer down in a powerful overhead blow, but Talon managed to block it with his blade. He would never have been able to do such a thing in a physical fight, but on the astral, power mattered far more than appearances, and Talonclaw was a powerful weapon indeed.

The spirit seemed taken aback for a moment and, in that moment, Aracos came back into the fight, leaving a trail of claw marks across the storm spirit's face that crackled with lightning in place of blood. The spirit tried to ignore the harassing attacks of the ally spirit to focus on Talon, but Aracos didn't let up, hitting the storm spirit at every opportunity, while Talon fended off each attack, and gave back another strike with his mageblade for each assault.

In a matter of moments, the storm spirit was enraged, hemorrhaging blue-white energy from multiple small wounds, laying about with its hammer, seeking to strike at its tormentors, who leapt away at the speed of thought, or else blocked its attacks with more powerful weapons of their own. Aracos raked talons across the spirit's chest and, when the storm spirit drew back for an attack, Talon took the opening and thrust Talonclaw directly into the creature's very heart. There was a clap of thunder and a flash of lightning, and the storm spirit vanished. The dark clouds of its manifestation began to break up and Talon looked to the Stallion, which was making its way out over the city. It was almost out of sight of the hotel, and Zoller could do little else but fume and vent his anger against the guards with him. Having seen his spirit defeated so quickly, Talon doubted Zoller would try coming after them astrally himself.

He looked over to where the other astral magician had hovered, observing the battle. The elf looked back at Talon for a moment, gave a slight bow in the air, then zipped away at the speed of thought, vanishing from sight. Talon wondered what was the elf's interest in the whole thing, but he wasn't going to get any answers at the moment.

"Stay in the astral and keep watch in case Zoller tries to send any watchers or other spirits after us," Talon told Aracos. *"I'll take care of the chopper."*

"Done," Aracos said.

Talon easily caught up with the Stallion and slid back into his physical body. As he stirred, Boom clapped him on the shoulder.

"Nice job with the storm spirit."

"Thanks," he said. "We shouldn't have any more trouble from Zoller for now. I've got Aracos watching in case he tries anything else clever."

"We should be at the landing zone in about twenty minutes," Val said.

"Good, I'm going to call Brackhaus and arrange to deliver our cargo. Then we can wrap this up and go home."

Boom leaned back in his seat and rested his hands

on his knees. "Not totally smooth sailing," he said, "but not half bad."

"Are you kidding?" Hammer said from beside him. "That was probably the easiest hundred grand we ever made."

"Yeah," Talon said, as he activated the head's up display for his headware and told it to dial the number Brackhaus had given them, "but don't forget it's not over yet."

11

Speren watched the end of the battle with the storm spirit with great interest. These shadowrunners were bold, and there was nothing he could really do to stop them in his astral form. Not that he wanted to at the moment. Clearly, the runners were hired to do exactly what Prince Jenna had dispatched Speren to Germany to accomplish: to recover the artifact. He wondered how much the shadowrunners knew about their intended targets. Not much, he suspected. Fixers rarely told runners more than they had to.

Although the involvement of the shadowrunners was an unexpected complication, it wasn't necessarily an unwelcome one. For one thing, it had solved Speren's problem of locating and recovering his quarry. The runners might have escaped for the time being, but the hunt was far from over.

With a gesture of respect to their magician for the skill with which he and his familiar dispatched Zoller's storm spirit, Speren sped back to his physical body, which still sat quietly in a chair in the auction room. The guests continued to mill around, although more of them had taken seats, waiting for things to begin. Speren knew there would be no auction tonight. Though part of him wanted to stay and watch the fixer Rashid and Zoller squirm their way out of this, opportunity called. He stood, stretched, and then quietly withdrew from the room, heading toward the bank of elevators off the lobby of the hotel.

He stepped into the elevator and touched the button for the twelfth floor. As the elevator ascended, Speren caught his reflection in the polished brass plate around the controls. He closed his eyes, whispering under his breath in Sperethiel, the language of his people, as he drew on the magical energies all around him and wove a minor spell.

When he opened his eyes and regarded his reflection again, he looked, not like a proud and fierce elven paladin, but like one of the uniformed security guards who'd accompanied Zoller to the roof. He stepped out of the elevator and made his way briskly down the hall to Zoller's suite. The door still stood open, and three other security guards were on hand, one of them standing outside the door, keeping watch. Speren gave the man a cursory nod and walked into the room like he belonged there. The two other guards were looking around the place, no doubt searching for any clues the runners might have left behind. Perfect.

Speren went over to where Zoller's hearth spirit had struck the ork shadowrunner with his saber. Sure enough, there was a small dark blood stain on the carpet. Speren had noted it even as he'd watched the fight. He knelt down beside the bloodstain and took a dagger from his boot-top. His illusion made the finely jeweled blade look like a utilitarian jackknife in his hands.

"Hans?" one of the other guards asked in German, "what have you got there?"

"Blood," Silverblade replied in the same language, keeping his voice low. Since he hadn't heard the guard's voice, his spell couldn't replicate it perfectly. Hopefully, they wouldn't notice. "Herr Zoller will want to see it." He quickly and efficiently cut out a square of carpet with the blood stain on it, then stood, pocketing it.

"But we were ordered . . ." The guard's eyes narrowed for a moment, looking at Speren intently. "You, you're not . . ."

Speren realized the man had seen through the spell. Unfortunate. Before the startled security guard could even begin to voice his concerns, Speren moved with blinding speed. He leapt between the two guards in the room and over the bed on the far side. He had to time things exactly right. He called forth a spell in his mind, gathering in the power.

The guard who noticed his disguise shouted a warning, which brought the guard in the hall running into the room. Perfect, Speren thought again, loosing his spell.

The invisible wave of magical energy surged out and blossomed into a sphere of power around the three guards. Speren tightly controlled the energies unleashed, because he did not want to be caught inadvertently in his own spell. The sleep spell instantly sent the three men into unconsciousness, their bodies sagging to the floor without a sound even as they reached for their weapons. Speren stepped over their limp forms, wasting no time leaving the room and heading back to the elevators.

Just as he was entering the elevator car, his sharp hearing picked up the sounds of the others coming down from the stairwell. By the time they figured out what had happened, he would be out of the hotel and lost in the teeming populace of the Megaplex. With good luck on his side, Zoller would take the intruder as a compatriot of the shadowrunners who'd escaped him, not another competitor for the artifact.

He reached into his pocket to finger the piece of carpeting. Zoller would eventually guess what took place in the hotel suite, and would realize that his one opportunity for finding the artifact and Dr. Goronay was gone. Although he was unaware of it, Zoller had given Speren the key to finding the shadowrunners and their purloined treasures. It would take very little for a magician of Speren's skill to track them down. Then he would deal with them and complete his mission.

12

The Hughes Stallion angled away from the wealthy riverside district of Essen, heading north and west, toward some of the burned-out industrial areas that still awaited the rebuilding and revitalization promised by corporations like Saeder-Krupp. They flew fairly low, near enough to the tallest buildings to make following them on radar difficult. Talon opened up a comm channel to Trouble.

"How's the air traffic control?" he asked.

"Null sheen," she said. "They haven't picked you up, and my smart frame should see that they don't. I doubt Zoller will notify the police that his illegal artifact has been stolen from him. Even if the hotel reports it, we should be long gone by the time they start checking."

"Let's hope so," Talon said. "Good work. Keep an eye on the authorities for any signs of trouble. We're almost to the rendezvous point now."

"I'll meet you there," Trouble replied. "Out."

The chopper flew smoothly for a while longer, until they reached a virtually abandoned area of Essen that Val had scouted out earlier. There were no signs of any pursuit, either aerial or astral. Val killed the running lights on the Stallion and brought it down onto the cracked and weed-choked parking lot of an old industrial complex, now rusting quietly away from years of neglect. The surrounding area was soaked with toxic levels of chemicals, leaking from old dumping and storage sites that dated back to the twentieth century. Until the area got cleaned up—an expensive and time-consuming process—nobody but the most desperate bothered to come here. That probably included shadowrunners, Talon thought as the chopper landed.

Val powered down the engine, and the rotors slowed to a stop. In a matter of minutes, there was no sound in the cabin except the faint, chill breeze outside.

"Look sharp, everyone," Talon said. "Our Johnson should be along any time now." He turned back to where Boom sat with Dr. Goronay. "How's he doing?" he asked.

"Still out cold," Boom said. "That spell you hit him with really put his lights out. You sure he's going to be okay?"

Talon shifted his perceptions to the astral plane to see the archeologist's aura. The glow was not as strong as he would have expected, but it was stable and showed no signs of any immediate danger. There was a kind of erosion of Goronay's life force, however. That was odd, even for a man his age.

"He'll be all right," Talon said, letting his vision slip back to the normal world, "but he's definitely given his body a beating. There are signs of long-term systemic abuse of some kind in his aura. I'd almost guess drugs, or maybe beetles."

"Why would an old guy like him be jacking beetles?" Boom asked.

Talon shrugged. BTLs, or "Better Than Life" chips, were simsense programs that provided an artificial high, experiences heightened to the point of causing damage to both body and mind if they were abused. BTLs were tremendously addictive. Talon remembered Val's story about how she got hooked on them, as so many street kids, and even adults, did. Still, it seemed out of character for a man like Goronay, whose whole life was about archeology and a quest for knowledge. Still, a BTL addiction could explain how the Runenthing and Zoller had gotten their hooks into him.

A bright light filled the vacant lot, coming from the halogen lamps of a high-class Eurocar. The team was immediately alert, hands hovering close to their weapons, as the car pulled into the lot and cruised slowly up to the Stallion. It stopped some ten meters away, but did not extinguish its headlights. The rear door opened and a dark figure stepped out, silhouetted by the lights as it moved.

Talon turned to Boom. "That's our cue," he said, motioning for the troll to bring the unconscious doctor. He hefted the bag containing the crystal and slid open the door of the Stallion. A glance at Hammer was sufficient to tell him to keep watch for anything suspicious. Talon knew he could count on the big ork to watch their backs. He also sent a mental head's up to Aracos, telling the spirit to watch for any signs of trouble in astral space.

Together, he and Boom climbed out of the chopper, Boom carrying Dr. Goronay over his shoulder like a sack of grain. They began walking toward the dark figure as it also came toward them. As they approached, Talon could make out more of the man's features: the immaculate suit, so out of place in the crumbling ruins; the perfectly coifed hair and the stony features, betraying no emotion or trace of the man's thoughts.

"Herr Brackhaus," Talon said, greeting their Mr. Johnson.

"Talon." He acknowledged them with a nod. "I see you have brought the doctor as well. Well done. You have the artifact?"

Talon held the carrying bag open so Brackhaus could see inside. The Johnson glanced at the rosy crystal, gleaming in the halogen lights, and nodded. Talon pulled the bag closed.

"We'll just turn them over to you and collect the rest of our fee," Talon said.

"I'm afraid there's been a change of plans," Brackhaus said. Talon instantly tensed, fearing a trap, but Brackhaus raised a hand in a gesture of holding.

"Nothing to be concerned about," he said smoothly. "Quite the contrary. My employer is most pleased with your work, and would like for the materials to be delivered directly to him as soon as possible. He has requested that you accompany me to the meeting, Herr Talon, and has said that you may bring one other along, if you wish. He will give you the remainder of your fee, with a generous bonus for your good work and the cost of your time."

Was Brackhaus serious? He couldn't possibly . . .

"By your 'employer' do you mean . . ."

"Yes," Brackhaus replied, "I do. Will you honor his request?"

Put that way, it sounded less like a request and more like a formal command, which, Talon supposed, it was, in a way. There was a saying among shadowrunners: "Never deal with a dragon." On the other hand, there was an equally valid saying that applied here: "What do you give a dragon? Anything he wants." Especially when the dragon was Lofwyr, master of the world's largest megacorp. If Lofwyr wanted to meet Talon, then who was Talon to refuse? Besides, it sounded like his team wasn't going to see the rest of their fee unless he went along with the dragon's request.

"I would be honored," Talon said.

"Excellent," Brackhaus replied. "Since my employer has asked that we return with all possible speed, we shall use the helicopter, while your associates can be delivered anywhere they'd like."

"Thank you," Talon said, "but we've made our own arrangements." Trouble should be waiting nearby with the van to pick up the team. Even if he did have to go along with Lofwyr's whims, Talon didn't like the idea of putting his entire team in the hands of the dragon's servants.

"As you wish," Brackhaus said. He raised his right hand and waved. The passenger-side door of the Eurocar opened, and a man dressed in a jacket with the Saeder-Krupp logo on the breast and shoulder stepped out. He wore a reversed baseball cap and a pair of mirrored sunglasses, despite the fact that it was nighttime. Talon could see the telltale gleam of a datajack port behind his ear as the man came toward them.

"My pilot will take the controls," Brackhaus said. It was not a request.

Talon turned back to Boom. "Put Dr. Goronay back in the chopper and tell Hammer to wait here." Then he walked over to the Stallion and pulled himself up to the cockpit.

"What's going on?" Val asked.

"Brackhaus' boss wants us to deliver the goods in person and we need to use the chopper. You and Hammer will stay here and wait for Trouble to come pick you up."

"His boss, you mean . . ." Her eyes widened a bit.

"Yeah," Talon said, "Lofwyr only wants me and one other. Brackhaus has his own pilot, so you and Hammer have to stay here."

"I don't like this," Val said.

"I know. I'm not crazy about it either, but what choice do we have?"

"It could be a trap."

Talon shrugged. "Why would Lofwyr bother? If he wanted us dead, he could have sent an elite S-K squad to meet us instead of Brackhaus. Hell, he could probably do it in twenty different ways we couldn't even think of until it was too late. I know it's risky, but it's the only way we're going to see the rest of our money, and besides . . ."

"Besides what?"

"We're talking about a chance to meet *Lofwyr* here! That's not something that comes along every day. I wouldn't pass this up for twice what he's paying us."

Val slowly unplugged the lead from her datajack, studying Talon's face the whole time.

"You're a strange man, Talon."

"So I've been told."

Val and Hammer stepped down from the Stallion, and Brackhaus' pilot took his seat in the cockpit and jacked into the control systems. As he powered up the rotors, Talon turned back to Brackhaus with a slight bow, gesturing toward the cabin.

"After you, Herr Brackhaus."

"*Danke*, Herr Talon." Brackhaus stepped up into the cabin, followed by Talon. He pulled the door closed, and the helicopter began to rise into the air. The Eurocar backed away slowly, then turned and drove out of the vacant lot, leaving Hammer and Val alone, to be swallowed up by the shadows.

The chopper rose up high over the buildings below, then turned and headed back on a course for the Ruhr River and the heart of Essen. From the faint radio chatter coming from the cockpit, Talon could tell that, this time, they were following a pre-filed flight plan with Essen air traffic control. He briefly wondered how Saeder-Krupp would explain a flight coming from the middle of an abandoned area with no heliport, then decided that S-K probably didn't have to explain much of anything in Germany, if it chose not to.

Brackhaus sat near the cockpit, quietly composed, making no effort at conversation. For most of the flight, they rode in silence, Talon and Boom sitting together and the unconscious Dr. Goronay in the back of the chopper.

Eventually, the massive Saeder-Krupp Ruhr arcology building came into sight. Even from kilometers away, it was an impressive sight. Rising like an ancient medieval castle above the smaller buildings surrounding it, the arcology was more than two hundred stories tall, and covered almost ten square city blocks, rising up like a truncated pyramid. The sides of the building were covered in black macroglass, giving the whole structure a glossy black surface that gleamed wetly in the city lights of Essen. Along the top of the building glowed the Saeder-Krupp name and logo, a reclining black dragon against a neon-red background. Lights glimmered from the numerous landing pads placed at different levels, and spotlights cast shimmering cones of illumination along the building's sides and from the roof.

Though not quite as large as the ill-fated Renraku arcology in Seattle, the S-K arcology still housed nearly seventy thousand employees and their families, like a small, self-contained city. It was completed sometime in 2058, Talon recalled, having seen a trideo broadcast of the dedication ceremonies. He recalled the corporate commentators mentioning how Saeder-Krupp had managed to finish their arcology project before Renraku completed theirs, even though S-K began more than a year later. A definite public relations coup for the megacorp.

As the Stallion banked toward the arcology, Boom leaned in close to Talon and spoke softly. "So, chummer, have you ever met a dragon?"

"Yeah," Talon said, "but it wasn't a very friendly meeting. The dragon had . . . issues."

"The only one I ever met was Dunkelzahn," Boom said, glancing out the window. "He's the one who really got me started in the shadow-biz in Boston. Saw something other than muscle in me, I guess. Showed me I could be more than that. Nice guy."

Somehow Talon didn't think the same could be said of Lofwyr. Still, he hoped this experience with a dragon would be more like Boom's than his own had been.

The arcology loomed to fill Talon's entire field of vision as the helicopter came in on its final approach. They touched down gently on one of the rooftop helipads, the others already occupied by corporate helos and tilt-rotor aircraft to convey S-K personnel to various points throughout the plex. As they landed, Dr. Goronay stirred and moaned slightly. Boom took the doctor's arm and shook it gently.

"Wakey, wakey," he said.

Goronay stirred and opened his eyes. He looked over at Boom and Talon in confusion and muttered something in Russian. Talon didn't speak it, and didn't have a Russian language chip on him.

"Wake up, Doctor," he said firmly. "We'll carry you if we have to, but it would be better if you can walk."

"Where . . . ?" Goronay began.

"Saeder-Krupp HQ," Talon said. "We have some business to conclude here."

If Goronay was concerned over the prospect of being forcibly brought back into the presence of his patrons, he certainly didn't show it. In fact, the doctor seemed somewhat befuddled, but he offered no resistance and did what he was told.

Brackhaus opened the door of the helicopter and stepped down, waiting for Talon, Boom, and Goronay to do the same. The doctor was a touch unsteady on his feet, but managed to get his bearings with a little help from Boom. Then Brackhaus led them to a bank of elevators on the rooftop. Taking a credstick from his pocket, he slotted it into the port next to one of the elevators. A light immediately went on over the port and the elevator doors slid open smoothly.

"Gentlemen," he said with a wave. They all stepped into the elevator, followed by Brackhaus. Talon noticed there were no visible controls. As soon as the doors closed, Brackhaus said "executive level," and the elevator began to move quickly. It slowed and came to a stop with a gentle bump, and the doors opened again to reveal a long corridor lined with doors. The walls were a pale cream color and the hallway was carpeted in deep burgundy, with dark wood trim. Talon was willing to bet it was real wood, too, not synthetic. Everything in the place, from the doors to the brass fittings and nameplates to the faint spicy scent of herbal air freshener, spoke of power and wealth. This was where the real high-rollers of the world's most powerful megacorp operated.

Talon was quite certain that they were being scanned by an infinite array of state-of-the-art sensors as they walked down the corridor. He itched to use his astral senses to check out the place, but he resisted the urge. Any use of his magical abilities might bring a sudden and brutal response from the unseen S-K security forces. Instead, Talon did his very best to keep himself looking as calm and unthreatening as possible.

The corridor ended and opened up into a pleasant reception area. Talon had lived in smaller apartments than the room, which was spacious, with one wall to the left made up of macroglass windows that afforded a spectacular view of the Ruhr River and the city sprawling more than two hundred stories below. Two other walls were the same cream color as the hallway, while the wall opposite where they entered was paneled in dark finished wood. A number of couches and small end tables were placed precisely around the room, and there was a set of bronze double-doors set into the wood-paneled wall. They were each carved with the image of a dragon coiled atop an ornate ledge, so that the two dragons faced each other.

Talon smiled to himself, thinking Lofwyr was nothing if not stylish.

Sitting to the right of the doors was a curved desk that blended in with the decor. Coming around from behind it was a striking human woman dressed in a sharp business pants suit of dark blue, with a short jacket and a lighter blue blouse. A belt of silver disks encircled her slim waist, and she wore tasteful silver earrings. Her hair was ash-blond, pulled back from her face into a pony tail, and perfectly coifed. Talon noticed that her eyes matched the color of her blouse and that her smile was almost perfectly white. For some reason he couldn't explain, he found himself reminded of a predator baring its fangs when he saw her smile. Perhaps it was the dark-uniformed security guards flanking either side of the hall through which they entered.

"Hello," she said. "I'm Karen Montejac, the President's personal assistant. I must ask you to surrender your weapons."

Talon and Boom glanced at each other, then Talon reached, slowly, under his coat and withdrew his Ares Viper. He made a careful show of removing the clip from the weapon before handing it over to Montejac. Boom did the same with his Predator. One of the guards waved a hand-held scanner over Boom from head to foot.

"He's clean," the guard said. He did the same over Talon, pausing at his waist.

"I'm afraid you must surrender *all* your weapons, sir," Montejac said in a firm tone, her gaze falling on the jeweled dagger hilt barely visible beneath his coat.

"No," Talon said, quietly.

"Excuse me?"

"Talon, give them the bloody dagger!" Boom hissed under his breath.

"No," Talon repeated. "I won't surrender my mageblade." His gun was one thing, that was protocol, but Talonclaw was more than just a weapon, it was bonded to Talon magically, almost a part of him. He'd worked a long time to make it, to enchant it as an embodiment of his will and his magical power. He wouldn't surrender it easily. Besides, what did they think he would do with it in Lofwyr's presence? Even a mageblade was of little use against the power of a great dragon.

"Sir," Montejac began, her eyes narrowing dangerously. Then she stopped and cocked her head, as if listening to a voice no one else could hear. She nodded, almost unconsciously, and turned back to Talon and the others.

"You may enter," she said. "He is expecting you."

Talon swallowed and nodded. Brackhaus stepped forward and pushed open the bronzed doors, allowing Talon, Boom, and Goronay to enter, followed closely by the unobtrusive security guards.

Dominating the room was the sprawling body of the great golden dragon, making Talon feel quite small and insignificant in comparison. As he stood looking at the shimmering, awesome shape of Lofwyr, he heard a voice speaking in his mind.

"Welcome, Talon. I've been looking forward to this meeting."

13

The "corner office" of the Saeder-Krupp arcology was a vast room by necessity. One could easily have landed a mid-sized VTOL inside it, with plenty of space to maneuver. In fact, in many ways it less resembled an office than a hangar, or perhaps a cavernous den where a dragon would feel more at home.

Two adjoining walls were floor-to-ceiling armored macroglass, with adjustable tint and opacity, currently set to provide a clear view of the Ruhr River and the light-dappled cityscape of the surrounding megaplex. Beyond them was a broad balcony of shaped ferrocrete that provided an area large enough for a small aircraft—or a large dragon—to take off and land. Talon suspected that the macroglass walls retracted to allow the dragon a means of entry and exit, since there was no way he could fit through even the wide double doors leading in from the reception area.

The wall in which those doors were set was of pale stone, carved with elaborate bas-reliefs that looked medieval in style. No noble knights slaying dragons on them, however. They could very well have been authentic, looted from some castle or other ruin in

Europe during the work of the Restoration. The floor was a seamless slab of dark marble, smooth and cool, although the air in the room was fairly warm.

The wall off to the right of the doors drew the most interest. The entire surface was covered with a sensitive film of ruthenium polymers, turning the whole wall into a giant trideo screen. On that screen were dozens of different "windows" showing video footage, computer graphics, and scrolling lists of text and numbers. Talon recognized a couple of major international news channels, along with the stock indices for Tokyo, London, and Boston. The rest was just a meaningless jumble of sounds and images overlapping, too much information at once for his senses to make heads or tails out of it.

In the midst of the room, lying curled up like a giant house cat, was by far the largest dragon Talon had ever seen. Not that he'd seen many. Most people gladly went their whole lives never getting any closer to an actual dragon than on the trideo. Talon had met only one other during his years in the shadows, and that creature was a child compared to the majestic shape he saw before him. It wasn't until he looked on Lofwyr, resting in his own lair, that Talon understood where the term "great dragon" came from.

Even curled up like he was, bat-like wings furled tightly against his back, back spines lying flat, with his sharp, reptilian head close to the floor, Lofwyr was huge. The dragon's golden scales shimmered in the light coming from the upper corners of the room as his sides heaved slowly, in and out, like great bellows. The air was filled with the dry, musty scent of a reptile house. Talon was reminded of a lizard, sunning itself on a rock, as he saw Lofwyr bathed in the glow of the track lighting from above.

As Talon, Boom, and their escort entered the room, the dragon raised up his head and forelimbs and stretched, another catlike gesture, spreading his wings so the tips brushed up against the far walls of the room. One look from Lofwyr's golden eyes reminded Talon that this was no mere lizard, but a creature of formidable intelligence, who single-handedly controlled the world's largest megacorp.

"Welcome, Talon, I've been looking forward to meeting you," Lofwyr said. The dragon's mouth did not move, nor did Talon hear any sound. Instead, Lofwyr's voice spoke directly into his mind. It was similar to the way in which he and Aracos communicated, only that bond was deeper and more personal. Talon felt none of the same warmth or friendship in Lofwyr's thought-voice nor, he suspected, could he shut out the dragon's words, had he wanted to. He found the sensation profoundly disturbing, but did his best to suppress any outward sign of it.

"And I see you've brought the wayward Dr. Goronay. Greetings, Doctor. I've followed your career with some interest."

Goronay seemed to have come out of his stupor upon seeing Lofwyr and now shrank back from the dragon's glittering gaze. It occurred to Talon that when Lofwyr had awakened some fifty years ago, Goronay was only a child and Talon and his friends had yet to be born. How long had the great dragon slumbered before that time, and how long had he lived before entering his long sleep preceding the birth of the Sixth World? The sheer weight of Lofwyr's experience, all that the dragon had seen and done, was like a palpable aura surrounding him. Little wonder he commanded such respect, his fearsome physical qualities aside.

"You have also brought the crystal?" the dragon said. Talon suddenly realized he'd been standing like an idiot with his mouth hanging open the entire time Lofwyr was speaking. He felt the dragon's attention on him as he recovered and nodded quickly.

"Yes," he said. "Yes, we have." He reached into the shoulder bag he carried and withdrew the rosy-colored crystal, which gleamed in the light.

"Excellent," the dragon's thought-voice hissed through his mind. *"Brackhaus, guards, leave us."*

Mr. Brackhaus gave a short bow, then he and the security guards silently withdrew, pulling the doors shut behind them. They closed with a thunk that echoed in the cavernous space.

"Bring the crystal to me," Lofwyr said in Talon's mind. Talon found himself moving to obey before he even thought about it. He went forward until the great dragon towered overhead, only about three more paces away. He could see the armored scales ripple with every breath, every slight movement.

"Place it there," Lofwyr said, and Talon carefully set the crystal heart on the marble floor, then backed away from it. Lofwyr's wedge-shaped head dipped down, hovering over the crystal. In the back of his mind, Talon heard strange, alien words whispering as the dragon shifted his neck to look at the crystal from different angles, the golden eyes narrowing, looking at things beyond the range of human vision. Lofwyr's features were completely unreadable, at

least to anyone other than another dragon. Finally, he raised his head again and turned to look at his three visitors.

"Now then, Doctor," he said in a purring tone of thought, *"perhaps you would care to explain why you murdered one of your own students to remove this bauble?"*

Goronay's face had gone ashen, and sweat broke out on his brow. Talon certainly didn't envy him at that moment.

"I . . . I . . ." he stammered, "I don't know . . . that is to say, I'm not completely sure, but . . ."

There was a mental sigh from Lofwyr as the doctor continued to stammer and stumble over his words. The poor man looked close to a collapse.

"Very well. I can see I shall have to follow a more expedient path." Lofwyr's eyes narrowed and focused on Dr. Goronay. The old archeologist stood paralyzed, trapped in the dragon's gaze like a terrified sparrow confronting a cobra. His own eyes widened and his mouth opened, but only strangled, meaningless noises emerged. Both Talon and Boom flinched at the treatment Lofwyr was giving their prisoner. Part of Talon was tempted to use his astral senses to see what it was Lofwyr was doing, but his own good sense told him it was best not to interfere in the dragon's business.

Suddenly, Dr. Goronay threw his head back and gave a terrible cry, whether of pain or anger, Talon couldn't tell. The doctor grabbed his balding head with his right hand and pointed his left at Lofwyr, forefinger extended in accusation.

"Monster! Defiler!" he shouted. "You will not

break me! I am a true servant of the gods! Death!" he cried. "Death to all tyrants!"

As Goronay spoke, the rosy crystal on the floor in front of Lofwyr began to glow brightly. Talon looked quickly from the crystal to the golden dragon looming overhead.

"Lofwyr . . ." he started to call out. Then, an arc of pinkish lightning exploded from the crystal, striking the great dragon in the chest. Caught off guard by the sudden energy surge, Lofwyr threw back his head and roared in pain, a sound that seemed to shake the entire room. Talon had never heard anything so terrible as the dragon's pain-laden roar. Lofwyr's entire body was awash in arcs of energy, from his head to the tips of his outstretched wings and tail. Goronay was still babbling and shouting taunts and insults at the dragon as Lofwyr began to thrash his head and tail in pain.

"Talon, look out!" Boom yelled. He grabbed Talon and pulled him back and down as the dragon slammed his tail into one of the macroglass windows, which were designed to withstand the impact of a rocket launcher. It shattered on impact, sending shards flying across the room.

Goronay was laughing like a madman, practically gibbering. "Yes! Yes!" he shouted. "Now you will pay! Now you will feel the suffering you have inflicted on others! The judgment of the gods is upon you, serpent! The twilight of the gods is upon us all!" The old archeologist was almost dancing with glee.

Gods, Talon thought, he's completely insane.

Lofwyr thrashed his head forward, opened his massive jaws with a roar and loosed a gout of flames that engulfed Goronay. The doctor's laughter turned into a scream that was quickly drowned out by the roar of the flames. The room began to fill with acrid smoke and the horrible smell of roasting flesh as Goronay was incinerated by the blast. Talon, lying some four meters away, could feel the terrible heat of the flames, like the backwash of a rocket, as Goronay's remains collapsed to the floor.

However, the death of the mad archeologist did nothing to stop the assault of the crystalline artifact on the great dragon. The crimson glow around Lofwyr intensified, bolts of energy coruscating over his scaly hide, a blinding beam of radiance arcing between his chest and the crystal on the floor. The dragon appeared helpless to strike out at the crystal, or to do anything else to end his torment. The glow was growing brighter and brighter, until it was painful to look at. Talon glanced up from the floor and, for a moment, locked eyes with the great dragon. The pain he saw reflected in Lofwyr's gaze was dizzying, as was the choking smoke and the heat of the lingering flames in the room. Talon felt almost faint and closed his eyes tightly against the sight of it. The sound of the dragon's cries echoed in his mind.

Aracos! he called out with his thoughts. *Help!*

Then, Lofwyr threw his great head back and roared again, a sound that tore through Talon like a blade. The crystal heart expended a final burst of energy, filling the room with a blinding pinkish light. When the glow faded, Lofwyr's body twitched, then slowly toppled toward the floor, landing with a crashing thud. Boom lifted his arm from where it had been protectively clasped over Talon and pushed himself up with the other, looking over at the dragon's body, stretched out on the marble floor, silent and motionless.

"Holy shit," he whispered. "I think we just killed Lofwyr."

Talon was still trying to get his bearings. His head was spinning. He started to push himself to his feet, swaying slightly. Then he felt a familiar presence and a voice spoke into his mind.

"Boss, what's . . . holy shit!" Aracos said as he appeared in astral space nearby. "Is that . . . is that Lofwyr? What the hell happened?"

"I don't fragging know," Talon said. The inside of his head felt like it had been scrubbed out with sandpaper. He walked over to where the crystal rested on the floor and bent down to look at it. The stone had gone from a dusky rose to dull gray. He reached out and touched it gently. Despite the spectacular display of energy just moments before, it was cool.

"Talon, what the frag are you doing?" Boom asked. "That thing just took out fraggin' *Lofwyr*. Leave it alone! We've got to get out of here. Listen!"

Talon stopped and cocked his head. The room they were in was clearly soundproofed, but even the most sophisticated soundproofing couldn't block out the high whine that came from outside.

"Alarms," he said, somewhat absently. He picked up the crystal and looked over at Lofwyr's body, then back at the crystal, then over at Boom.

"This thing may have killed the most powerful being on Earth," Talon began, as though in a daze, "and we're standing here, holding the smoking gun."

"Right," Boom said, "so let's get the hell out of here!"

"I'm with him, boss," Aracos said. *"We need to vamoose, right now!"*

"Right," Talon said, getting his bearings at last. "Let's go." He only briefly considered staying and trying to explain what happened to Saeder-Krupp security. It hardly mattered that he and Boom weren't at fault. S-K would be out for blood, and a couple of shadowrunners made for excellent scapegoats. He and Boom would simply disappear until the corp decided to pin the attack against Lofwyr on them, at which point there would be a showy trial and an equally quick execution, assuming they weren't simply "killed while trying to escape." Talon wasn't about to let that happen.

He moved over to the macroglass window broken by Lofwyr's thrashing.

"Boom," he said, and the troll kicked the window hard, sending the remaining glass flying outward. Talon could hear pounding on the double doors: security forces trying to break in. He and Boom stepped out onto the landing platform outside the office. It was empty of any vehicles they could use to escape. The side of the arcology was sheer glass and steel rising up more than a dozen stories above them, with a sheer drop of nearly two hundred stories below. Peering over the edge, Talon briefly considered their chances of reaching the ground safely, then looked up at the rooftop helipad where they'd landed. Odds were that the Hughes Stallion that brought them was still there.

"Which way?" Boom asked.

"Neither one appeals to me," Talon replied.

Just then, the doors into Lofwyr's office opened with a dull boom, followed by Karen Montejac and a group of dark-uniformed Saeder-Krupp security men pouring into the room.

"Master!" Montejac cried out in alarm at the sight of Lofwyr's motionless body.

One of the guards immediately spotted the broken window and pointed toward the landing pad.

"There they are!" he shouted.

"We just ran out of options," Talon told Boom. "Jump!" He hopped up onto the edge of the platform and gestured to Boom as two of the guards rushed at the broken window, their submachine guns at the ready. Boom followed quickly and took Talon's hand, then the two of them leapt from the platform as the guards opened fire, rounds ricocheting and pinging off the ferrocrete.

"I fraggin' haaaaaate thiiiiiiiis," Boom yelled as they plunged through the air. Talon spoke arcane words, and a faint shimmer filled the air around them, slowing their fall and guiding them away from the sloped sides of the building.

As they fell Aracos materialized nearby in the form of a golden-feathered hawk, his voice speaking into Talon's mind.

"Boss, that chica with the guards is a wendigo, and a shaman. She's got some sort of illusion on her to make her look human. And she's starting to cast a spell!"

"Protect us," Talon told his ally, as he focused on doing the same. Glancing up, he saw Karen Montejac leaning over the side of the landing platform, her long hair blowing in the wind. She was gesturing and her mouth moved, but the wind carried away all traces of the sound. The effects of her chant were felt, however, when her spell impacted against Talon's shielding. It was a fairly powerful one, but Talon's shields, combined with Aracos' own sorcerous abilities, were enough to protect them from its effects. Talon sincerely hoped Montejac wouldn't try something like that again. He angled their descent to use some of the lower landing platforms of the arcology as cover. If Montejac couldn't see them, then she couldn't use magic against them.

In a few moments, they touched down on the plaza surrounding the arcology. Saeder-Krupp security forces were already swarming out of the building. Talon spoke another mystic phrase and waved his hand over himself and Boom, creating the illusion that they looked like nondescript security guards in dark uniforms. Aracos vanished back into the astral plane, invisible and undetectable to the physical senses.

"Let's play this nice and easy," Talon said to Boom. "We just blend in and walk out of here." They headed for the perimeter of the plaza, hoping to blend in with the other guards on alert throughout the area. Talon only hoped that Saeder-Krupp's magical security resources were spread as thin as those of most megacorporations. He couldn't conceal the effects of his spell on the astral plane; any astral magician who spotted them would know something was up.

They made it almost to the perimeter gate before a security patrol van screeched to a halt in front of them. The doors opened and security guards spilled out, calling "Halt!" as they raised their weapons.

Talon and Boom were already moving. Talon concentrated and swung his hand like he was lobbing a grenade at the guards. There was a soundless explosion, causing a faint ripple in the air that expanded outward from the center of the patrol car to surround all the guards. They collapsed where they stood as Boom rushed forward. He tossed the unconscious guards out of the van and squeezed into the driver's seat. Talon climbed into the passenger side, and Boom took off toward the gates.

"You okay?" he asked Talon as they sped away.

Talon nodded wearily. "Yeah, but all the spells are starting to wear me out."

"Just hang on for now," Boom said. They came at the gates at top speed. Security guards stood their ground and tried to stop the van. Bullets cracked the windshield and pinged off the body. Talon felt one impact against his shoulder. The ballistic lining of his coat stopped the round from penetrating, but it still felt like getting slammed by a troll wielding a baseball bat. He looked at the gates and clutched Boom's arm.

"Frag, the gates! We aren't going to be able to break through them in this thing!"

"If you've got a better idea, I'd love to hear it!" Boom said.

"Aracos," Talon thought, *"aid me."* He could feel his ally's power feeding into his own. Concentrating with all his might, Talon cast the same spell he'd used to lower himself and Boom safely to the ground, this time on the van itself. The van was considerably

heavier, and it took everything Talon had, but he managed to levitate it. As the van rushed toward the gate, it suddenly lifted off the ground and was airborne. It flew up and over the gate and its security devices and tire-shredding spikes, then landed smoothly on the road outside. Boom laid the pedal to the metal and the tires squealed as they touched down, burning rubber to put as much distance between them and the arcology as possible.

"Hope you can handle it from here, chummer," Talon said wearily. "Cuz I'm done." He slumped back against the seat, nearly exhausted from all the rapid-fire spellcasting. He mentally told Aracos to keep watch for anyone trying to track them in astral space and to deal with them. Then he started to consider their next move.

Talon didn't believe what happened to Lofwyr was an accident. Someone *wanted* them to bring Dr. Goronay and the artifact to the dragon, as some kind of hit. And that meant someone had set them up. Talon didn't like to play the puppet in somebody else's show. Whoever they were, he was going to find them, and he was going to make them pay.

14

It took some time for Talon and Boom to be sure they had evaded the Saeder-Krupp security forces, at least for a little while. Talon was against using his headlink to try and warn the others about what had happened at the arcology. Cellular calls were too easily traced, and he was certain that S-K would be using all of its considerable resources to track them down. They were better off returning to the safe house and getting the rest of the team out of there. Talon was just glad they'd made their own arrangements in Essen, rather than relying on Herr Brackhaus; otherwise the location of the safe house would already be compromised.

Talon wondered about Brackhaus' involvement in this whole mess. It was possible the man knew nothing about it, that he really was simply acting under orders from Lofwyr or someone else in Saeder-Krupp. It was equally possible that he'd set Talon and his team up for a fall as part of some power struggle within the megacorporation. There was no way to be sure at the moment. Still, Talon fully intended to find out.

They'd quickly ditched the Saeder-Krupp security

van and stolen a good-sized minivan. If the corp had a means of tracing the van, they would find it soon enough, but minus the runners. Boom's skill in electronics came in handy for hot-wiring the van, and his driving prowess helped them maneuver around the city to keep from being spotted and picked up by the local authorities. Talon hoped Saeder-Krupp would try to handle things themselves before bringing in the police. Of course, the police worked largely for S-K anyway, but he still believed the corporate higher-ups would be reluctant to allow any word of what had happened at the arcology to leak out.

The Essen safe house was in an abandoned warehouse district in the city's former industrial area. As they pulled into the alleyway, Talon scanned the area for any signs of pursuit or a tail. His senses, both magical and mundane, detected none.

"Coast is clear," he told Boom. "Let's go."

They climbed out of the van and took the stairs two and three at a time up several flights. When Talon was a few steps from the door, he heard Aracos call out in his mind.

"Boss, trouble! That elf magician is here, he's . . ." Suddenly, the voice was cut off and Talon felt a sudden emptiness, an absence in his mind and spirit. Something had happened to Aracos.

"Boom!" he hissed quietly. "We've got company." He jerked his head toward the door. The troll leveled the submachine gun he'd taken from an unconscious Saeder-Krupp guard, while Talon drew his mageblade with one hand and readied a spell with the other.

With practiced precision, Boom kicked the door open, his gun moving to cover the room while Talon went in low, senses alert for a potential target. Then they stopped in their tracks and froze.

What they saw were Trouble, Val, and Hammer, every one of them unconscious. They'd been secured to chairs with heavy plastic strips, the kind used by police to restrain prisoners. All save for Hammer, who was bound to some stout pipes protruding from the floor. Their mouths were covered with silvery tape.

Their captor stood in the middle of the room, behind the chair holding Trouble. In his left hand he held a slim pistol, most likely a Slivergun, with its deadly plastic flechettes. In his right hand was a slim-bladed silver sword, its edge pressed near Trouble's pale, exposed throat. His thin, cruel face wore an arrogant expression of triumph, and he radiated calm, despite the situation.

"Welcome back," the elf said in a quiet, firm voice. "I was beginning to wonder if you would return at all. Lower your weapons, or this lovely dies."

Talon glanced over at Boom and lowered Talonclaw, but did not sheath it. Boom slowly lowered his Ingram, never taking his eyes off the elf.

"Who are you, and what did you do to Aracos?" Talon asked.

The elf gave a slight bow, sweeping his Slivergun in the air in front of him. "I am called Silverblade," he said. "You need not be concerned. Your familiar is only disrupted temporarily, although I could just as easily have destroyed it. And I assure you, I have more than enough power to deal with the both of you, if I don't get what I want."

"And what is it you want?" Talon asked, as if he didn't already know.

"I'm interested in Dr. Goronay, and the artifact you appropriated from Herr Zoller and his friends earlier this evening."

Talon shrugged and gave him a weary smile. "Then you're out of luck, chummer. The good Dr. Goronay freaked out completely and has a new career as a pile of ash on the floor of Lofwyr's office. As for the artifact . . ." He took the bag off his shoulder and slowly upended it, dumping the gray, cracked crystal out into his hand. "It managed to take out Lofwyr himself in one shot, and every Saeder-Krupp security agent in Europe is probably looking for it, and us, right about now."

The elf's eyes widened and Talon could see the calm facade crack a bit.

"The crystal . . . attacked Lofwyr?" he asked incredulously.

"Attacked and very possibly killed," Talon replied. "When we left him, he was lying on the floor. I couldn't tell if he was stunned, hurt, or dead, but he didn't look very good."

"Impossible," Silverblade said.

Talon shrugged. "Believe what you like. You're a mage, and I'm sure you're already reading my aura. Go ahead and check to see if I'm lying. I won't try and hide anything from you. At this point, I've got nothing to lose." Talon let his masking drop, revealing his true aura to Silverblade. It was a calculated risk, since it would allow the elf to know just how powerful, and how tired, Talon was, but it was important that the elf know he was telling the truth.

Silverblade's eyes narrowed as he weighed Talon's words. "This puts matters in a different light," he said slowly.

"Glad you think so," Boom muttered.

Talon decided to try and press the advantage. "Look, I don't know who you are, or who you're working for, but you're after what's about to become the hottest bit of property in all of Europe, possibly the entire world. And as much as I'd like to continue this conversation, we've really got to get out of here before Saeder-Krupp manages to track us down. You found us, and that means they could be here any fragging minute too. Now, do you want to take it up with them, or can we just go our separate ways?"

"Unfortunately, I still have orders to recover the artifact," Silverblade said.

"You're welcome to try, but do you really think you can smuggle it out of Germany? Especially with S-K security watching all the ports of exit?"

"I have my own means out of this charming little region," Silverblade said. "And as for Saeder-Krupp, I hardly think they—" The elf mage suddenly glanced to one side, as if he saw something invisible to normal vision. Boom started to make a move, but Talon grabbed the troll's arm.

"No!" he said. "There's something there."

Silverblade removed his sword from Trouble's throat and slashed at empty air. Suddenly, a loud hissing and gurgling noise filled the room and things began to materialize out of the shadows of the loft.

"Elementals!" Talon said. "We're under attack!"

Two spirits appeared in the room: one a mass of dark, smoky vapor that exuded a noxious odor, like rotten eggs; the other a gurgling, vaguely humanoid blob of water that seemed to form from beads of moisture in the air. Silverblade slashed and parried with another that could not be seen.

"There's a fire spirit in the astral," he said, "and a magician controlling them. I think Saeder-Krupp has found you."

"Boom, get the others out of here!" Talon said. "We'll hold off the spirits as long as we can!" The troll looked from Talon to Silverblade, then back to his friend, then he went into action. He grabbed Trouble and Val, chairs and all, and headed out of the room. Talon shifted his attention to the astral plane and leapt into the fray to help Silverblade.

As astral space unfolded all around him, he could see the auras of the three spirits—the material air and water elementals and the astral fire elemental Silverblade was dealing with. He could also see the hovering astral form of a dwarf clad in flowing robes edged with faintly glowing mystic symbols, the mage directing the spirits. Although nothing on the dwarf's person indicated it, Talon was sure he must work for Saeder-Krupp, and that meant some kind of backup wouldn't be far behind.

The air spirit tried to cut off Boom's retreat from the room. Talon swung at it with his mageblade, striking at it from the astral as well as on the physical plane. Although physically the spirit was nothing more than a cloud of mist, the astral form of Talonclaw connected with its astral body, leaving a long black rent in its structure. The spirit recoiled slightly from the touch of the mageblade, then regrouped and began moving back in on Talon.

A horrible stench flowed over him as the spirit tried to smother him with its substance. Talon fought down the urge to retch from the terrible odor and set about with Talonclaw, slashing at the spirit wherever he could. He coughed and his eyes began to burn and tear. The assault of the elemental was worse than tear gas, and it was only Talon's astral senses that let him see at all through the stinging and watering of his eyes. His attacks were having some effect. The air elemental recoiled more and more from each swing of the enchanted dagger, tears and rents showing in the fabric of its astral form.

Suddenly, Talon felt something cold and slimy coil around his ankles. The water spirit! The liquid began to flow up and over him as the air elemental backed away. Talon slashed at the water elemental with his mageblade, but the spirit continued to flow until it covered him completely. Talon tried to take a deep breath, but only managed a quick gasp of the fetid air before the spirit engulfed him, surrounding him with a bubble of water. Talon fought back as the elemental began to exert pressure on him, trying to squeeze the air from his lungs. It was like dropping to the bottom of an ocean, the water pressure increasing more and more. Talon thrust out with his dagger, and the enchantment allowed it to wound what was only water, but the spirit fought tenaciously.

Talon's vision started to swim as his lungs burned for oxygen. He fought the need to exhale, since he knew the spirit would force all the air from his body if he did. He felt the water recede from the hand holding Talonclaw, and he tried to cut into the spirit elsewhere. He was starting to black out.

Suddenly, a gleaming silver blade sliced through the bubble of water around him. The water parted and fell away as the magical forces that allowed it to defy gravity were dispelled. The spirit's vital force broke up and its manifestation became ordinary water, leaving Talon sopping wet, but able to gasp for a breath of air before the air elemental tried to move in again.

Silverblade went back to back with Talon, holding his sword in front of him like a shield.

"Deal with the air spirit," the elf said over his shoulder. "I'll take the magician."

"Right," Talon said. The air elemental tried to engulf him as well, but this time Talon was ready for that tactic. He stabbed out with his mageblade and sliced upward, nearly cleaving the spirit in two. Any other creature would have fled, but elementals knew only obedience to their masters, and the spirit kept coming. Another thrust of Talonclaw finished it, leaving only a faint lingering trace of its foul odor in the air.

Talon turned in time to see Silverblade fend off a spell from the astral mage. An arc of blue-white lightning leapt through the astral plane at the elf, but it broke like a wave against his personal shields, unable to reach him. Silverblade charged forward and slashed with his sword, drawing a cry of pain from the mage as he cut him across the shoulder. He came in for another thrust, but the astral mage moved too quickly. He zipped away, passing through the substance of the wall, and vanished before the blow could connect.

The elf cursed as the mage disappeared from sight. He and Talon quickly cast about for signs of any other foes.

"Gone," Silverblade said.

"Yeah, but he'll be back," Talon replied, "and with reinforcements. We need to get out of here right now." He lowered his dagger. "Thanks, I appreciate you stepping in back there."

The elf nodded. "Since we've now been seen together, and that mage will doubtless report back to his superiors about my presence here, it would seem that our fates are linked for the time being . . ."

Talon extended his hand. "Talon," he said.

The elf ignored it. "I am Speren Silverblade, a paladin of Tir Tairngire." He sheathed his sword. "As you have said, we should go from here as quickly as possible. I have transportation, but nothing that can accommodate you all."

"We've got something," Talon said. "Probably not as high-class as you're used to, but I'm sure you'll manage."

"Of course."

"You want to help me wake everyone up and get them into the van?" Talon asked. "What did you use on them anyway?"

"A simple sleep spell," Silverblade said with a shrug. "It should be easy enough to wake them, then we can be on our way."

"Do you have someplace in particular in mind?"

"I do," Silverblade said. "Assuming you are willing to trust me?"

Talon studied the elf's expression for a moment. He seemed sincere about wanting to help them out, for the time being, but Talon didn't trust him any more than he could have thrown Lofwyr, and he was sure the feeling was mutual.

"Like you said," Talon told him, "it doesn't look like we've got much choice in the matter. Let's go."

15

Prince Jenna Ni'Ferra was *not* a happy woman.

"They did *what*?" she said. "What do you mean 'they may have killed Lofwyr'? How can that be?"

"I can only relate what they have told me, my Prince," Speren said carefully. Prince Jenna's ire was something to be wary of, even over an encrypted communications link thousands of kilometers away. He had wasted no time in communicating with his Prince in Tir Tairngire once he'd guided the shadowrunners to a Tir safe house in Essen and made sure they would stay there. He had excused himself to the other room, where he made use of a sophisticated miniaturized transmitter setup. Connected to a concealed satellite dish on the roof, the transmitter used secret Tir Tairngire comsats to route his transmissions back to the Royal Palace.

It was a risk using the transmitter, here in Saeder-Krupp's own backyard, with the corporation's security forces stirred up like an angry hornets' nest, but Speren had little choice. The situation was unprecedented, and he needed to pass on what he'd learned so far to his Prince, to protect Tir Tairngire's interests, at the very least.

"What exactly happened?" Prince Jenna asked over the link. Her voice was calmer after her initial shock and surprise. Though she, like many in Tir Tairngire, held no love for Lofwyr, Jenna respected the great dragon's power and position. An assault and possible assassination were no small matter.

"I tracked the location of the artifact and the archeologist who stole it," Speren said. "It led me to individuals trying to sell the artifact on the black market. However, a group of shadowrunners, apparently in Lofwyr's employ, managed to seize the artifact and Dr. Goronay and spirit them away. Two of them were summoned into Lofwyr's presence, where the artifact—a crystal carved with runes—surrounded the dragon in some sort of energy field. In his throes, Lofwyr slew the scientist, then collapsed. The shadowrunners do not know if he was dead or merely stunned. They took the crystal and ran, fearing for their lives. Saeder-Krupp is hunting for them now."

"What is your position?" Jenna asked.

Speren swallowed a bit before replying. "I used magic to track the shadowrunners to their hiding place. There I captured three of them, but I did not locate the crystal or Dr. Goronay. Shortly thereafter, the other runners returned from the meeting with Lofwyr. Saeder-Krupp security managed to track them and saw me with them. We fought off their magical scouts, and I brought them here. Since we'd been seen together, I thought it wise to ally with them for the time being, at least until I could find out more about what they've done and what can be done about it. I can still acquire the crystal, but it appears that whatever enchantment lay within it is now gone. Dr. Goronay is gone, ashes on the floor of Lofwyr's lair. What remains of the crystal is in the possession of the shadowrunner's mage. My Prince, what is your command?"

Speren paused to hear Jenna's orders. He heard his Prince curse softly over the link.

"*Makanagee*," she said under her breath. "Idiots. And Lofwyr, of all the possible targets . . . Speren, do you believe this attack against Lofwyr was planned in some way?"

"Yes, my Prince," he said without hesitation. "Accidents do not happen to the likes of Lofwyr. From what I have learned so far, I believe that someone has used these shadowrunners as catspaws to reach Lofwyr and attack him."

"I tend to agree," Jenna said. "If this is so, then the threat may end there. The attack has been carried out and we must deal with the consequences. Still, there may be a greater threat, if this attack against Lofwyr is only the first step in a more complex plan. In either case, the Council must know more about this. I have told them about Goronay's project and the discovery of the artifact. I will inform them of the attack on one of our own members now. You will continue to investigate this matter. Work with these shadowrunners so long as they are useful."

Jenna paused for a moment, then said, "I cannot offer you aid in this matter, Speren. Once news of this reaches the Council, there will be much to concern us. If the dragon is dead . . ." She left the rest unsaid.

"I understand, my Prince," he replied. Speren knew what the death of a great dragon meant for the world. When Dunkelzahn was assassinated, it threw most of North America into chaos. There were riots throughout the United Canadian American States, and Tir Tairngire was forced to close its borders even tighter. The fallout from Dunkelzahn's death was still being felt the world over. His will had redistributed considerable wealth, made and broken fortunes, and triggered a corporate war.

Dunkelzahn was a powerful dragon, more powerful than most suspected. But Lofwyr . . . Lofwyr was by far the world's wealthiest individual. His power and influence reached everywhere. His fortune was virtually immeasurable, and his schemes legendary. If Lofwyr truly was dead, his demise could trigger events that would make the passing of Dunkelzahn look trivial by comparison. Such a revelation could shatter the Corporate Court, perhaps even plunge the whole world into war.

Speren felt the weight of responsibility heavily on his shoulders. If his homeland was to survive the coming storm, they would need all the information possible. Tir Tairngire was probably the first power to learn of the attack on Lofwyr, even before the other nine megacorporations of the Corporate Court. It was vital to maintain that edge.

"I will continue my investigation, my Prince, and report again when I have more information."

"Very well," Jenna Ni'Ferra said. *"Ozidano teheron, milessaratish. Imo medaron co versakhan."*

Speren bowed his head at the formal dismissal. "I leave my life behind, my Prince. At your command, I am the death of your enemies."

Then he broke the connection.

* * *

The safe house to which the elven paladin brought Talon's team was an inconspicuous townhouse in one of the better sections of Essen. The Tir government owned the entire building, through a series of blinds and intermediaries, of course. The appearance that the townhouse was regularly rented out was maintained, though the apartments were actually inhabited only occasionally, by Tir agents in need of them.

Talon and his friends sat in the large main room of one of those apartments, considering their options in light of recent events. Things looked pretty grim.

"Remind me never to jinx a shadowrun again," said Harlan Hammerand, massaging his temples as he sat on the edge of a couch. He'd been the last to wake up from the effects of Silverblade's sleep spell and he seemed the worst hit by it, still a bit groggy and grumbling accordingly. Talon had brought them all up to date on what happened since they'd left the meet site with Brackhaus in the chopper: about the crystal and the mysterious attack on Lofwyr, their flight from the Saeder-Krupp arcology, and their encounter with Silverblade. The question that remained was, what were they going to do now?

"The first thing we need is information," Talon said. "We need to know what exactly happened to Lofwyr and whether or not Saeder-Krupp is still looking for us. We also need to know who set us up to get at Lofwyr."

"Are you sure it's a set-up?" Val asked.

Talon nodded. "Has to be. I can't believe it was all an accident. No, Goronay was primed by somebody. I'm pretty sure that whatever that crystal did to Lofwyr, Goronay set it off before he was killed."

"Maybe Goronay was behind it, then," Hammer said.

"No way," Boom replied. "You shoulda heard this guy, Hammer. He was completely off his nut, totally gone. There's no way he coulda planned and pulled off something like this."

"Besides," Talon interjected, "if Goronay was behind it, why go through the whole set-up of stealing the crystal in the first place? I agree with Boom. He was completely out of his head when we were in Lofwyr's lair. I think somebody set him up, the same as us."

"Some kind of conditioning?" Trouble asked.

Talon nodded. "Could have been. Or magical influence, although I doubt something like that would get past Lofwyr's security."

"Why even bother with all this drek?" Hammer said. "Why do we care who wanted to cack the dragon? Why don't we just get out of this fraggin' country and call it a day?"

"Well, for one thing, we have Saeder-Krupp security out looking for us." Talon began ticking off items on his fingers. "We can forget about any legit way out of Germany, and they've probably got most of the shadow-routes locked up, too. Secondly, even if we do leave, where on earth could we go where Saeder-Krupp can't find us? We're talking about the world's largest megacorp here. They've got resources that put national governments to shame, watchers in every major city, and one of the best intelligence networks around. If Saeder-Krupp needs scapegoats—and one way or another, I think they're going to—then they're going to keep looking for us.

"Lastly," he said, eyes gleaming with purpose, "*somebody* set us up to take the fall for bringing down Lofwyr. I don't like to be fragged with and I definitely don't like playing the fall guy. I want to find whoever it is and explain that to them . . . in great detail."

"What about this Silverblade guy?" Boom asked in a low voice, glancing quickly at the door to the other room. "Do you think we can trust him?"

"Trust him?" Talon shook his head. "No, but I think we can count on him to want to know what's going on nearly as much as we do. At least for now."

"Well, then," Trouble said, rising from the couch, "if it's information we need, I'm your girl." She picked up the carrying case holding her cyberdeck. "I just need to find a jackpoint in this place, and I can start digging."

"No," came a voice from the doorway. They all turned as one to see Speren Silverblade standing there. Several hands reached toward weapons before they realized who it was. Hammer slid his Ares Predator back into its holster slowly before taking his hand off the grip. Silverblade had appeared without a sound.

"What do you mean 'no'?" Trouble demanded, glaring at the elf.

"The term is a simple one," the elf replied. "You will not access the Matrix from this location until I am satisfied you will not give away our position to the enemy, and until I have a few more questions answered."

"Listen, fairy-boy!" Hammer said, rising from his spot on the couch. "Who died and made you king? You're not the boss of us! Hell, a while ago you were ready to kill us to get what you wanted."

"As long as you are here, you are under my protection," Silverblade said, with deliberate slowness. "And as long as you are here, you will do as I say, or else I will simply turn you over to Lofwyr's hunting dogs and be done with you."

Hammer started toward Silverblade, fists clenched. "You lousy, dandylion-chewing . . ."

"Hold it, Hammer." Talon put a hand on the ork's arm to keep him from launching himself at the elf. "Listen, Silverblade, we'll play it your way for now. We both want the same thing: to find out who wanted to knock off Lofwyr and why. If you want our help, you work with us. You may be used to playing lone wolf, but we're a team. We've got our own ways of doing things and we know our jobs."

"I certainly hope so," Silverblade said. "Because I would like to hire you."

"What?" chorused several voices at once.

Silverblade smiled smugly and walked over to an overstuffed chair in one corner of the room. He sat down like a piano player in front of an audience. He leaned back and regarded the gathered shadowrunners over steepled fingers before replying.

"Yes, I would like to retain the services of your team, Talon. As you have said, I am interested in uncovering more about this plot against Lofwyr, and those I serve cannot provide me with the resources I might need. Therefore, I must make do with what is available."

"We don't work for free," Talon said.

"Of course you don't." Silverblade smiled slightly. "In addition to having helped save your lives . . ."

"Only after you knocked us out," Hammer grumbled.

"In addition to that," Silverblade continued, "and the use of these facilities"—he took in the whole room with a sweep of his hand—"I am prepared to compensate you. How much did Saeder-Krupp owe you before the . . . unfortunate incident?"

"A quarter-million nuyen," Talon said, without missing a beat.

The elf raised one eyebrow in a quizzical look, then smiled again.

"Really? Then you're better-paid than I thought. Or perhaps you're merely lying to me."

"You think so?" Boom asked.

The elf shrugged. "It doesn't really matter. I will pay your team twenty thousand nuyen to assist me in uncovering information about the person or persons behind this plot and dealing with them."

"Negotiable based on possible risk," Talon said.

"You're not in much of a position to negotiate, Talon," Silverblade replied. "I can still simply leave you to your fate, but agreed."

"And you'll give us some leeway to handle investigations ourselves?" Talon asked.

"Under my supervision, of course."

Talon glanced over at his chummers. There was no need for discussion. He could see their concerns written clearly in their eyes and their expressions. He turned back to Silverblade.

"We'll do it," he said, "on two conditions."

The elf gave him a leering smile. "Which are?"

"First, *I'm* in charge of this team, not you. You may be paying the bills, but you're not calling the shots around here."

"Very well," Speren said slowly. "And the other?"

"You help me recover my familiar, which you disrupted. If we're going to do this, we're going to need all the help we can get."

"Agreed."

"All right then," Talon said. "Let's get to work."

Silverblade showed Talon to a basement room in the building, where various hermetic magical supplies were stored. Talon took careful note of them. The ritual supplies in the room were suitable for performing all kinds of ritual sorcery and summoning different elemental spirits. The floor of the room was slate, ideal for drawing and painting hermetic circles. The air was musty, filled with the scents of chalk dust, earth, dried spices, and herbs.

Together, he and Silverblade astrally projected onto the metaplanes, the distant astral dwelling places of the spirits, home of Talon's familiar Aracos. The astral journey to the metaplane of air to retrieve Aracos from his temporary banishment seemed like a short jaunt to Talon. But in the physical world, he awoke to discover that the remainder of the night and part of the next day had passed, about eight hours while they were in a trance state, their spirits journeying. He groaned and stretched, feeling his joints pop, then got slowly to his feet. He saw Silverblade stir and open his eyes before pulling his legs under him and standing gracefully. There was a shimmer in the air and Aracos materialized in the form of a gray-furred wolf, which turned and growled at the elf.

"I don't think he likes me," Silverblade said.

"Can't imagine why," Talon replied. He put a hand on Aracos' fur to soothe him.

"Just let me take one bite out of him, boss," the spirit spoke in Talon's mind.

"Sorry, chummer, but we need him for now," Talon answered. *"He's our new Johnson."* A feeling of disgust came back at him. Talon returned a mental shrug, as if to say "what can we do about it?"

"I assume you can keep him under control?" Silverblade said, with a nod toward Aracos.

"Don't worry," Talon said. "He only goes after the people I tell him to. Shall we rejoin the others?"

"After you," Speren said with a smile and a courtly bow.

Talon walked out of the room and let Aracos watch his back.

"About time you two got back," Boom said when they returned to the main room. In the hours that had gone by, Talon's team had transformed the place into a base of operations. Trouble sat in one of the padded chairs, her deck cradled in her lap, tapping out a steady rhythm on the keys. A cable was plugged into her datajack, and her head was lolled back, not unlike Talon's own journeying trance, although her journey took her into the depths of the German Matrix. Val was working on a drone that was partly broken down on a blanket spread out on the floor. Boom and Hammer were checking the team's weapons and had the trideo unit in one corner of the room tuned to a twenty-four-hour news channel.

"Did we miss anything?" Talon said.

"Not too much," Boom said, gesturing toward the trideo with the gun he was cleaning. "There hasn't been much about Lofwyr on the news. Saeder-Krupp put out a press release this morning that the dragon was involved in some high-level meetings and that he'd canceled a meeting with some skags from the megaplex government, but that's it, no mention of a disturbance, much less an attack. And no trid footage of the dragon, of course. Trouble's been digging almost since you tranced out. She's only jacked out once to have something to eat. She said she had some leads, but she wanted to wait to see where they went. She'll give everyone an update at once."

"No problems?"

"Not a one. Whatever else you can say about the Tir, they've got a nice safe house," Boom said. Silverblade pointedly ignored the left-handed compliment. "No sign of Saeder-Krupp security of any kind. Of course, I can't say for sure when it comes to spooks and mages checking things out."

Silverblade closed his deep green eyes for a moment, then opened them again.

"There are no disruptions of the building's wards and protections," he said. "No signs of any intrusion. If there had been any while we quested, I would have known of it. We remain undiscovered, for the time being."

"Good," Talon said. "Now, is there anything to eat in this place?"

After he'd polished off a couple of sandwiches put together from the house's well-stocked larder, he began to feel much more grounded. He was nearly always hungry after any long magical operation. Such things took a lot of energy, and food helped to replenish him and clear away the heady after-effects of using a lot of magic. As he finished up, he heard Trouble stir as she tapped a few final keys on her cyberdeck, logging off the Matrix with a flourish.

"Evening, boys," she said to Talon and Silverblade, looking up from her chair with a grin. "Looks like you chummers are just in time. I think I've got us a lead on who might be setting themselves up as dragonslayers."

16

"I've got good news and bad news," Trouble said to the rest of the team gathered around the room, all intently focused on her and the information she'd gathered.

"Good news first," Talon said.

"The good news is Lofwyr isn't dead. First thing I did was crack into Saeder-Krupp—not an easy task since their systems are seriously on alert, but I know a few back doors here and there." Talon doubted it was anywhere near as easy as Trouble made it sound, but she definitely knew her business. Trouble was one of the best deckers Talon had ever worked with, and that was saying a lot.

"What did you get?" he asked.

"It seems that Lofwyr managed to survive whatever the crystal tried to do to him, so we're not looking at another dead dragon."

"Great. What's the bad news?" Talon asked.

"The bad news is that Lofwyr isn't dead, but he hasn't regained consciousness since the crystal attacked him like you described. Saeder-Krupp has called in all sorts of paranaturalists and parabiologists for top-secret meetings and examinations, very hush-hush. Their preliminary findings are that the dragon is in some kind of coma. His life signs are stable, but at a very low level, and he's completely unresponsive. Of course, the findings are only preliminary, and nobody really knows a whole lot about dragon biology. A lot of it is probably guesswork on their part."

"So Lofwyr could bloody well be brain-dead, for all we know," Boom said.

"Right," Trouble said. "Which could be almost as bad, if not worse, than him being dead-dead. Rumors have already started up on the 'trix that something happened at the S-K arcology last night, but nobody knows what. Saeder-Krupp is keeping a tight lid on the whole thing: no leaks to the media, top security on the arcology. Still, some people have twigged onto the fact that *something* happened out at the arcology, but, of course, nobody's talking. Speculation is starting to run rampant. I already saw some posts from people saying they think whatever is happening is somehow connected to Dunkelzahn's assassination, that somebody may be gunning for great dragons."

"What about Dr. Goronay?" Silverblade inquired. It was the first time he'd spoken during the briefing, and Trouble glanced over at Talon for a second before answering. The elf was a stranger among them, but Trouble didn't allow that to affect her professionalism.

"It looks like Talon may be right. S-K had an autopsy done on what was left of Goronay after Lofwyr flamed him. From the sound of it, there wasn't a whole hell of a lot left, but they did find some of his cyberware, along with evidence that he may have been slotting BTLs, or something similar."

"Which suggests that he *was* conditioned by someone else somehow," Talon said.

"Right. The only question is who?" Boom said.

"That's where things start to get interesting," Trouble told him. "I figured that somebody must have hooked Goronay on BTLs, because none of the psych profile we dug up indicated any addictive behavior patterns or likelihood of getting involved in that drek. It also doesn't explain the stuff Talon and Boom said he was spouting when he went off. Somebody must have programmed that into him at some point.

"So I did some more digging, using BTL-based mind programming as my basic search parameter, looking for someone who might have had an ax to grind with Lofwyr, Saeder-Krupp, or even Goronay himself. Guess what I came up with."

"Runenthing," Talon said.

"Almost, but not quite. I found a file on the Shadowland boards about an organization that calls itself Winternight. Ever heard of them?"

"Yeah, I read that file," Talon said. "They're some sort of terrorist group, aren't they? Obsessed with bringing about the Norse 'twilight of the gods' so they can end this nasty world and start another one, right?"

"Got it in one," Trouble said. "Not only that but, according to the file, Winternight uses specialized BTL chips to brainwash people into working for them. The chips are completely addictive, and carry encoded subliminal programming instructions."

"The twilight of the gods," Boom said. "That's

what Goronay said before Lofwyr cracked him. He said 'The judgment of the gods is upon you, serpent. The twilight of the gods is upon us all.' "

"You're right!" Talon said. He was always impressed by Boom's memory. "That fits with Winternight's M.O. exactly."

"It gets better," Trouble went on. "Seems Winternight is heavily into Norse/Germanic mythology and imagery, not unlike der Runenthing. Apparently, there are suspected ties between Winternight and various German terrorist organizations, like Alt Welt, which oppose Saeder-Krupp's plans for European Restoration and support Europa Dividus."

"Brackhaus said that S-K had pegged Zoller as a member of Alt Welt," Talon said. "What if he was right? What if Zoller *does* have ties with Alt Welt in some way?"

"No," Silverblade broke in. "That is unlikely. Alt Welt does not even truly exist. The organization is a blind, a front organization used by different terrorist groups to cover their true activities in Europe and elsewhere. The most recent intelligence reports suggested that Alt Welt was being used as a cover for der Nachtmachen some years ago, but that organization is also defunct. A covert operation ended their involvement in European politics."

"Maybe somebody is still using Alt Welt as a front," Val put in, "somebody like this Winternight."

"Zoller is high up in Runenthing," Talon mused, "and S-K suspected him of involvement with Alt Welt, so it sounds like he's our link. Runenthing is strongly nationalistic and opposed to Saeder-Krupp's restoration plans. They're suspected of links to terrorist activities, and it was Zoller that Goronay came to with the crystal. We suspected Goronay was looking to sell it, but what if he was simply programmed to bring it to Zoller as part of the whole plan?"

"But then why did Zoller try to sell it himself?" Val asked.

"He set up the auction," Silverblade said, "but he did not actually try to sell the artifact. Zoller must have known that the artifact had some value to Lofwyr, that it would draw his personal attention. He must have also known that Lofwyr would not allow it to go missing, that he would arrange for agents—such as yourselves—to recover it. You did say that recovering Goronay and the crystal didn't seem as difficult as you originally thought."

"That's true," Talon mused, "but do you really think Zoller would go to such lengths, take those kind of risks, just to get at Lofwyr?"

"To overcome a dragon, you must think like a dragon, in mazes and plots," Silverblade returned.

"Maybe," Boom broke in, "but that doesn't explain everything. How the frag did Zoller know to co-opt Goronay in the first place? How did he know that the crystal would even be there? And, more importantly, how could he have put a spell on it capable of taking down Lofwyr?"

"That's a good point," Talon said. "I've never seen anything like the magic that attacked Lofwyr. It seemed to go right through his defenses. There's no way Zoller, or even his whole circle of magicians, could have cooked up a spell that powerful."

"Unless they have access to magical secrets unknown to you, alley runner," Silverblade said with a trace of smugness.

"If you want to compare wand-size, long ears, we can do it some other time," Talon retorted. "I know what I'm talking about, and I'm saying that I don't think the crystal's magic, whatever it is, came from Zoller. Still, I agree that Zoller and his group are our best possible lead. I think we should follow up on that. Trouble, why don't you and Val put Zoller under surveillance again. Find out whatever you can. If this really is some plan of his, then he should be following up on it, one way or another. Silverblade and I can take some time to look over the crystal and see if there's anything to be learned from it. Boom, you and Hammer . . ."

"I know, I know," the troll said. "We'll hold down the fort and check into the supplies for dinner."

Talon grinned. "Good man. Let's get to work, people."

The silvery sprite glided through the electron world of the Matrix like quicksilver, skating along datalines toward her destination at the speed of light. The computer system Heinrich Zoller used for his personal affairs wasn't anywhere near the league of the high-tech corporate machines Trouble was used to dealing with, but it was still the cutting edge in personal computer systems, which included defensive programs. If Talon was right, and Zoller was tied in with the whole mess in some way, then the fairly light security programs she encountered the first time in could have been camouflage for more sophisticated intrusion countermeasures.

She approached the Matrix icon representing Zoller's personal system. It looked like a dolmen, a standing stone, the sort you might see in dozens of places all over Europe. This particular "stone" stood roughly head-height and was carved with intricate patterns of Nordic runes. Trouble didn't know very much about runes, but she knew plenty about computer encryption systems. The runes represented an encryption lock-out on Zoller's system. She needed a password to get by it.

Fortunately, Trouble had a piece of software for just such a situation. She pulled a magnifying lens out of thin air and used it to examine the runes on the dolmen. As she peered through the glass, her program began invisibly searching for possible password combinations. In the dark ages of computing tech—back in the late twentieth century—such a search could have taken hours, but Trouble's cyberdeck was as far ahead of those clumsy machines as they were ahead of the abacus. Light pulsed in the optical circuitry of the deck, the program executed, and the runes began to resolve themselves into a recognizable pattern. Trouble input the password, and the "stone" split open to reveal a doorway inside.

She passed through into the system itself. The dolmen was far larger inside than it appeared, containing an entire large room that represented Zoller's computer system. The room was decorated in the same relentless Nordic motif as the dolmen, looking like an ancient meadhall. Dull, duller, dullest, Trouble thought as she looked around. She'd been inside Zoller's system once before, when she'd put her spybot frame in place, but this time the system was much more active, and much better protected. A large, black-furred wolf slept curled up near the fireplace in the hall. It wore a spiked iron collar and looked large enough to tear Trouble in half. Definitely some kind of protective ice. She'd have to be careful.

Trouble called up the system's activity log. She wanted to see what Zoller had been up to. He didn't use the system much. No surprise there. Members of der Runenthing—and Winternight, she recalled— didn't overly trust the Matrix or computer technology in general. They believed such things weakened those who used them, that the illusions created by the Matrix were a trick to lure honest folk into lives as sickly couch potatoes. In some ways, Trouble supposed they were right. Plenty of people went into the Matrix and preferred never to come out, living virtual lives in a place "better" than the harsh and dirty reality they'd left behind. She knew plenty of deckers like that, chummers who hadn't seen sunlight literally in years.

Still, as a modern businessman, Zoller couldn't entirely avoid the "evils" of the Matrix. All telecommunications went through the world computer grid and, as a magical consultant, Zoller needed to be available for his clients. His home system contained some very nice personal-assistant software that managed Zoller's calls and provided potential clients with information about his various services. It was the program that most interested Trouble. Its logs and databanks were represented by the collection of books and scrolls stacked up on one table in the virtual mead-hall. Trouble headed toward them, tiptoeing past the sleeping wolf. There she drew a slim silver wand and waved it over the table, sprinkling the papers with glittering electron fairy dust. Almost immediately, one of the scrolls began to glow faintly.

It was the most recent file. Trouble tapped it gently with her wand and it floated up into the air, where it unfurled for her to view it: a record of an email Zoller had received not long after Talon and Boom paid their fateful visit to Saeder-Krupp. It read: "Stage Two accomplished. Meet at the train yard for Stage Three. J."

Trouble downloaded the information to her cyberdeck, paying particularly close attention to the email address of the sender. She would try and track it down next. It looked like a temporary address, probably long gone by now, but there was always a chance someone had been sloppy, like Zoller not deleting his email files. Speaking of which . . . she thought, and made her way over to the waste bin at one end of the table. She might be able to recover some interesting things from Zoller's deleted files, with a little reconstruction work.

She had just begun sorting through the trash bin when there was a snort from the wolfhound by the fire. *Frag!* Trouble thought. She'd been in the system too long. The intrusion countermeasure had detected her. With startling suddenness, the black wolf sprang to life. It suddenly split in two, and there were two wolves where there was only one before. One howled and rushed off, nose to the ground. It was backtracking Trouble's data trail, trying to figure out the location from which she was decking. Once found, it would report that information to the system, and possibly trigger other IC. The other wolf snarled and leapt at the intruder, clearly trying to keep Trouble busy until the trace program could complete its work.

Fortunately, Trouble came into the system prepared. Her spritely form was clad in intricate silver armor that deflected the attack of the second wolf. She produced a satchel out of thin air and opened it to reveal a white rabbit, its pink nose twitching, eyes bright (Trouble was particularly proud of that little bit of programming).

"Okay, Bugs," she said, "go get 'im boy!" She tossed the rabbit onto the floor and it took off in a white blur, past the wolf tracking her trail. The rabbit stopped, practically in front of the wolf, and wiggled its cottony tail, as if taunting the wolf to catch it. The wolf left off following Trouble's trail and raced after the rabbit, which led it off into the depths of the Matrix. By the time the trace program's diagnostics figured out it was chasing after shadows, Trouble would be long gone.

She turned and met the attacking wolf with a shining silver sword in one hand. The time for subtlety was over. She slashed at the wolf as it charged, her blade cutting off one of its paws, revealing it to be solid silver and pixels inside. The wolf snarled and snapped at her, but it could not get through her armor, and her fairy wings carried her away before it could bring her down. She danced around the wolf, slashing and stabbing it with her blade, until finally the program came apart in silvery ribbons of code and crashed altogether.

Now, then, where was I? Trouble thought as she resumed rummaging through Zoller's trash.

Talon sat cross-legged on the floor of the basement room, opposite Silverblade. Between them on the floor sat the crystal. It remained dull and gray, with none of its former luster or the faint inner glow Talon had noticed before. Around them was drawn a warding circle, to protect the building against any magical energies they might accidentally unleash, though Talon doubted any ward could contain the kind of magical power he'd seen the crystal display.

"Are you ready?" asked Silverblade.

Talon nodded. "As I'm likely to be. Let's see what there is to see."

He took a deep breath and focused on his heartbeat, as he'd learned to do from his mentor so many years ago. He slipped easily into a light trance state, allowing his awareness to expand beyond the physical world into the realms of the astral plane. From the astral he could sense the forces of magic and the life force of living beings. To his magical sight, the warding circle appeared as an opalescent shimmering dome of light enclosing himself and Silverblade. The elf's own aura showed brightly around him; filled with magical power, bright with confidence, touched in places with hints of other emotions kept tightly controlled by the constraints of his duty. Talon could also see Aracos, in his wolf-form, standing nearby. His familiar would remain in astral form to better help study the magical crystal.

Talon turned his attention toward the crystal itself. Most non-living objects had no aura to speak of, only the emotional and magical imprints they picked up from being handled by living beings. As an enchanted item, the crystal should have had a strong aura of its own, but it was weak and barely visible. Whatever power resided in the crystal, most of it had fled.

"The aura is weak," Silverblade said quietly. "It looks like the crystal expended whatever enchantment it held all at once."

"Yes," Talon replied. "Not unlike a spell anchor of some kind." The spell anchor was a magical technique for "attaching" a spell to an item and setting it to activate when certain conditions were fulfilled, like a magical "time bomb" of sorts.

"Hmmm, perhaps. But an extraordinarily powerful spell anchor to be sure. No mere focus could have done what you described."

Talon peered more intently at the smoky-colored crystal, looking past its surface, trying to plumb its depths, to learn what secrets it held. *What are you?* he asked silently. *Where did you come from? And why did someone use you to get at Lofwyr?*

The smoky color of the crystal seemed to expand to fill his field of vision. It was as though he dove into the very substance of the crystal itself until he was immersed in it, surrounded by it. He was drawn down, down into the depths of it, until he felt he could almost drown in it.

Suddenly, Talon found himself soaring. He was flying, high above the ground, which stretched out below like a multicolored patchwork. His vision was amazingly sharp; he could still make out the details of small creatures moving far below. He could see some of them look up in awe, could feel the fear that radiated off them, like smoke rising from a flame. The wind was strong at his back and flowed over his wings and his body as he soared. The heat of the sun beat down on his back and his outstretched wings, and he luxuriated in the sensation for a while. It felt good to fly, stretching his muscles and feeling the air around him.

Then he spotted them, a small herd of creatures moving along the ground far below. They were what he was looking for: prey. Instantly, his eyes focused on them and he could see that they were some sort of cattle, a fine meal, indeed. His wings furled in and he dove toward the earth like an arrow from a bow. The animals sensed his approach, but far too late to do them any good. Some of them tried to run, beginning to stampede in their panic.

As the ground rushed up to meet him, Talon felt his mighty wings unfurl again, snapping out to catch the wind, his mighty tail acting as a rudder to keep him moving straight and upright as he pulled up out of his dive to fly close to the ground, so near the prey he could smell the strong scent of their hides. He opened his mouth and a geyser of flame erupted from it, washing over part of the herd. They screamed in pain and terror, then suddenly fell silent as they were seared by the flames.

Talon banked around and landed on the ground, mighty wing beats blowing away the last of the smoke from the half dozen or so charred cattle that lay on the ground. He leaned down and took a large bite out of one, biting off nearly half of the beast with his massive jaws. He chewed on it, still warm, felt the bones crunch under his teeth. He swallowed, savoring the taste, eager for the rest of his feast. Then a voice called out to him.

"Talon!"

Who dares interrupt my meal? he thought. He looked around, but saw no one. The voice came again, quickly followed by another.

"Talon!"

"Talon, can you hear us? What's going on? Hey, boss!"

Talon shook his head. What was he doing? What was going on? Just as suddenly as it began, the vision vanished and Talon found himself sitting on the floor of the basement room. Silverblade was shaking his shoulder while Aracos, materialized in wolf form, nuzzled his side and eyed the elven paladin with distrust.

"Wha . . . ?" Talon managed to gasp as he looked Silverblade in the eyes.

"Talon, what happened to you?" Silverblade asked. "We were studying the crystal and you fell deeper into trance. I couldn't bring you out of it."

"I . . . I'm not sure," Talon said. He told Silverblade and Aracos all that he'd seen during his vision. "It was almost like an astral quest," he said, "only I wasn't in control. It was like I was living somebody else's life."

"A dragon's life," Aracos said.

"Interesting," Silverblade mused. "I experienced none of this. All I could determine was that the stone once held powerful magical energies, most of which are gone now. I still can't tell exactly what its enchantment is for, or who might have enchanted it. Whoever it was, he is a more skilled sorcerer than

Zoller or any of his cronies. Did your vision give you any insights about the crystal?"

Talon shook his head. "Not really. The crystal didn't seem involved with it at all. At least, not that I can remember."

Just then, a tiny bell icon flashed in the upper right corner of Talon's field of vision. He mentally keyed his headcom to pick up.

"Talon here," he said aloud for Silverblade's benefit, holding up one hand to stay the elf's questions.

"It's Trouble. You two need to get up here. Zoller is on the move, and I think he can lead us to whoever is behind this."

17

The train yards were located in a particularly rundown area of Essen. Although trains were still used to move goods to different parts of the German Alliance, they were being supplanted by remote-piloted trucks and cargo-lifters. The train yard was dark and virtually silent but for the few sounds drifting from the distant inhabited areas of the city.

Talon and the others sat in their van on the outskirts of the yard. The van's lights were dark, its engine silent. Val sat in the driver's seat, jacked into the controls, her remote deck sitting on her lap. Trouble was in the front passenger seat. She also had her cyberdeck on her lap, but wasn't jacked in at the moment. Instead, she remained alert and kept watch for any signs of trouble outside.

In the back near the rear door was a launching rack for several remote-drones, along with the rest of the team. With Talon was Boom, Hammer, and Speren Silverblade, all of them dressed in dark clothing under armored jackets or long coats like those Talon and Speren wore. The elf wore his sword on his belt and Talon had his own mageblade sheathed at his side. They all carried sidearms—Boom and

Hammer had several guns each—and they checked them one last time.

"Ready?" Talon said, receiving nods from the others. "All right, let's go."

"Good luck," Trouble said from the front.

Talon slid the side door of the van open and the runners hopped down, moving quickly and quietly away from the van. Hammer applied a small pair of bolt-cutters to the chains holding the gate shut, and they slipped into the train yard. They moved across the open spaces, dashing from one place of concealment to another, hiding behind stacks of crates and the sides of buildings and supply bins as they moved.

Talon checked with the rest of the team over his headcom.

"Team Two, this is One, come in," he subvocalized through his cybernetic link-up. He could hear Trouble's response in his head.

"One, this is Two. We read you."

"We're almost in position. Val, what have you got?"

"They're definitely in that warehouse near the tracks," Val said. "I'm moving in for a closer look now."

"Be careful," Talon told her, then turned to the rest of the team. "Val's drone is heading into the warehouse for a closer look. Let's get into position and be ready to move."

"If these rune-magicians are tampering with magical forces, we had better watch the astral plane," Silverblade said quietly.

"Already taken care of," Talon replied. "*Aracos,*

how are things on the astral?" he sent to his familiar spirit.

"Not too good, boss. There's definitely signs of something nasty around here. Tough to say for sure out here, but I think somebody has been doing some major league mojo around here for a while. There's also something else, some kind of power building up, but I can't say for sure what it is. I'll keep watching."

"Good," Talon said. *"Let me know the second you see something else."*

"Aracos says there are signs in the astral of magic being worked here before," he told the others. "And that they may be working magic now, building up for some kind of ritual."

"Then we should see about interrupting their plans," Silverblade said, resting one hand on the hilt of his magesword.

"I'm in," Val said over the commlink, routed to speak to the whole team. She had sent a tiny Renraku arachnid drone in to check out the warehouse beforehand. Normally, Talon would have simply used astral projection to scout the warehouse himself, or sent Aracos to do it, but with Zoller and his magical cronies about, they couldn't risk using magic until absolutely necessary, for fear of being detected. The spider-drone was small enough to go unnoticed, and able to fit into tight quarters.

"Zoller's here all right," Val continued. "He's inside the warehouse with eight other people. They're all dressed up like something out of a fantasy simflick, with cloaks and furs and drek like that. They're standing around a circle drawn out on the floor with magical-looking symbols around the outside edge. They've also got some company."

"Show me," Talon said. Val opened a link to Talon's headware and transmitted a low-resolution video of what the drone was seeing. It imposed itself over his field of vision, and he could see the room exactly as Val described it.

"There's some kind of metallic cylinder in the middle of the circle," Val said, "and they've got people chained to it, three of them. All elves." Silverblade's face darkened and a dangerous light flashed in his eyes at this announcement. "They look like squatters or people they picked up off the street," she said, "and they look like they've been doped up or something to keep them from fighting. Frag, I think we've wandered onto the set of some kind of freaky magical production."

"Nine of them," Boom said, "probably all mages. Can we take that many?"

"We'll need some help," Talon said. He turned to Silverblade. "Spirits?" he asked quietly.

The elf nodded. "It might even the odds enough if we sent elementals against the magicians inside, especially if they don't have any spirits present for the ritual. If they do, then our spirits can keep them occupied."

"They've also got no muscle," Hammer said. "From what Val said, it's just those mages. Mages may be tough, but they're not immune to flying lead, either."

"So we do this?" Talon asked.

"Damn straight," Boom grunted. "I'm not standing around while these fraggers do whatever they're doing, not to mention the fact that Zoller may have set us up."

"Same here," Hammer put in.

"I will not ignore my people in danger," Silverblade said. "Zoller and his cronies must pay."

"All right then," Talon said. "Let's do it. Regular magician-drill, chummers. Silverblade, you're with me. We keep spirits hammering them, and we protect everyone from incoming spells. Don't spellcast unless you have to. There's no point wasting effort against their defenses." The elf nodded.

"Team Two," Talon said over the commlink, "we're going in. Fire up the reinforcements. We'll do the same."

"Roger that," Val responded.

Talon closed his eyes and whispered words of power under his breath. He sent out the call through astral space into the depths of the elemental planes, the dwelling place of the spirits bound to serve him. In a few moments, the air around Talon shimmered faintly, like the air above a roadway in the desert. Three of Talon's elementals were present, awaiting his commands. He opened his eyes and saw Silverblade surrounded by a similar faint shimmering. The elven mage called up four of his own elementals to aid them against the rune-magicians gathered in the warehouse. Talon hoped it was enough.

"At my command," he sent to the spirits, *"attack the humans inside the warehouse. Do not kill them unless you must, and leave this human alive."* He sent a mental image of Zoller to them. He wanted the German magician alive for questioning.

"We obey," the spirits responded.

"Aracos," he called, *"is the warehouse warded?"*

"Nope, I don't see anything from out here. Of course, there may be wards inside the walls or something. Want me to . . ."

"No," Talon said, *we can't risk warning them. We'll deal with it when we get there."*

Talon heard a faint humming and looked up to see one of Val's rotor-drones hovering overhead. The drone was shaped like a tapered cylinder with a rounded top, from which sprouted the rotor blades that kept it aloft. It was armor-plated, and its "chin" held a machine gun on a swivel mount, giving it a wide arc of fire. Like most highly technological items, it was also fairly resistant to magic.

"Boom, you're with me," Talon said. "Hammer, you and Silverblade take the back. Let's move."

The runners split into pairs, with Hammer and the elf mage working their way around to the back of the warehouse. Talon and Boom headed for the sliding loading doors in front, while Val's drone headed for the roof, its dark hull nearly invisible in the shadows.

"Two, what are they up to inside?" Talon asked as they neared the doors.

"Looks like they're getting started," Val replied. "They're standing in a circle around the column and meditating or something."

When they reached the doors, Boom placed a small shaped-charge against the door panel.

"Set for ten seconds," Talon said.

"In place," Hammer's voice said over the comm.

"On my mark," Talon said. "Mark." Boom hit the countdown on the charge, and the two of them moved back. The timer ticked off the final seconds before the charge went off.

The small shaped charge blew through the reinforced sheet metal of the warehouse door like it was paper, leaving a jagged hole large enough for Boom and Talon to move through.

"Go!" Talon said. Boom pulled a small, metallic sphere from his belt, pulled the pin and tossed it through the opening before the smoke cleared. Two loud bangs sounded within seconds of each other as the stun grenades Boom and Hammer hurled into the room went off together. The shadowrunners immediately rushed into the warehouse.

As Talon hoped, the suddenness of their attack and the effects of the stun grenades had the runemagicians reeling. They had been about to begin their ritual, but now everything was in chaos and they were having difficulty knowing which way to turn. He could see some of them starting to gather their wits and preparing spells. Leveling the Narcoject gun he carried, Talon fired at one of the magicians, his dart catching him in the shoulder. The fast-acting neurostun chemical immediately caused the mage to collapse, his eyes rolling back in his head as he hit the floor.

Talon saw the others firing at the confused mages, and two more went down from the effects of the neurostun.

Two dark clouds materialized out of the air, flickering from within with eerie blue light. They immediately engulfed two of the rune magicians, cutting off their chants and cries, which changed to coughing and gagging noises as the spellcasters gasped for breath in the relentless grip of the air elementals. Talon saw his water elemental materialize and attack another mage, surrounding him in a globule of water. Bubbles poured from the startled magician's mouth as the spirit forced the air from his lungs. That was more than half of the circle out of action already.

The remaining magicians wasted no time before mounting a counterattack. Talon saw Zoller raise his arms as he shouted out magical words, power shimmering in the air between his hands. A bolt of green fire shot out at Talon, but the flames seemed to strike an invisible shield in the air. They flowed around Talon and he could feel their heat, but his own magical shielding held against the force of the spell. He saw one of the other mages hurl a spell at Hammer, only to have it blocked by Silverblade's defenses. The remaining magicians also hurled spells. Talon was able to block another with help from Aracos, but the fourth struck Boom and sent the troll reeling, his armored jacket smoking from the impact of a stream of acid.

Then there was a crash as Val's rotor drone came through the rooftop skylight, sending shards of broken plexiglass raining down. The drone hovered above the fight and trained its machine gun down toward the startled magicians. The gun chattered and bullets slammed into two of the magicians, nearly cutting them in half. They collapsed to the ground in pools of blood. The tide had quickly turned back to the shadowrunners. Talon was sure they could handle the Runenthing now. There were only three of them capable of fighting back at the moment, including Zoller.

Talon ran through the melee and rushed Zoller, who tried to ready another spell. He wasn't quite fast enough, and Talon slammed into him like a linebacker, sending them both rolling on the floor. He jammed an arm against Zoller's windpipe to cut off whatever incantation he was starting and brought Talonclaw up against his exposed throat.

"You've got some explaining to do, fragger!" Talon said as he pinned Zoller down. "All right!" he yelled to the remaining magicians. "We've got your boss! Give up now or he's gonna be speaking spells through a second mouth!"

The fighting died down as the remaining magicians raised their hands and were covered by the other shadowrunners. The magicians entrapped by the elementals had passed out from lack of oxygen, and the spirits withdrew, awaiting further orders from their summoner.

"Boss!" Aracos said in Talon's mind. *"One of those rune magicians has some kind of protective spell up around him. There's something weird about him. Watch out."*

Just then, one of the dark-robed figures took a step forward, and Hammer turned to cover him.

"I'm afraid you're mistaken, Talon," the man said in deep, unaccented English. "Herr Zoller is not the leader of this circle. I am, and you've chosen the wrong time to interfere."

The robed figure raised a hand and Hammer fired a burst from his Ingram. The bullets spattered off an invisible wall that seemed to spring up between them and their target, leaving the man unmoved. He gestured, and Val's rotor-drone was swatted out of the air like an insect struck by a giant, invisible hand. It smashed against the wall, then dropped to the ground as a pile of useless junk.

Talon dragged Zoller to his feet, still holding Talonclaw pressed against his neck as Boom, Hammer, and Silverblade all opened up on the mysterious figure with their guns. Bullets ricocheted and bounced off the invisible barrier, but none of them reached their mark. The figure drew back his hood to reveal a face with refined Aryan features and dark blond hair. His eyes, however, were a deep amber color, unlike any human eyes Talon had ever seen, but they reminded him of other eyes, inhuman eyes, he'd seen recently.

"Poor things," the man said, like a father lecturing his children. "You have no idea what you have stumbled into, have you?" He took a step toward Talon.

"Stop right there," Talon said, "or Zoller's still toast!"

"Ah, well that is a problem," the man returned. "Allow me to relieve you of it." He raised a hand.

"Master, no!" Zoller cried out, "I've served you well! I've . . . argh!"

"Holy frag!" Talon said as the man gestured lightly and Zoller's entire body began to melt away in Talon's grip. The form of the Runenthing magician flowed and shifted out of Talon's hands, his dark robes collapsing into a heap on the ferrocrete floor. Something stirred from inside them, the cloth rustling to reveal a large toad. It croaked, then hopped away from the stunned Talon.

"Now then," the mystery man said calmly, "we can talk without interruption. I had hoped to use these fools to augment the ritual I wanted to perform tonight, but I suppose they can still do so, in a way." He gestured again and chains leapt from their hanging places along the walls and ceiling struts to entrap the remaining Runenthing members. The chains dragged them to the foot of the metallic cylinder where the elven prisoners were bound. Some of them cried out, but were flogged for their efforts until they fell silent, mewling and whimpering.

"Do you consider their lives worth your efforts?" the robed man asked, gesturing toward the elven prisoners, who remained in their drug-hazed state.

"I will fight to protect any of my people from the like of you!" Silverblade spat.

"Will you, paladin? And what do you know of me? I, who know your race far better than you can imagine?"

"You set us up!" Talon said. "You set us up to take down Lofwyr for you."

"Yes," the man replied. "And it worked far better than I'd imagined. My brother's own greed and curiosity always did get the better of him."

"Your . . . brother?" Talon said.

"Of course." The man smiled. "Who else could possibly have crafted a spell to strike a blow against one of the mightiest of great dragons except for another?"

The man seemed to shrug, and his body suddenly expanded. The dark robe ripped and tore as his body stretched. Leathery wings sprang from his back as his arms and legs elongated, becoming scaly. His neck stretched impossibly and his face distorted, elongating and becoming a snout filled with dagger-like teeth. It stretched up, up, until it nearly reached the roof of the warehouse. In an instant, Talon and his team were faced with a gigantic golden-scaled dragon.

"I am Alamais!" the dragon's thought-voice echoed in their minds. *"And you, my little puppets, have chosen a poor time to try and cut your strings."*

Faced with the dragon, Talon wanted only to run, to escape. But for some reason, he couldn't move. He couldn't do anything but stare in horrified fascination at the creature that loomed overhead.

"Aracos, run!" he thought to his ally. *"Get out of here and back to Trouble and Val!"* He couldn't tell if the spirit obeyed, for all his attention was focused on the looming form of the dragon.

"Still, your timing is fortunate," Alamais said. *"You will have an opportunity to witness the completion of my latest work."*

The chains holding the elves to the metal cylinder fell away, dropping them to the floor. Talon could see, printed on the side of the metal, radioactive warning labels and markings in German, along with the Saeder-Krupp logo.

Oh my gods, he thought. *It's a nuke!*

"Now," Alamais' thought-voice said, *"prepare for your final journey."*

Talon felt a surge of magical power from the dragon overcoming his will, overcoming his defenses and driving him down into darkness. He tried to fight against it, but it was too powerful. He felt his grip on consciousness fading, then everything went black.

18

In his dreams, Talon soared. He imagined once again he was a mighty creature, flying high over the Earth. The ground below stretched out in all directions like a fantastic patchwork. The air flowed over his wings as he glided on the thermal currents, supported by the power of his magic. The magic flowed as strongly as the warm air itself.

Magic was everywhere, a part of everything. He could sense its flow as clearly as he sensed everything else, his perceptions expanded far beyond those of a mere human. To Talon, it was like a blind man given the gift of sight, except in his case it was more than just one sense, it was many. It was clear vision and hearing, a sense of smell that could pick up odors of grass, flowers, and animals far below, a sense of emotion, of space and time, of magic and thought. All the sensory impressions were so intense as to be nearly overwhelming.

He approached the majestic peaks of some mountains, feeling the winds change. The temperature dropped and he could sense the flow of powerful magic around these mountains, his home. He circled around a broad plateau on the tallest peak before slowly gliding in for a landing there. Folding his wings close to his body, he then made his way into the dark cave opening that awaited him.

The interior of the cave was cool and dark, a pleasant contrast to the warmth and sunlight outside. Its stone walls were worn smooth from centuries of erosion and, Talon sensed, from subtle and careful shaping through magic. Embedded in the walls were crystals, some mere flecks, others the size of a human's entire torso, all the colors of the rainbow, all of them gleaming in the light coming from the mouth of the cave. They were beautiful; more than that, they were powerful. Talon could sense the energies inherent in each of the crystals, the auras that flickered around them, shedding a warm astral light in the cavern.

In the center of the cave was a deep pit dug into the warm sand, a cool and comfortable place to rest. Scattered around the pit were gleaming objects: sacks spilling over with gold and silver coins, sparkling gemstones, trinkets, and jewelry forged by small and clever hands. Mementos and tokens from those paying homage and those foolish enough to challenge him. Each represented a memory, and Talon found he liked to view them and recall those memories often.

He moved to rest from his travels when he heard a sound outside the cavern. A loud roar shook the air, making crystals vibrate and hum. The sound of it was unmistakable: a challenge. Anger fired Talon's blood as he turned and left the cavern to find out who dared to challenge him on his own ground. The roar spoke to the predator instinct within him and called him to answer, called him to battle.

Leaving the cave, he threw back his head and roared an answer to the challenge. He could see the challenger now as he approached: another male, large and powerful. His scaly hide gleamed golden in the sunlight, his wings glinted as they caught the light. His teeth were like daggers and his talons like swords. But Talon was not afraid. He had been challenged and to show fear was to admit defeat. He would not be overcome by this challenger, especially not by this one. With a mighty sweep of his wings, he took to the air to meet the challenge.

They would use no spells, no magic or power except the strength of their own muscles, the sharpness of their own weapons and the cunning of their own minds. It was the way of things, and had been since the beginning of memory. There would be no quarter, and no mercy. Talon rushed forward to meet his foe.

"*Boss!*" a voice called to him. It seemed familiar somehow, but Talon ignored it in the rush of battle.

"*Boss!*" it came again. "*Talon, you've got to listen to me! You've got to wake up! But don't move, and don't open your eyes. Listen to me, boss, you've got to wake up!*"

Talon felt a feathery touch on his face and stirred. The image of the battle faded and he found himself listening to the voice that spoke in his mind.

"*Hmmm? Aracos?*" he thought.

"*Yeah, it's me,*" the spirit said. "*Listen, boss, stay very still. Don't let them know you're awake.*"

Talon nearly bolted completely awake as memory of recent events flooded back into his mind.

"Alamais! The dragon . . ."

"Yeah," Aracos said. "I thought you and the others were goners for sure. Last thing I saw before I took off was the dragon getting ready to cast some kind of spell. I thought for a second he was going to frag everybody, but he must have just put you to sleep. I could still sense you through our link."

"What happened?" Talon asked. "Where are we?" He was completely awake now, although he obeyed his ally's counsel and kept outwardly calm, neither moving nor opening his eyes. He could feel the cold weight of chains around his wrists and he could feel a faint vibration and swaying from the floor. They were moving.

"You're on a train, headed for Berlin," Aracos said. "You, Boom, Hammer, and that Silverblade guy are chained up to the bomb Alamais and his Runenthing buddies were playing around with."

"A nuke," Talon said.

"Looks like. There are a couple of guards in the train car with us, but it looks like they're mundanes. There's also some kind of enchantment on the bomb, but I can't make heads or tails of it. I've never seen anything like it before."

"You sure the guards are mundanes?" Talon asked. "They couldn't be masking from your sight?"

"Could be," Aracos replied. "But they're not astrally aware, so they can't see me at all."

Good. Talon focused his concentration, relaxing his body even more. He needed a better look at things, without opening his eyes or giving away that he was awake. He went into a trance and allowed his astral form to slip free of his physical body, leaving it virtually comatose. That would keep the guards focused while he and Aracos got some things done.

As he entered the astral plane, Talon saw his ally standing beside his physical body in wolf form. He could also see the others, chained as he was to the metallic cylinder of the nuke inside the train car. Their auras showed that they were unconscious, but otherwise unharmed. There was some kind of spell affecting them, most likely keeping them knocked out for the rest of the trip.

There were two other men in the car. They wore body armor and carried rifles cradled in their arms. They also wore heavy-looking swords at their waists. Both men were heavily bearded and Nordic-looking. Talon noticed that both of them had some cyberware; dark patches in their aura showed the presence of artificial implants in their heads. They didn't appear to have any other implants to speak of, but that didn't mean they weren't dangerous.

"What's the situation?" Talon asked his familiar spirit.

"After the dragon KOed the rest of you, I went back to the van with Trouble and Val and we got the frag out of there. Val sent up another drone to keep an eye on things at the train yard, and we saw them load you on the train with the bomb. I could tell you were still alive at least, so we needed to get you out of here. Val pulled in some favors and got us the use of a chopper. She and Trouble are following the train while I slipped in to find out how you were doing. Now we've got to get you all out of this place."

"Easier said than done," Talon said. *"The others still aren't awake. Did you remove the sleeping spell from me?"*

Aracos shook his shaggy head. *"Wasn't me,"* he said. *"There wasn't any spell on you when I got here."*

"Hmmm," Talon mused. *"Well, I can try to deal with the spell on the others, but I've got to be on the physical plane for that, which means dealing with the guards."*

"I think you and I can handle the guards," Aracos said. *"There's only two of them, and they don't know you're awake. Doesn't look like they've got any magical protection."*

"True. Okay, here's the plan."

A few moments later, Talon's astral form returned to his physical body. He carefully pretended to remain unconscious, but kept in mind where he'd last seen the guards. Any moment now, Aracos would go into action.

Talon heard a deep growl from one side of the train car and then one of the guards saying something to the other in German. Talon didn't have his German chip active, but by the tone of surprise in the guard's voice, it wasn't too hard to guess what he'd said. Talon opened his eyes and went into action.

As they'd planned, the guards had turned to look in surprise at the ghostly wolf that suddenly appeared behind them. Talon concentrated and focused on the two men. One of them heard a faint noise from the chains as Talon moved and started to turn back, but he was too late. Talon's spell struck both guards instantly and overcame their wills, forcing them down into unconsciousness much like his own chained companions.

"*Nice job*," Aracos said.

Talon held his hands up in front of his face, staring intently at the chains.

"Shatter," he whispered, focusing a bolt of magical force against the chains. They broke apart with a popping sound and clattered to the floor. As he got up, Talon checked his headware systems. They were all operating normally. His chronometer showed that he'd been out for a few hours. He opened up a channel on his commlink.

"Team Two, this is One. Over," he said quietly.

"Thank God!" he heard over the link. "One, this is Two. What's your situation?" Trouble asked.

"Could be better," Talon replied. "I'm loose, and Aracos and I have taken care of our guards. The others are still out. I'm going to try to wake them. How are things from your end?"

"We're keeping up," Val broke in. "This bird can pace the train you're on all day long, but we haven't exactly got unlimited fuel. You're also headed through some fairly rough terrain, which is making things kind of interesting. You want us to come down and pick you up?"

"Sounds good to me," Talon said. "How do you want to work it?"

"Rooftop pickup's probably our best bet," Val said. "We can lower you a ladder and pace the train."

"All right. I'll signal when we're ready."

"Roger that," Val said and Talon closed the link.

Bending down near where Boom lay, he focused his senses on the astral plane once more and examined the aura of the spell around his friend. It was a powerful one, very powerful. He'd never seen anything quite like it before. But then, this was the magic of a dragon, probably a great dragon. Still, he had to try and break the spell. There was no way he could get the others out while they were unconscious.

"Aracos, I need your help here," he called to his familiar.

Aracos settled on Talon's shoulder in his falcon form. "Looks tough," was all he said after examining the spell.

"I know." Talon held his hands out over Boom's head and chest and focused on breaking the spell. He threw his own will against the spell's energies, drawing on Aracos' power as well. The spell was powerful, more powerful than anything Talon had encountered before. All his efforts were having no effect. But he had to overcome it, or else leave everyone else behind, and that was something Talon was not willing to do.

He redoubled his effort, focusing on the structure of the spell, on pulling it apart. Sweat beaded on his forehead and he could hear the blood roaring in his ears. Then something broke. He felt the spell yield, grabbed onto that slight weakness and pushed with all his strength. The seconds ticked by like hours, but the spell slowly dissolved and his companions began to awaken.

"Look sharp," Talon told them. "We're getting out of here in a hurry. We're on a train bound for Berlin and riding with some nasty company." He jerked his chin toward the tapered cylinder of the bomb. Almost immediately, the others were fully awake and ready.

"So how are we getting out?" Boom asked.

"Val and Trouble are following in a chopper," Talon explained. "They can pick us up off the roof."

"What about one of your air spirits? Couldn't they help us out?"

Talon shook his head. "I can't feel any of my servitor elementals. Alamais must have completely disrupted them somehow. How about you, Silverblade?"

The elf likewise shook his head. "No, nothing."

"Then we're on our own," Talon said.

"And unarmed," Hammer added.

For the first time, Talon noticed that they'd been relieved of their weapons and ammo belts. His hand automatically went to his side and found Talonclaw was missing.

"Damn!" he said. "Well, there's nothing we can do about it right now. First order of business is getting out of here." Talon moved toward the door at the side of the car. "This looks like the only way out."

"As far as I could tell," Aracos told him. "But it looks like it has some electronics hooked up to it."

"An alarm." Talon examined the edge of the door. Aracos was right, there were hints of some sophisticated electronic circuitry there. "Boom, take a look at this," he said.

The troll bent down to examine the door. Despite his brutish appearance, Boom had become quite adept with electronics over the years. Still, he shook his head after a few moments.

"Sophisticated stuff," he said. "No way I can defeat it without at least some tools."

"Can we open the door?" Talon asked.

Boom flexed his massive arms a couple times. "Null sweat there, but we'll definitely set off an alarm if we do."

"No choice," Talon said. "Let's do it." He opened up a commlink and told Val and Trouble to get ready.

"Hurry it up, Talon," came Val's voice. "You're headed for a tunnel and we'll have to go around it. If you go through, it could be a little while before we catch up to you again."

"If we wait, somebody might come to check on us," Talon said. He looked over at Boom. "Okay, do it, chummer."

Boom grabbed the handle of the door in his huge hands, firmly planted his feet, and yanked. The door groaned in protest for a moment, followed by the sound of a snap as it slid open, letting a howling blast of frigid air into the train car.

From the open door, the runners could see it was still night, and they were speeding along through rocky, hilly terrain. Without hesitation, Boom leaned out the door and reached for the ladder mounted on the side of the car. He swung out into the darkness and began climbing.

"Go," Talon told the others. "I'll go last." Hammer nodded and followed Boom, leaving Talon, Silverblade, and Aracos alone in the train car with the unconscious guards and the dark shape of the bomb.

"You next," Talon told the elf.

"Afraid to turn your back to me?" Silverblade said.

"No, I just want to make sure you get off this thing. We still may need your help."

The elf gave a short bow from the waist before

leaning out and grabbing the ladder. Then Talon followed him out as Aracos shifted back into his astral form.

"Team One, we have you on visual," Val said to Talon over his headcom. "We're coming in." As Talon clambered up the ladder toward the roof of the car, wind whipping his long coat around him, he could see the running lights of the helicopter as it began to descend toward the train. As he reached the roof where the others crouched, the chopper began to lower a rope ladder from the open cargo door in the side. Val carefully piloted it to bring the swinging ladder close to the roof of the train.

"Almost, almost," Boom said as the rope ladder drew closer. The big troll shot out one hand in a lightning grab and managed to snatch the end of the ladder out of the air.

"Got it!" he said. "You sure this thing'll hold me?" he yelled to Talon.

Talon paused to listen for a second. "Val says yes!" he shouted back. "Now get going!"

Hammer held the end of the ladder as Hammer clapped him once on the shoulder and started climbing. "You next, elf-boy," he said to Silverblade when Hammer reached the chopper. The elf didn't bother to argue, but simply grabbed the ladder and started climbing with great agility.

"You're next, Talon," the troll said.

"But . . ."

"No buts! Someone needs to hold this thing stable and there's no way you can do it for me. I'll follow you up. Now get going!"

"Better hurry things up, Talon," Val said. "We're

coming up on that tunnel mighty fast." Talon could see the high hills looming ahead of the train.

"All right," he said, grabbing hold of the ladder, then started climbing up toward the chopper.

The ladder bucked and swayed in the wind as Val fought to keep the helicopter steady and stable near the train. Talon had to climb slowly to keep his grip, and once he almost slipped and fell. Looking down at the ground, rushing past at well over sixty klicks per hour, he wasn't eager to see if his magic could break his fall in time.

"Talon!" Val's voice came over his commlink. "We've got company! Two bogies coming in fast!" Talon looked behind the train, but he couldn't see anything: no running lights or signs of aircraft.

Then he spotted them. They had no lights, only broad black wings spreading out from slim, muscular bodies. Whiplike tails tipped with poisonous stingers coiled in the air, and their long, thin necks supported small, reptilian heads, jaws filled with needle-like teeth. The two wyverns were coming right at them, their hunting cries carrying over the sound of the train.

19

"Boom! Get up here!" Talon yelled down as the wyverns closed in. Each of the flying creatures was nearly as long as the helicopter that hovered less than ten meters above the train cutting its way through Germany toward Berlin. They opened their fanged maws to give loud hunting cries as they closed in.

"Talon, we've got no heavy weapons on this bird," Val said over his headlink. "We'll try to hold them off. Get the hell up here!"

From the open side-door of the helicopter, Harlan Hammarand leaned out, clutching an Ingram submachine gun. The gun roared as he fired several bursts in the direction of the wyverns. There was no indication he'd hit them. The creatures barely slowed their approach as they started to bank around to either side of the chopper. Their tails were tipped with wicked-looking stingers.

A wyvern came rushing in at Talon, its tail poised to strike. Talon kicked off the rope ladder and hung on for dear life as he swung to the side. The stabbing tail barb barely missed him, and the wyvern started to come around again. Its companion swooped down at Boom, who was standing on the roof of the speeding train. The troll dropped to the roof in a roll to avoid the creature's sting, but nearly flung himself off the roof in the process. He grabbed the edge of the roof with one of his massive hands just as his body went over the side.

Without Boom to anchor the rope ladder, the end flapped loosely in the wind as the chopper rose slightly upward. Hammer's gun roared again as he fired at the wyverns, but the creatures were remarkably fast and maneuverable for all their size, their heavy scales like armor. Again, there were no signs of significant injury from either beast.

"We need to get back down to Boom!" Talon said to Val. "Can you lower us?"

"We don't have a lot of time, Talon. That tunnel is coming up fast. We haven't got more than a minute or two."

"We can't leave Boom behind. We've got to get down there. Lower this thing!"

"I'm bringing us in," Val said. "Try and keep those things off our tail."

"Aracos," Talon thought, *"try and distract one of the wyverns, keep it away from the chopper."*

"Will do," the spirit answered.

One of the wyverns was coming around for another shot at Talon. Suddenly it banked and turned away, as if something unseen had buzzed in front of it. Wyverns were sensitive to the astral plane, like most Awakened creatures, so it could perceive Aracos even when the spirit was in astral form. Talon knew that Aracos was far swifter and more maneuverable in his astral form than the wyverns, so he should be able to keep the creature busy for a little while at least.

Meanwhile, the other wyvern was still trying to get at Boom. Talon turned and focused his attention on the beast as it banked around for another run at the train. He concentrated and drew magical energy to him, focusing it into a bolt of pure power. He pointed at the wyvern and shouted a magical phrase over the shrieking of the wind. The manabolt slammed into the creature with the force of an oncoming train. The wyvern shrieked in pain and pulled up at the last moment, flying over the top of the train and missing Boom completely. Still, the spell didn't incapacitate the creature, and it kept on coming, this time headed straight for Talon.

Talon started another spell, even knowing there was no way he'd be in time. The wyvern's stinger caught him in the right thigh and Talon cried out in pain, nearly losing his grip on the ladder. He could feel a terrible burning sensation spreading out from his leg as the wyvern's venom took effect. It was like that part of his body was on fire, a fire that was rapidly spreading outward. The injured wyvern drew back and prepared to stab a second time to finish its prey.

There was a loud crack and a jet of flames shot from the open door of the helicopter, striking the wyvern full in the chest. Speren Silverblade stood in the doorway, fire flowing from his outstretched hand like a flame-thrower. The creature wailed as withering flames flowed over it, burning exposed skin and flesh. The creature fell back, beating its wings furiously to stay aloft, and the train and the chopper pulled ahead, leaving the wyvern behind.

Talon struggled to retain his grip on the rope ladder. His leg was starting to go numb, and he was afraid he would lose consciousness.

"Talon . . ." Val started to say over the commlink.

"Don't worry about me," he snapped, gritting his teeth, "just get us down there to pick up Boom!" The chopper started to drop down in response to his order.

Talon could see Boom struggle back onto the roof of the train, hand over hand, lying flat as the wind tore across it. The hills were looming high overhead as the train headed for the dark mouth of the tunnel opening.

"Grab the ladder!" Talon yelled. Boom levered himself up and reached for the flailing end of the rope ladder, but even his huge troll arms weren't long enough. It flapped just out of reach. Val was trying to pull the chopper into a better position to give Boom another shot, but Talon wasn't sure there'd be time.

"Boss, I can't hold these lizards off any more," Aracos said. *"They're headed your way again."* Wyverns were nothing if not persistent, and they were not renowned for their intelligence. Talon glanced back to see the forms heading for the chopper like bat-winged fighter planes.

Ignoring the burning pain of the wyvern's toxin, Talon gestured tightly with one hand, focusing on the end of the ladder. Power flowed, and he gasped out words of power to shape it to his will. An invisible hand seized hold of the ladder and pulled the end of it toward Boom's outstretched arm. The troll grabbed hold as the hills seemed to rush up at them.

"Val, pull us up!" Talon said. The chopper pulled up sharply, lifting Boom off the roof of the train. The engine whined as they fought to clear the steep hillside, Boom's feet lifting mere meters off the ground as the train plunged into the darkness of the tunnel.

"Incoming!" Talon heard Val say as the wyverns arced in toward the chopper again. The damn things were amazingly persistent and stubborn. Boom was starting to climb up the ladder toward Talon as he began concentrating on another spell.

"Aracos, aid me," Talon commanded.

He was getting tired of this. The wyvern's poison burned in him like a fever. All the rapid-fire spellcasting was making him feel dizzy and lightheaded, and he was battered and bruised from hanging on to the rope ladder. He took all his anger toward the situation, toward Alamais, and toward being set up and hung out to dry, and compressed it into a glowing sphere in one outstretched hand. It burned white-hot at its core, a fire of anger and pain. As the wyvern arced in, Talon hurled the sphere at it with all his might.

The sphere streaked out like a tiny meteor and struck the oncoming wyvern dead center. There was a massive boom and a detonation that nearly knocked Talon off the ladder he clung to. The little ball blossomed into a massive sphere of flames that engulfed the wyvern completely. The creature let out a shriek of pain that echoed through the hills, then died out as the flames did too. The wyvern dropped toward the ground, its flesh covered in burns, parts of its wingflaps burned away entirely by the blast.

Talon watched the creature fall with a certain fascination, then glanced down as he felt something tap him on the foot.

"Start climbing!" Boom shouted from directly below him. Talon nodded numbly and started up the ladder as quickly as he could. The blast seemed to startle the other wyvern, but it had not yet given up the chase. Talon wasn't sure he could manage another spell, but he had to try. He got to the open door of the helicopter, and Hammer's strong arm reached out to help haul him aboard. Speren Silverblade stood near the doorway, obviously readying another spell of his own as Boom clambered aboard close behind Talon. Once in, he hugged the floor of the chopper for a moment in sheer relief.

Talon leaned over the big troll to look out the door as the wyvern closed in. He wasn't done yet, and for some reason didn't want to show weakness in front of Silverblade anyway. He gathered power to him again and shaped it into a spell. Almost at the same moment, he and Silverblade loosed their spells on the oncoming creature. The twin manabolts stabbed out like magical lasers. The bolts struck the wyvern and sundered its life force, killing it almost instantly as the creature's uncomprehending mind was overwhelmed. The wyvern dropped from the sky like a stone, crashing into a copse of trees on the hillside below.

Silverblade slumped against the side of the chopper, holding onto a wall-staple with one hand. Hammer quickly moved to pull the door closed as Boom carefully rolled Talon off of him.

"Talon was hit," Boom said with concern as Talon slumped limply to the floor. The last spell seemed to have taken it out of him. Boom lifted Talon like a parent would lift a small child and moved him to one of the bench seats. The ragged hole in the leg of Talon's jeans was covered in blood.

Trouble came back from the cockpit with medkit in hand as Boom tore open Talon's jeans to expose the wound.

Silverblade waved Trouble off, "I have a spell . . ." he began to say, but Boom interrupted him with one raised hand.

"Wouldn't worry about it," the troll said, crouched over talon. "Take a look at this."

Both Trouble and Silverblade leaned over Boom's shoulder to see the hole in Talon's leg nearly closed. Even as they watched, the wound appeared to shrink, until only a small, tender-looking spot remained. Boom reached out and placed one big hand over his friend's forehead.

"He's got no fever, and his pulse seems normal."

"His aura is strong and undisturbed," Silverblade said, shaking his head. "How is this possible? I've never seen a human recover from any injury like that. Wyvern venom is among the most fatal there is."

"I've seen Talon pull off some pretty amazing healing spells," Trouble said, "but not while he was unconscious. Aracos?"

There was a shimmering in the air, and Talon's familiar spirit appeared at his master's side in wolf form. *"Wasn't me,"* the spirit's thought-voice said. *"I've never seen anything like it."*

Talon groaned and began to stir.

"Oh, frag," he muttered, his eyes fluttering open. "Did we get it?"

"And then some," Boom said, touching him gently on the shoulder. "Those wyverns aren't going to be bothering anyone anymore. How are you doing?"

Talon blinked a couple of times. "Fine, I think. In fact, I feel pretty good. Way better than I should after all that spellcasting and . . ." Suddenly he sat bolt upright, one hand reaching for his leg. "The wyvern," he said, "it stung . . ." He stopped and his eyes widened as his fingers brushed across unblemished skin beneath his bloody clothing.

"Almost completely healed," Boom said. "And it looks like the venom isn't affecting you either."

"But how?" Talon asked, a look of confusion on his face.

"That's what we were going to ask you," Trouble replied. "We don't know. None of us do. Guess you've got a guardian angel or something, chummer."

"We're going to need one," Silverblade broke in. "There's still the matter of Alamais and whatever he's planning. Alamais is obviously working with Winternight, or perhaps using them for some purpose of his own, and they have control of a nuclear weapon. The devastation they could inflict is immense."

Talon glanced at his teammates and read the expressions on their faces.

"He's right. Whatever Alamais is planning, we can't let him get away with it. The dragon set us up to take out Lofwyr, but there's got to be more to it than that. If we can find out what Alamais is doing, maybe get word to Saeder-Krupp, we can tip them off."

"Do you really think S-K would believe us?" Boom asked.

"I don't know, but we've got to try. If anyone wants out of this, now's a good time to say so. We can drop you off, and you can find your own way back to Boston or wherever. No hard feelings, no questions asked." He looked from one face crowded around him to another.

"I follow the needs of my people," Silverblade said first. "Alamais is a monster, and what he is planning must be stopped."

"I'm not looking to play hero," Hammer said. "But I don't like being set up, either. The dragon used us, and we've got a rep to protect. If we can take him down and clear ourselves with Saeder-Krupp at the same time, I say we do it."

"Same here," Trouble said. "We're the only ones who know about the dragon's plan so far. We've got to do something."

Talon looked over at Boom, who answered with an expressive shrug. "Hey, probably nothing good on the trid tonight anyway. I mean, who wants to live a long and safe life, right? Count me in."

"How about you, Val?" Talon called up to the cockpit. There was a moment of pregnant silence.

"Haven't been to Berlin in a long time," Val said. "It'll be just like old times."

"All right," Talon said. "Let's do this. If Alamais thinks we're history, he's sadly mistaken."

20

As Val explained, the Free City of Berlin was almost pure anarchy. Even by the lax standards of some North American metroplexes, Berlin was practically an open city. Val brought the team in to the Schönefeld Airport, where she knew some people in the smuggling business. They were able to land at the airport with only a quick conversation over the comm system, and they skipped customs and immigration altogether, even though all visitors to Berlin were supposed to be issued a green card and pass a customs inspection.

"They say that, but nobody really bothers with it," Val said. "The government—such as it is—hasn't got the money to clean up the streets, much less pay people to handle customs inspections. The private contractors who do run the airport couldn't care less what people bring into the city, so long as they don't try to blow up the airport itself. That's probably one reason why Winternight came here; Berlin is one of the only cities in Europe where you could cart a nuclear bomb in on a freight train and nobody would even notice."

They were situated for the moment in a room off the hangar where the helicopter sat, planning their next move. They knew the train they had been on was bound for Berlin, thanks to some Matrix work by Trouble. Unfortunately, they didn't know exactly what had been done with Winternight's "cargo" once it arrived.

"The Berlin Matrix is a nightmare," Trouble said, massaging her forehead with one hand. "It's such a mess that the legitimate users can't get anything useful out of it more than half the time, to say nothing of pirating. Also, Winternight didn't exactly file a manifest for their cargo, or what they were planning to do with it. We're not going to be able to track them down that way."

"We don't need to," Talon said. "Remember, when Alamais clocked us, he or his flunkies must have taken our mageblades, along with the rest of our gear." He gestured to Silverblade, who sat quietly at one end of the table. "They've probably still got them, and Silverblade and I are still connected to those blades magically. We can track down their location on the astral plane and follow the trail right to wherever Winternight is hiding out."

"The only concern is what sort of magical security Winternight has on their headquarters," Silverblade added. "If the dragon is behind them, as seems to be the case, then their magical defenses could be truly formidable, perhaps more than we can handle."

"I think we can do it," Talon said.

"Are you sure, Talon?" Trouble asked. "We're talking about a great dragon here. I don't know much about this Alamais, there's not much about him on the 'trix, but it seems like his claim to be Lofwyr's brother is true. And if so, that makes him one fragging tough dragon, backed up by a fanatical terrorist organization. Don't you think just maybe this is out of our league?"

"What would you suggest?" Talon asked her.

Trouble shrugged. "I don't know. Maybe we can contact the authorities . . ."

"In Berlin?" Val was incredulous. "What authorities? The whole city is run by gangs and criminals, Trouble. What are they going to do about a group like Winternight?"

"Then, what about contacting Saeder-Krupp, telling them what we know?"

Talon shook his head. "Saeder-Krupp thinks we were in on the hit against Lofwyr. They're looking for a scapegoat. Why should they believe us? They would simply track us down and interrogate the drek out of us to get at the truth. By the time we could convince them, it might be too late. No, if we're going to do something about this, we've got to do it ourselves. Call me crazy, but I think we can handle whatever else Alamais has up his scaly sleeve."

"Okay, you're crazy," Boom said with a smile. "Now that we've established that, count me in. If we're going to have any chance of figuring out Winternight's plans, we'd better get started."

"Right," Talon said. "Here's what we'll do. Silverblade and I will go astral and try to track down our blades. That might tell us where Winternight is, or at least where some of them are."

Silverblade nodded without comment.

"Trouble, get back on the 'trix and get the buzz on what's happening in the city. Find out if there's anything Winternight might target—something that could attract terrorists with a bomb they're itching to use."

"Sure, nothing to it," Trouble quipped. "I'm on it."

"Val, use any contacts you've still got in Berlin and get the same scan. See what you can find out about Winternight, but don't give away too much about who we're looking for. Try checking up on Alt Welt or Runenthing. The local groups might have ties. While you're at it, see if you can scrounge us some heavier weaponry. I have a feeling we're going to need it. Boom, you and Hammer . . ."

"I know," the troll said. "We cool our heels and keep an eye out for trouble until it's time to kick some butt."

Talon grinned. "Right in one. You can also try checking up on some of your contacts to find out what they know about the Saeder-Krupp situation. If something's going down in the corporate sector, we need to know about it."

"Got it," Boom said.

"Okay people, let's get to work."

It didn't take Val long to arrange a place for the team to crash and set things up. Smugglers were regular visitors to Berlin, and the shadows of the city worked to accommodate those who brought needed supplies and other goods across the walls from the outside world. Val's friends provided a tiny apartment, but it had the necessary amenities, including a jackpoint Trouble could use to access the Berlin Matrix.

Talon and Speren would use one of the apartment's two bedrooms to begin their astral journey.

The bed was little more than a cot, and Talon pushed it against one wall to make room on the floor for them both to lie down. Hammer and the others could keep watch over their physical bodies while their astral forms went looking for their stolen magical weapons.

"Are you actually prepared to take on a great dragon?" Silverblade asked as they pushed the remaining beat-up pieces of furniture out of the way.

"I'm hoping it doesn't come to that," Talon said. "But I will if I have to. Whatever Alamais is up to, it affects a lot more than just us. I want Saeder-Krupp off my back, but I don't want the deaths of the people Winternight is planning to kill on my conscience."

"Conscience," Speren muttered. "And here I thought that term was incompatible with being a shadowrunner."

"Some shadowrunners would agree with you, but I'm not one of them. We do what we must to survive in the shadows, but that doesn't mean we have no honor or decency."

"More words I never expected to hear from a shadowrunner's lips," Silverblade said. "But you say you do this because you must. Why? I can understand about some of your companions not having any other choice, but what about you, Talon? With your skills you could write your own ticket working for any number of corporations or other organizations."

"Like the government, you mean?" Talon said. "Sorry, I nearly went the wagemage route once. I've got no interest in going that way again."

"So instead, you use your abilities to be a more effective criminal?"

"Says the government spy," Talon said with a smile. "Chummer, I run the shadows because all I've ever seen the big noises do is use people: corporations, governments, policlubs, syndicates, all the fat cats. They take what they want and when they're done with you, they spit out what's left. You might call me a mercenary, and that's true. I work for whoever pays me. I don't work for people out of a sense of loyalty or devotion to a cause, I work because they pay me. In my view that doesn't make me any different from a high-priced corporate mage head-hunting for the best salary, or even the political-climbing government spook. It just makes me more honest. I know how the game works, and I play by my own rules. When it comes right down to it, Silverblade, you and I are a lot more alike than you may think."

"Perhaps," the elf said.

"What about you? What's your angle, paladin? Patriotism?"

"In part," Silverblade said. "Like many elves, I was not born in Tir Tairngire. The place doesn't really matter. It was a city like so many in this world: dirty, downtrodden, and hopeless, especially for those not fortunate enough to be born human. My mother was human . . ."

His voice took on a distant quality as he relived the old memories. "She wanted more than anything for me to be able to live in the elven homeland, away from the violence and the hunger and the despair of where she came from. She sacrificed everything to make that happen. In the Land of Promise, I found hope, and acceptance and a new life, like a dream come true. And I think every day of those of my people who also dream of such a life and never find it. I serve Tir Tairngire out of gratitude for what she has done for me, and to protect my people from those who would see us destroyed."

"A noble cause," Talon said. "Too bad Tir Tairngire only provides opportunities for some and not others."

"Are we to be expected to save the world?"

"Chummer, in my experience, you can't save the world. You can only hope to improve your little corner of it for a while. But for me, that's enough. Right now, I want to find my mageblade and figure out what that dragon is up to. You up for it?"

"Of course."

"Then let's go."

They stretched out on the floor side by side, settling down as comfortably as the worn hardwood and thin carpeting would allow. Talon closed his eyes and regulated his breathing in slow, even breaths. He let all the muscles of his body relax and allowed his awareness of it to recede until his astral body slipped free of the bonds of his material self and he found himself hovering above his body, which still lay on the floor. Silverblade's astral form hovered nearby, the two of them casting a faint glow from their auras in the dimly lit room.

Arcos appeared near Talon in the form of a golden-winged hawk, his aura glowing brightly.

"Ready to go," the spirit said.

Talon focused his awareness on his enchanted dagger. He concentrated on the feeling of the cool, chain-wrapped hilt pressed against his palm, on the keen edge of the rune-marked blade, on the fiery gleam of the opal set into the pommel, and on the steady glow of its aura. He saw his connection to Talonclaw like a faintly glowing thread, connected to his aura and stretching out through the astral plane toward his mageblade. Once he had the thread firmly in sight, he glanced over at Silverblade.

"Ready?" he asked.

"Yes," Silverblade said. "I can see the connection to Argentine."

"Let's go then, and try and stick together."

The three astral forms passed up and through the roof of the small apartment and out into the city beyond. The light of dawn was coloring the horizon, and the city below was starting to wake from the night's slumber, people warily crawling out from behind whatever shelter they'd taken during the night. The nighttime predators, both human and otherwise, took shelter from the growing light, retiring to their own dens. The glowing threads guided their way as they took flight over Berlin and headed northward, toward the center of the city.

Following the trail through the astral plane was painstaking. Normally, Talon's astral form could have traversed the city from one end to the other in a matter of moments, using the blinding speed available to astral travelers, but such speeds make following the complex twists and turns the trail took all but impossible. Still, they traveled far more quickly than they could have in the physical world. In only a matter of hours, they reached what Talon hoped was their destination.

It was a fairly nondescript building in the city, in what Talon guessed was a working-class neighborhood, though it was difficult to tell with Berlin. The building was two stories and built like a concrete bunker. There was a broad sign over the doorway. The language was a meaningless jumble of abstract symbols to someone in the astral, but Talon did notice what looked like a wolf's head on the sign. The magical trail to Talonclaw led inside and did not emerge, so he surmised that his mageblade was somewhere within.

"Aracos, take a look at this place physically," he told his familiar. The spirit materialized in hawk form on the physical plane near the roof, then took wing, making a fly-by around the outside of the building. Talon wished Aracos had a less distinctive form at that moment, but there was nothing to be done about it. He and Silverblade couldn't read abstract things like text from the astral, so Aracos had to serve as their physical "eyes."

"Place is called the Wolfsschanze, boss," the spirit said in Talon's thoughts. He memorized the name, although he didn't speak German, and his language chip wouldn't interface with his astral form anyway. He'd have Trouble check up on it later.

"What does your spirit report?" Silverblade asked, a note of impatience in his voice. Talon filled him in.

"The Wolf's Lair," Silverblade said.

"What's that?"

"Wolfsschanze, it's German for 'wolf's lair.' It was the name Adolf Hitler gave to his secret bunker during World War II, more than a hundred years ago."

"Charming," Talon said. "I didn't know you were a student of ancient history."

"I'm not. But this place is known to us as a regular

meeting place for sympathizers of the Humanis Policlub in Germany. They're ultra right-wing German nationalists and neo-Nazis opposed to the 'pollution' of the pure Aryan race with metahuman genes."

"Frag," Talon said. "Humanis—just what we needed."

"It's very possible the group has been co-opted by Winternight, become another of their front organizations. Or perhaps they aren't even aware they're being used. Members of organizations like this are given to mindless obedience to their leaders. They don't question orders."

"Either way, they've got our mageblades, which means they might have some leads about what Winternight is up to. We should take a look inside."

"Agreed," Silverblade said, "but cautiously."

The two of them moved toward the upper story of the building and carefully probed the walls.

"Warded," Talon said. "I'll bet that's not standard Humanis-issue."

"Not necessarily. The Humanis have been known to work with magicians. Racism is hardly limited to the mundane. Still, I agree that it is unusual."

"If we bust through this, whoever put it here will know we've come calling. But we need to get a look inside this place," Talon mused. He turned to Silverblade. "I assume you're familiar with the concept of spoofing wards?"

The elf smiled, smug satisfaction lighting up his aura. "Astral counter-intrusion measures? We practically invented them."

"Of course," Talon said. "Let's try it, then. Aracos, you wait out here and be on the lookout for any unexpected company. Let me know if anyone shows up."

"Got it," the spirit said.

Talon and Speren pressed their astral hands out against the ward, which followed the contours of the building's own walls. They probed with their magical senses, studying the structure and aura of the wards. Every magical ward contained the owner's astral signature, a kind of psychic and magical "fingerprint" that was unique to each individual worker of the arts of magic. A ward automatically recognized the aura of its creator, allowing him or her to pass through the barrier as if it weren't even there. A while back, magicians seeking a means of defeating wards came up with a way of adjusting their own aura to match the "signature" of the ward's creator, allowing them to slip through undetected. It was considerably more difficult than simply breaking the ward down, but it had the benefit of leaving the ward intact and keeping its creator ignorant of any trespass.

Talon studied the ward carefully, taking in its essence, getting a feel for its energy. Then he began altering his own aura, like a musician tuning an instrument, going up and down the scales, looking for exactly the right pitch. He zeroed in on the signature and felt the ward begin to give slightly under his touch. With a few minor adjustments to his aura, he matched the correct signature exactly, and the ward allowed him to pass. About the same time, Silverblade did the same and they both slipped through the magical barrier as if it were no more than mist.

The second floor of the Wolf's Lair was apparently set up as living space for the proprietor and whomever he chose to have as guests. The quarters were paramilitary in style, and the only decorations were Humanis neo-Nazi propaganda posters and flags mounted on the bare walls. The ongoing atmosphere of hatred and bigotry in the place tainted the astral plane within. Talon felt like he was swimming through polluted waters as he floated through the ether inside the building.

There were no signs of any other magical defenses within, for which Talon was grateful. They probably figured the wards were sufficient to dissuade casual intruders and alert them to anyone else. The two magicians made a quick survey of the top floor and found it inhabited by nearly a dozen Humanis club members, most of them asleep or just waking up to perform morning calisthenics, like so many soldiers in an army barracks. The mageblades were locked up in a safe, inside what Talon took to be the proprietor's office.

"Seen enough?" he asked Silverblade.

"Yes," the elf replied.

"Let's head back, then, and get the rest of the team. I'm feeling a hankering for some German food. How about you?"

21

One kick from Boom was enough to break in the back door of the Wolf's Lair, then the shadowrunners poured into the room.

Boom and Hammer took point, with the ork mercenary crouching down low and Boom firing high over his head. The two Humanis members, in their tight-fitting T-shirts and flat-top crewcuts, never even knew what hit them. Boom was packing a pump-action shotgun loaded with gel rounds and Hammer used an Ares Predator, loaded with the same ammo, instead of his usual explosive or armor-piercing rounds. Talon was insistent that they avoid unnecessary casualties. Hammer expressed his opinion when it came to showing mercy to Humanis goons, but he went along with Talon's plan. Even though they were firing non-lethal ammo, both of the policlubbers would have some nasty bruises and maybe some fractures when they finally came to.

Hammer and Boom moved out into the room, covering the doors and windows. Talon and Silverblade followed close behind. Talon carried a Narcoject pistol. Silverblade had a slim-profile Baretta loaded with gel rounds, although he preferred to rely on magic to deal with his opponents quickly and quietly.

Behind Talon and Silverblade hovered a small drone, about the size and shape of a thick garbage-can lid, equipped with a powerful lifting fan, along with a suite of sensors and a swivel-mounted gun. Val controlled the drone from their nearby transportation, while Trouble coordinated communications and kept an eye on the local grid for any sign of calls to the authorities or—more importantly—calls for help elsewhere. Talon was hoping that the raid would lead someone to call a higher-up for instructions, allowing Trouble to track down the number.

The runners hit the back stairs up to the second floor. Another Humanis goon appeared at the top of the stairs, submachine gun blazing, firing a burst of 9mm rounds down at the intruders. They certainly weren't using gel rounds. Boom stepped in front of Talon as a living shield, and Talon could hear a loud "thunk" as one of the rounds impacted against the troll. Hammer flattened himself against the wall to avoid the burst and fired two shots from his Predator in return. The guard slumped over the railing of the stairwell, his weapon clattering down the stairs. Hammer wasted no time and kept on moving.

"You okay?" Talon asked Boom.

The troll nodded with a grunt. "No problem. Take more than that to get through all this armor. 'Sides, I'm pretty tough." Boom's own hide was natural armor strong enough to protect him against some weapons. That, plus the heavy armored jacket he wore, was enough to reduce the impact of even a 9mm round to nothing more than a bad bruise.

At the top of the stairs, Hammer and Boom covered each other as doors opened along the hall. Humanis members, alerted by the sounds of gunfire, began to pour out of their rooms, weapons at the ready. Boom grabbed the unconscious goon slumped over the railing with one massive hand, hefted him like he was no more than a sack of grain, and threw him at the oncoming Humanis members. Several of them went down in a heap, blocking the doorway.

Hammer pulled a small silvery sphere hanging from his combat vest, yanked the pin out with his teeth, and tossed it down the hall. Trailing white smoke as it went, the gas grenade went off with a dull "wumph," sending a cloud of thick white vapor spreading through the entire hallway. Talon could hear coughing and choking, along with voices cursing and yelling in German. From behind them on the stairs, Talon heard Val's drone cough out a staccato burst of gunfire, probably keeping any reinforcements from downstairs at bay.

Boom and Hammer fired into the gas cloud, picking off policlubbers as they tried to stagger out into clearer air. Talon and Silverblade moved up behind them into the hallway.

"Under control," Hammer pronounced, looking over the scene.

"One of the polis managed to get a window open before he passed out, boss," Aracos sent to Talon from his position in the astral.

"Wiz," Talon replied. *"Makes things that much easier. Let's do it."*

Talon raised his hands and spoke a short phrase, drawing slightly from Aracos' power to augment his own. A strong wind sprang up from where Talon gestured and blew down the corridor. It swept away the stun gas, which blew out the open window, then died away as Talon lowered his arms. There were nearly a dozen policlubbers scattered in the corridor, most of them unconscious or nearly so. Some were fully dressed, but others were wearing only their underwear, obviously awakened from sleep by the melee before being stunned. The doors of the barracks rooms were open, and Hammer and Boom moved to cover them.

As Hammer approached one of the doors, a shot rang out, splintering wood off the door frame. The ork pulled back fast enough to avoid being hit, and flattened himself against the wall next to the door. He looked like he was about to rush the room, but Talon held up a hand and shook his head. If there was a gunman holed up in the room, rushing through the doorway would only give him a better shot at one of the runners. Talon thought there was a better way to handle it.

"Aracos, take out the gunman in there, but leave him alive and able to talk."

"You got it." His ally spirit gave a wolfish grin and faded from sight, passing through the wall. A moment later, Talon heard a yell and another gunshot, a growl and a momentary scuffle. After a few more seconds passed, he nodded to Hammer and Boom and waved them toward the room. They wasted no time going in. Talon and Silverblade followed.

Lying on his back on the floor was an older human. He was dressed similarly to the others they'd seen, and had iron-gray hair in a short crewcut.

Perched atop his chest was a large wolf. There was a bloody bite-mark on his arm and his pistol lay about a meter away, just out of reach. The man eyed the slavering wolf with a look of terror in his eyes.

"Good work," Talon said to Aracos, coming around to ruffle the fur behind his familiar's ears.

"Who are you?" the man asked in German. Talon was glad he'd jacked his German language chip before hand. He bent down to look the man in the face. The icy blue eyes stared back, wide with anger and fear.

"We're asking the questions here," Talon told him. "First, what's the combination to the safe?"

The man looked like he wanted to spit. "Trog-lover!" he growled. "You won't get anything from me!"

"We're wasting time here, chummer," Boom said in his best "dumb troll" voice. "Let me rip one of his arms off, that'll get us some answers."

"Do your worst, subhuman! All of you are dead men anyway. You don't know who you're dealing with here."

Boom took a step toward the policlubber, apparently intent on carrying out his threat. He grabbed the man by the front of his shirt and lifted him bodily off the floor as Aracos hopped off his chest. The policlubber probably outweighed Talon by a good fifteen kilos of solid muscle, but Boom picked him up like he was a small child and pinned them against the wall.

"No, chummer, you don't know who *you're* dealing with here. You know, I don't much like it when scum like you thinks I'm beneath them. It makes me mad, and when I get mad, I start to break things."

Some of the man's bravado faded when he was face to face with three meters of angry troll pinning him to the wall and backed up by a gun-wielding ork and a grim-looking elf, to say nothing of Talon or the fierce wolf at his side.

Talon came up next to Boom.

"You're right, chummer. We're wasting time. I was hoping to do this the easy way, but . . ." He shrugged and reached out to touch the man's forehead with the fingertips of his right hand. The man almost immediately began squirming and struggling, but Boom's iron grip kept him from escaping.

"What are you . . . ?" the man sputtered. "No. No! Stop! You can't . . ."

Talon spoke the words of a spell and the protests fell silent. In an instant he was inside the policlubber's excuse for a mind. His mind probe spell reached out, sifting and probing through the man's thoughts and memories.

Well, well, Talon thought. *What have we here?* He continued probing for a few moments, isolating some other pieces of information, in addition to the combination of the safe. Then he withdrew from the gibbering policlubber's mind. He started to come out of the fugue state almost immediately as Boom turned to Talon.

"All finished?"

Talon nodded.

"Good." Boom pulled back and punched the man in the face hard enough to crack the plaster wall behind his head. Then he let go of the man's shirt and allowed him to slide down to the floor, unconscious, with blood dripping from his broken nose to stain the clean white shirt he wore.

Talon went over to the safe and knelt down, quickly going through the combination. With a tug, he pulled open the safe door. Inside were Talonclaw and Argentine. Talon reached in and retrieved his mageblade, then handed Silverblade his sword. The safe also contained some hardcopy deutchmarks and nuyen, which Talon and Hammer loaded into a backpack. They could use the money to help defer some of their expenses, and Talon rather liked the idea of the Humanis Policlub helping to fund their run against Winternight.

"Team One, this is Two," Trouble's voice said over Talon's headlink. "Word's out to some of the locals about your visit. You can expect some company in a few minutes from the sound of it."

"It's a wrap up here," Talon said. "We're heading home. Start doing some digging. According to our friend's memories here, Mitsuhama is sponsoring some kind of benefit concert in Berlin. Find out everything you can about it."

"Okay," Trouble replied. "Do you think it ties in with Winternight?"

"I do. More importantly, our target does, too. Team One out."

Talon opened up a channel to Val.

"Yo, Val, are we clear?"

"All clear downstairs," the rigger said. "And all clear on the street, although you're starting to draw some local attention. Time to go, chummers."

"Took the words right out of my mouth," Talon said. "Get ready, we're coming down."

He turned back to the rest of the team. "Let's go."

Hammer and Boom headed for the door as Aracos faded back into the astral plane. Silverblade stood for a moment over the unconscious body of the Humanis ringleader, one hand resting on the hilt of his sheathed sword.

"Do you always show your enemies such mercy?" Silverblade asked.

"I don't kill everyone who gets in my way, if that's what you mean," Talon said, slipping Talonclaw's sheath onto his belt. "As for mercy, I wouldn't exactly say leaving him alive is merciful. He and his boys just got shown up by a gang of 'trog-lovers' and 'sub-humans,' as he so eloquently put it. Not to mention that they've seriously disappointed Winternight. I'd wager that this here skag won't be top-dog with the Humanis around here much longer, and *they'll* do things to him that would take me days to think up."

"Why, Talon," Silverblade said with a sardonic smile, "you could almost be an elf."

"Thanks." That was about the nicest thing Talon had ever heard Silverblade say about anybody. He decided not to spoil the compliment with a comeback. Instead, he simply gestured toward the door with a mock bow.

"After you," he said.

"As it should be," Silverblade returned as he moved past Talon and through the door like royalty leaving an audience.

So much for not spoiling a nice moment, Talon thought.

The shadowrunners left the Wolf's Lair quickly and

ran to the alley where Val was waiting in the van. As soon as they were all inside, Val pulled the van out into the street, to the blaring of horns from oncoming cars. Then they were off.

"Man, I miss driving in Germany," she said with a grin as she swerved to cut off another car and turned the corner, flipping off the driver as he blared his horn at them. "Cities like Boston just aren't much of a challenge."

Talon never thought he'd hear anyone say that about his hometown, but he had to admit that driving in Berlin was more like a demolition derby than anywhere he'd ever seen. Plenty of cars and trucks on the street looked more like armored rigs than simple passenger vehicles. Val certainly seemed to be enjoying herself.

"So, was there anything inside that Neanderthal's underdeveloped excuse for a brain?" Silverblade asked once they were underway.

"A few things of interest," Talon said. "First off, said neanderthal is none other than Klaus Kühnen, the head of the local Humanis chapter. That's his place we just trashed, and his men."

"Couldn'ta happened to a nicer guy," Hammer rumbled, while Boom grinned.

"Seems ol' Klaus has some ties with Winternight," Talon continued, "only he doesn't know it. Winternight supplies him with some of their tech, particularly a kind of simsense chip that inspires berserker rages; great for Humanis gangs to use when they're out hunting some metahuman skulls to bust. Winternight has Klaus convinced they're some kind of ultra right-wing Germanic nationalist organization opposed to metahumans. They work through fronts like Alt Welt and der Runenthing. Klaus doesn't even know that Winternight really exists."

"Doesn't sound like he has much information of use then," Silverblade said.

"Not quite," Talon replied. "There was one thing. Seems that the skag who gave our mageblades to Klaus for safekeeping was none other than our old buddy Zoller."

"Zoller?" Boom said. "But Alamais turned him into a frog!"

"Maybe Alamais' spell wasn't permanent," Talon said, "and Zoller is back working for his old boss, or else it was and somebody's pretending to be Zoller. Three guesses who that could be."

"Alamais," Silverblade said.

"Whoever it is, he's got all the earmarks of a Winternight shaman. Apparently, there's something going down very soon in Berlin. Herr Zoller got some extra muscle from Kühnen's Humanis cell to beef up his own followers. Kühnen thought he had something big planned."

"Something involving a stolen nuclear weapon," Silverblade said. "But what? And more importantly, where?"

"Let's find out," Talon said, and keyed open his headlink. "Trouble, you there?"

"Right here," she said.

"Hang on, let me put you on the speaker," Talon said. He leaned past the passenger seat and activated the portable receiver that rested there. The speaker on it crackled a bit before Trouble's voice came through.

"We on?" she asked.

"Loud and clear," Talon said. "What did you get on that concert so far?"

"Some very interesting stuff. You were right, the entertainment division of Mitsuhama Computer Technologies is sponsoring a big benefit concert in Berlin tonight, in cooperation with DeMeKo, the big European media corp. It's part of a multinational world tour by some of the hottest bands and performers out there. I think you're also right about it being a likely target for Winternight."

"Why is that?" Silverblade asked.

"Three reasons. First, part of the concert is a benefit for charities in Berlin. Second, the guest list includes the VP of MCT Europe, Ryu Takahashi; the President of DeMeKo, Wolfgang Osterwald; and the VP of Saeder-Krupp Deutchland, Karl-Heinze Berninger."

"And the third reason?" Silverblade asked.

"The name of the show," trouble said, "is 'Ragnarock, the Concert of the Century.' If you were Winternight, could *you* pass up on irony like that?"

"But why a concert? And why this concert?" Hammer asked.

"Simple," Boom said. "Think about it. This show is a big Mitsuhama production supporting Berlin, which everyone knows hacks off Lofwyr. Alamais has already struck at S-K by attacking Lofwyr. While the dragon is out of commission, his Winternight chummers set off a stolen S-K nuclear weapon at a major concert in the heart of Germany, sponsored by S-K's chief rival in the heavy industries business. Of course, with everything going on after the attack on

Lofwyr, you can bet that Herr Berninger will cancel his appearance at the concert. So a nuke that could only belong to Saeder-Krupp goes off, killing two major rival execs, and handing MCT a PR nightmare, while the S-K exec is mysteriously absent. What would that look like to you?"

"Retaliation," Talon said, "for the attack on Lofwyr."

"Right, a magical attack, and guess who's the Number Two corp in magic R&D?"

"Mitsuhama," Silverblade said. "So Mitsuhama thinks they've been attacked by Saeder-Krupp. They retaliate . . ."

"And, boom! Pretty soon you've got a major corporate war," Boom said.

"But they'll figure it out," Val chimed in from the driver's seat. "I mean, Saeder-Krupp will tell them . . ."

"What?" Boom said. "That they're innocent? Do you really think MCT, or any other corp, will believe them? By the time the megacorps decide to trust each other and start putting the pieces together, they may already be too deep in the conflict to pull out without risking a major loss. At the very least, things will go on for a while, maybe long enough for Winternight to keep stoking the flames."

"So they're trying to trigger a final war, a real Ragnarock," Trouble said.

Talon nodded grimly. "That's what it looks like. Trouble, dig up everything else you can about this concert. I want everything there is to know about it. If we're going to have a snowball's chance in hell of stopping Winternight, we're going to need it."

22

The crowd gathered for the Ragnarock concert was like a sea of humanity, with waves of anticipation rippling through it as the time neared for the show to begin. As he moved unnoticed through the crowd, Talon hoped that the terrorists were planning to take advantage of the powerful swell of emotion he could feel rising off the concert-goers, like heat rising from asphalt in summer. Winternight had a lot of magicians, and they knew the power of unleashed emotion. Hopefully, they wouldn't act until the mood of the crowd built a little further.

The massive stadium was usually used for sporting events. Now the playing field below had been converted into a giant stage for the Ragnarock concert. Tens of thousands of fans were gathered in the stands above, most of them clad in street leathers and denim, gleaming with chains and metal studs. Talon also spotted more than a few well-off corporate kids and twenty-somethings doing their best to look like they fit in with the rest. The stadium lights were on, but the shadows in the stands were heavy and it was nearly impossible to see more than a dozen or so meters, much less across the stadium to the other side.

It was like looking for a needle in a haystack, Talon thought as he made his way up the stairs to one of the tunnel entrances to the outer ring of the stadium. Winternight could hide an army in this crowd and he'd never spot them. Pulling the collar of his long coat close around his neck, Talon mentally keyed open his headcom.

"Come in, team," he said. "Give me an update. Anything?"

"Nothing unusual on the fly-bys," Val said. "I've run four passes over the stadium and scanned to the limits of the sensors on this thing. There's just too many bodies and too much electronic gear down there to get any kind of accurate reading. Not to mention that Winternight could be using magic to hide themselves."

"Same thing from down here," Trouble said. "The scanning gear in the van is limited, and we're not in the best position out here. Can't pick up any signs of the nuke or of Zoller, or Alamais, or whoever he is."

"What about Silverblade?" Talon asked.

"He's still out-of-body," Trouble responded. "At least, as far as I can tell. I'll let you know as soon as he's back."

"We've got nothing, so far," Boom said. "Security's pretty tight. We're lucky you were able to get us past it with those invisibility spells." Fortunately, the hired security forces didn't include a lot of magicians to spot-check everyone coming through the gates, so the guards didn't notice a few invisible shadowrunners slipping past them, avoiding the metal detectors and weapons sniffers.

"How about getting into the backstage areas?"

Talon said. It was certainly possible Winternight might have something set up there.

"Working on it," Boom said.

Talon sent his thoughts out into the astral plane. *"Aracos, anything yet?"*

"Got a possibility," the spirit replied. *"but it's hard to be sure. There's a lot of emotional static floating around in the astral from all these people getting it up about the show. But I can sense some faint magical emanations coming from understage."*

"Under the stage?" Talon echoed. He glanced back down into the stadium. The stage was built up on the field below like a multi-tiered structure of its own. The "backstage" area would actually be in the hollow space underneath.

"Do you know what kind of magic?"

"Can't tell. It could just be some kind of special effect preparation for the show . . ."

That was certainly a possibility. Trouble's research showed that a local magical company was being employed to provide magical illusions as part of the stage show, so . . .

"Wait a sec," Talon said to himself, then into the commlink. "Trouble, that company doing the stage effects. Do they have their own staff of mages or do they contract out?"

"Checking . . . nope, they're not too big. Looks like they subcontract most of their magical work."

"Zoller. Zoller's a magical consultant. Winternight could be using his credentials to get backstage."

"Talon," came Silverblade's voice over the link. "There's something going on below the stage. The area is warded, and I didn't want to attempt to penetrate it, lest I should warn whoever set up the ward. But no other area of the stadium is warded."

Talon circuited the link to the rest of the team, to include them all in the conversation. "Okay, folks, it looks like our targets are down in the understage area. That puts them smack in the middle of the stadium, the perfect place to set up their bomb. We've got to get down there. Meet up at tunnel G of the outer ring." Talon headed up the stairs at a jog as the stadium lights dimmed and the floodlights illuminated the stage.

The show was starting, and Talon knew they didn't have much time.

"Ladies and gentlemen! And all you other assorted mutants!" a voice boomed out over the PA system. "Welcome to the concert of the century! Welcome and bear witness to . . . the coming . . . of . . . RAGNAROCK!" A deafening cheer went up from the crowd as they went wild. There was an explosion of light and sound on the stage as flares went off, spotlights swung in, and the first band went into a slamming shag metal guitar solo that seemed to make the walls vibrate.

As Talon turned the corner and headed to meet up with the rest of his team, he paused for a moment and looked out over the stadium.

Chummer, Talon said silently to the faceless announcer, *I sure as hell hope you're wrong*.

23

Heinrich Zoller stepped over the bodies of the security guards and directed his hirelings to place the bomb under the stage. His master had been merciful in restoring him after his initial failure. Zoller would not disappoint him again. Soon he would be the one to strike the spark that would ignite the glory of Ragnarok, and he would reap his reward. Out of the flames, he would be reborn, a new god to reign over the new world that would come about, under the guidance of his master, of course.

He opened the side panel of the bomb, setting the controls for a countdown. His Humanis hirelings had no idea of the nature of the device they were planting, of course. They thought it was a more conventional explosive intended to strike a blow against foreign corporations who would pollute German purity with their presence and their ideas. That was true, to a point, but they did not know how powerful the blast would be, or that Germany would be the first battleground of the final war. Zoller's true servants, members of Winternight, knew what was coming, but they faced it gladly, knowing they would be rewarded in the world to come, the world that would rise from the ashes of the old.

He placed a finger on the control switch.

"Master, all is in readiness," he thought.

"*Excellent,*" his Master's voice responded. "*You have done well, Heinrich. You will be of great service to me in times to come.*"

"Thank you, Master." Zoller pushed the button and the ten-minute countdown began. Now there was no turning back.

24

Talon met up with the rest of the team in the outer corridor of the stadium. Boom and Hammer arrived first, weapons carefully concealed beneath long coats and armored jackets. Trouble and Silverblade followed close behind, slipping in from the outside with the aid of Silverblade's magic. Talon could feel a faint magical presence nearby as they approached. A glance with his astral senses told him that Silverblade still had one of Val's drones concealed with an invisibility spell, keeping it hidden from sight.

"What's the plan?" Hammer asked.

"We hit them fast and hard, but don't forget they've got an active nuke with them. Trouble, do you think you can disarm it?"

Trouble nodded. "If it's electronic, I can shut it down."

"Good," Talon said. "Let's head for the understage area. If any local guards get in the way, let me or Silverblade take them down. We don't want to raise an alarm and we don't want any unnecessary casualties." They weren't packing gel rounds this time. "Save the heavy firepower for Winternight. Everybody link in on the comm and let's go."

They headed along the corridor to the stairs that would take them down to the bottom level of the stadium. A pair of uniformed guards stood at the entrance as they approached. Talon signalled the others to hang back. The guards turned and spotted the team just as Talon gestured, and a soundless, unseen explosion seemed to ripple the air around them. The guards collapsed where they were, sliding to the ground in a heap. Boom and Hammer quickly dragged them out of sight, and then the team hit the stairs.

Hammer took point, with Talon and Silverblade close behind. The elf drew his silvery sword with one hand, and held his pistol in the other. Talon did the same, drawing Talonclaw and keeping his Ares Slivergun close at hand in case his spells weren't enough to handle whatever awaited them below. Trouble and Boom brought up the rear, with Val's combat drone hovering behind them. Boom could see—and shoot—clearly over the heads of everyone in front of him.

"The ward is at the bottom of the stairs, boss," Aracos said to Talon.

"We're going to have to break through the ward to get Aracos in," Talon said quietly to Silverblade.

The elf nodded. "Shouldn't be difficult."

"But it may take time," Talon said, "and it'll warn whoever set it up."

"Send your familiar away then," Silverblade said, raising a hand before Talon could object. "Call it back from within the barrier. The ward cannot block its entrance from the metaplanes."

Talon nodded. *"Aracos, you got that?"*

"I don't like it," the spirit replied. *"What if you need me while I'm gone?"*

"Can't be helped, chummer. It's the best way."

"Okay," Aracos said. *"See you soon."* Aracos faded from the astral plane, vanishing back into the depths of the mysterious metaplanes he called home.

When they reached the bottom of the stairs, the team automatically fanned out. Boom and Hammer took point at the closed double-doors, along with Val's hovering drone. Talon and Silverblade came next, with Trouble bringing up the rear, a slim automatic pistol at the ready. None of them spoke this close to their goal, communicating mostly in gestures, meaningful glances, and body language. No words were needed.

When they were in position, Boom and Hammer glanced back at Talon, who gave the nod. The two metahumans hurled themselves at the heavy doors, which flew open with a shriek of protesting metal and a loud "bang!" Boom and Hammer both rolled with the force of the impact, coming up on their feet a few meters inside the doors while spraying the room with gunfire. Val's drone whined and accelerated forward; Talon and the others followed close behind.

Compared to Boom and Hammer's jacked-up reflexes, Talon felt almost like he was moving in slow-motion. Fortunately, the other people in the room seemed to be having a similar experience. Heinrich Zoller stood near the middle of the backstage area, next to the silvery cylinder of the bomb. Around him were nearly a dozen men wearing dark clothing and carrying compact submachine guns. The bodies of several security guards and concert personnel lay scattered on the floor in puddles of blood, the red soaking into the ground.

The sudden appearance of the shadowrunners seemed to catch their opponents off guard. Talon saw several of the men go down as Hammer and Boom raked the area with gunfire. The men were obviously wearing some sort of body armor, but it wasn't enough to deal with a full burst of well-aimed gunfire.

Moving with nearly equal speed, Silverblade sprang forward like a striking snake, his sword flashing out and connecting with Zoller. Droplets of blood flew through the air, and Zoller cried out in pain as the enchanted blade left a deep cut along his left arm. He managed to pull back at the last moment, which was probably all that kept his arm from being severed by the blow.

"Elven mongrel!" he growled. "You will pay for that!" Zoller's body seemed to twist and swell like putty. His clothes ripped and tore as he morphed into the shape of a massive black bear, the size of a troll, which towered over Silverblade. The bear threw back its head and roared before launching itself at the elf in a storm of fang and claw. The two of them went down on the ground in a struggling mass.

"*Aracos, now!*" Talon called out. He felt his ally responding, but then he felt something else—a surge of power from the astral plane. Trouble rushed forward to reach the bomb, while Val's drone laid down covering fire from its chin-mounted machine gun.

Bullets tore up the ground and stitched across some of the gunmen, their velocity lifting the men almost bodily off the ground before sending them tumbling back down.

Talon opened his senses to the astral to see Aracos appearing close by. As he did, he also spotted something else, something enormous, that towered over the entire room, only barely fitting into the enclosed space. It reached out one massive claw and struck at the spirit.

Aracos shrieked in pain as the claws tore into his astral body like swords. Talon could feel his familiar's psychic cries through the mental link they shared. Aracos retreated backward, moving behind Talon as the massive astral form of the great dragon Alamais loomed overhead.

Talon looked up into the burning eyes of the spirit-dragon as it spread its wings, parts of its phantom form passing easily through the shimmering ward around the room, indicating that Zoller had not been the only one to erect the ward.

"So," the dragon's thought-voice echoed in Talon's mind. *"You have survived. You are more fortunate than any mere mortal deserves to be, Talon. Still you should have left when you had the opportunity. This game is nearly over. In minutes this bomb will explode. You cannot disarm it, for only I know the codes to do so. The blame will fall on others, and the corporate wolves seeking to devour this land will fall upon each other instead. More importantly, my triumph over Lofwyr will be sealed."*

The dragon paused and bent its serpentine head forward.

"It is only a pity that you will not be able to see it all, little one. It will be quite glorious."

A voice responded to Alamais' taunt from deep inside Talon, but it was not his own.

"I think not, brother," it said.

25

"*Lofwyr?*" Alamais said in a confused tone.

"*Yes,*" Lofwyr's thought-voice replied. "*Really, Alamais, did you think your little plan was going to succeed, here, of all places? Did you think you could challenge me and win?*"

The giant shape of Alamais' astral form peered all around the room. "*Where are you?*"

"*Right here,*" Lofwyr said. Talon could hear the thought-voice, which seemed to echo inside him. It was coming from inside him. Lofwyr was speaking through him somehow!

"*Clever,*" Alamais mused aloud. "*Very clever, brother, hiding your astral form in the aura of this human. I would never have expected you to sink so low.*"

"*Interesting words, coming from you,*" Lofwyr replied. "*You who would ally yourself with anarchists and agitators who seek to bring about the end of everything. To use them as part of your challenge to me.*"

"*I do not ally,*" Alamais said, glaring at Talon. "*I control. The deluded plans of Winternight do not concern me, only their usefulness in carrying out my design. You should understand that.*"

"I do. It is you who never adapted well to controlling events behind the scenes, then or now."

"We should not be 'behind the scenes,'" Alamais sneered, his thought-voice dripping contempt. *"We should rule! As is our right!"*

"Times have changed," Lofwyr said. *"But you have always been unable to see that. The Young Races are not what they once were, nor are we. If you seek power in this Age, then you must learn the new rules of the game."*

"I follow the rules of our kind," Alamais spat, *"and I have challenged you, to prove you unworthy of the position you hold. Playing games of wealth and influence with the Young Races has softened you, Lofwyr."*

Talon was feeling dizzy. The sheer speed and volume of the mental communication between the two dragons was making his head pound. All around him the fight against Alamais' hirelings continued. Talon saw Boom and Hammer laying down covering fire against the remaining men, who'd taken cover behind crates and shipping containers.

Near the gleaming cylinder of the bomb, Silverblade struggled with Zoller in bear form. The elf's cheek was bleeding from claw marks, and his sword was red with the blood of his enemy. Zoller roared his defiance, seemingly lost within the mind of a pain-maddened beast, attacking like a storm of claws and teeth. Silverblade continued to fight calmly, his icy facade unaffected. His sword wove a net of gleaming silver around his body, fending off the bear's attacks, slowly driving his opponent back.

Hovering overhead, unnoticed by those on the physical plane, the astral form of Alamais glared down at him.

"In a way, I am pleased that you are here, Lofwyr," Alamais said. "It gives me the opportunity to deal with you personally rather than though intermediaries. It will make the final victory all the sweeter."

"Your trap was never a danger to me," Lofwyr replied. "I knew this challenge would arise from the moment Dunkelzahn left me his crystal. The only questions were who would make it and when it would come. Honestly, I never expected it to be you. I thought you had learned better."

"I have," Alamais said. "As you shall see."

"I have seen no proof yet, brother. If you mean to challenge me, then do so."

"The challenge is already offered," Alamais said. "Our battle is joined. I will prove myself the superior."

As Talon looked up in awe at the hovering form of the great dragon, he heard Lofwyr's voice in his mind speaking to him alone.

"Human, I must overcome Alamais, and I require your aid. You are currently my anchor in this plane. Without your compliance, my power will be weakened. Will you combine your power with mine to overcome my brother?"

"What if—"

"NO!" Lofwyr said. "The decision must be now! There is no time to waste! Will you aid me?"

Talon hesitated still. Lofwyr was perhaps the most influential being on Earth. He was also known as a schemer of the first order, with little regard for the lives of mere mortals. It was entirely possible the dragon was lying to him, in which case he might not survive. Lofwyr had already used him to get Alamais out into the open where he could confront him. What if the dragon considered Talon merely a pawn? Still, if Alamais wasn't overcome, there was a strong chance he would be able to keep the rest of Talon's team from disarming the bomb, even in his astral form. Lofwyr was the only force that could possibly hold his brother at bay. In the end, Talon knew he had only one choice.

"*I agree,*" he said.

"*So be it,*" came the reply.

"*Alamais! You have challenged me!*" Lofwyr said. "*I accept.*"

Talon felt a powerful surge of energy ripple through his body, like when he astral projected; only this was far more profound, far more powerful. He felt his astral form separate from his physical body and begin to expand, stretching outward, taking on a different shape. Wings sprouted and unfurled from his back, and a long serpentine neck stretched out. Golden scales gleamed along the surface of the great spirit-shape—as massive as that of Alamais—as it seemed to expand out of Talon's body in all directions. Blue sparks shot from where Lofwyr's wings brushed against the wards surrounding the understage area, and the wards shattered like prismatic glass, the shards raining down on the astral plane before dissolving like ice on a hot skillet. Lofwyr reared up, in his full majesty, to confront his brother dragon.

But it wasn't Lofwyr alone. Talon's astral body was a part of it, as if he and the dragon were merged as one, their spirits intermixed. Talon could see things as Lofwyr saw them. Together as one, Talon and Lofwyr rose up to face Alamais.

The two dragons lifted up through the ceiling of

the understage and through the massive stage itself. Talon was vaguely aware of the band playing there, wailing out some sort of thrash metal tune, and he could feel the aroused emotions of the crowd in the stands as they shouted and cheered.

Alamais let forth a roar and charged at him. The two dragons slammed into each other, locked in battle. Talon could feel the dragon's claws cutting into him while Alamais tried to bring his jaws close to Talon's neck. He twisted around (or was it Lofwyr who did that?) and slashed at Alamais, pushing him away and drawing a howl of pain from the dragon.

There was no subtlety to the battle, and little honor. Neither dragon tried to cast spells or use any abilities apart from tooth and claw, pure brute force, and cunning. Alamais spread his astral wings and swooped in, attempting to rake with his rear claws as his jaws snapped shut near Lofwyr's tail. Lofwyr whipped it aside at the last moment, but Alamais scored a hit along his flank and Talon recoiled from the pain.

"Do not fail me," Lofwyr said in his thoughts. *"We must overcome him!"*

Lofwyr responded by turning and slashing at Alamais with his foreclaws, but the other dragon danced away before the strike could hit. Lofwyr lunged forward with a snap of his jaws, forcing Alamais back further. He kept up the offensive, becoming a whirlwind of teeth and claws, pressing the other dragon hard.

"Which of us has become soft, Alamais?" Lofwyr taunted as he pressed the attack.

Talon suddenly became aware of the fact that the

noise of the crowd had stopped. As the battle raged on between the two dragons, he noticed that only the band kept playing; the crowd was almost utterly silent, all eyes fixed on the stage with rapt attention.

No, not gazing at the stage, but above the stage.

They can see us! Talon realized. Both dragons were focused so strongly on battle, and so powerful were their astral forms, that they were visible to people in the physical world! He heard the screams and cheers of the crowd at what they thought was the greatest special effect they'd ever seen: two giant, spectral dragons battling in mid-air over the stage. The driving beat of the music filled the air all around them as the band played on, oblivious to the display taking place just overhead.

Lofwyr rushed forward and crashed into Alamais, locking him in combat. He lunged and bit at Alamais' exposed flank, while Alamais sank his teeth into Lofwyr's shoulder. Talon felt the primal taste of spirit-blood on his tongue and the flame of pain spreading out from his shoulder. The dragons began slashing and biting at each other like pain-maddened animals. Talon felt like he might drown in the red-haze of Lofwyr's fury, but he fought to stay apart from it.

The dragons were too evenly matched. Talon wasn't certain Lofwyr could win this battle. Alamais seemed like his equal in every way. If Lofwyr couldn't defeat his brother, they were well and truly done. There had to be some other way he could help . . .

"*Aracos!*" Talon thought, calling to his familiar. "*Tell Silverblade to get ready. This is what we're going to do . . ."* He explained things to Aracos as quickly as possible.

"Got it, boss," the spirit said.

Talon turned his attention to Lofwyr, still struggling with Alamais. Both astral forms suffered a multitude of small wounds inflicted by the claws and teeth of the other. Talon focused with all his strength to reach through Lofwyr's rage and reach him.

"Lofwyr!" he said. *"Drive Alamais down below the stage!"*

"How dare you—" the outraged dragon began to say.

Talon cut him off. *"We don't have time to discuss it! Just do it!"*

"I see the idea in your thoughts," Lofwyr said. *"We strike!"* Together as one, the dragon and Talon twisted into a roll, shifting Alamais below them. Lofwyr reared back with a roar, then slammed into Alamais with all of his strength, furling his own wings and pushing with his will, driving the two dragons down toward the stage again. Talon heard the music swell to a crescendo as the band members felt something vast and powerful pass through them. The crowd was on its feet, screaming and shouting.

The two astral forms passed through the stage, and Talon felt his astral presence separate from Lofwyr's, resolving into his normal familiar shape. He saw Silverblade, locked in combat with Zoller's bear form, plant one booted foot against the bear's chest and shove it backward as he yanked his bloodied sword out of its body. The bear stumbled back and collapsed to the ground, shifting back into the form of Zoller, who lay in a widening pool of his own blood.

Talon's astral form hovered in the air as the two struggling dragons hit the solid earth below the stage and stopped falling, with Alamais on the bottom. He drew Talonclaw's astral form from its sheath at his waist, feeling the blade's magical power, and kept his attention focused on the action taking place below, seeing Silverblade and Aracos do the same.

"You're weakening, Lofwyr!" Alamais sneered. "Your little helper has abandoned you and you've hidden too long inside a human's shell! Now we finish this!"

"I agree," Lofwyr replied.

"Now!" Talon said, and he, Silverblade, and Aracos rushed forward.

As Alamais was about to strike, he became aware of the other threats. Talon plunged his enchanted dagger into the dragon's side. Alamais' astral body was weaker than his physical form; the blade bit deep into the scaly hide. Silverblade held Argentine in both hands and thrust the sword into the dragon's other side, and Aracos raked spiritual talons across Alamais' head.

The great dragon roared in rage and pain. Then Lofwyr reared back his head and struck with the speed of a cobra, his mighty fangs gripping Alamais' throat.

"Traitor!" Alamais shrieked. "You involve others in our duel . . ."

"No more than you have already done," Lofwyr replied. "You were the first to bring pawns into the game, which allows me to do the same. Now, our duel is done, brother. Unless you want me to finish you now."

"And what will the others think of your victory?" Alamais said.

Talon could almost hear Lofwyr's smile. *"They will only say that I understand how to use all my resources to achieve victory, Alamais. Now, this is ended. How it ends is up to you, but it is over."*

"We've got less than two minutes!" Trouble said, crouched near the bomb. "I can't get past the security lock-outs. I don't think we're gonna make it."

"What shall it be?" Lofwyr said. There was a long pause, and Talon held his breath. Alamais lifted his head up and looked at Lofwyr, who released his grip on his brother's throat. Something Talon couldn't understand seemed to pass between them, then Lofwyr allowed his brother to rise. Alamais stood and spread his wings, bowing his head.

"This victory goes to you, brother," he said.

Talon's astral form manifested near where Trouble worked. She looked up and saw him, a ghostly image of his physical self.

"I can't do it," she said. "I'm sorry."

"Ah, but you can," Lofwyr's voice said in her mind, and the minds of everyone in the room. *"If you follow my instructions."*

Trouble glanced at Talon in confusion for a second. He merely nodded assuringly.

"Do it," he said.

Trouble nodded and followed the instructions Lofwyr spoke into her mind. She entered the codes with steady hands and pressed the switch.

The countdown stopped at 00:00:28. The shadowrunners breathed a collective sigh of relief.

"The challenge is done," Lofwyr said. Alamais' head dipped low toward the ground again.

"It is so," he replied. *"The game is over."*

"Game?" Talon said. "You're telling me this was all just some kind of game?"

"*A game far beyond anything you could imagine, human,*" Alamais said in a dangerous tone, glancing over at Talon.

"*No mere game,*" Lofwyr said. "*A challenge, one I was obliged to answer. Alamais, you did well, better than I expected. You may yet learn.*"

Talon turned toward Lofwyr.

"You fragger! You knew about this all along, didn't you? You *used* us!"

There was a shimmer in the air as the great dragons made their astral forms visible to all present. Trouble gave a quiet gasp as the vast, golden-scaled forms appeared, glaring down at Talon with burning, fathomless eyes.

"*You sound surprised, Talon,*" Lofwyr's thought-voice said. "*But you offer yourself to be used every day. That is what makes you shadowrunners so . . . useful.*"

"Then you did know about Alamais."

"*Not precisely. I knew that I would face a challenge from others of my kind once I inherited the Crystal of Memory from Dunkelzahn, but not precisely who would challenge me, or when. I noticed the magical trap Alamais laid within the crystal unearthed by Dr. Goronay, a mere bauble from times long past.*"

"But one likely to attract your attention," Alamais interjected. Lofwyr ignored the interruption and continued.

"*I was not fooled by Alamais' trap, but I triggered it and allowed him to believe it had affected me, while I placed my astral form inside of you, Talon. I knew that you would eventually seek out Alamais and give me the opportunity to confront him, and challenge him directly, when the time was right. You should be pleased, Talon. Few humans have experienced the honor I granted you."*

"All right, so I'm honored," Talon said. "What happens now?"

Lofwyr turned to Alamais, who gave what looked like the draconic equivalent of a shrug.

"Lofwyr has won this challenge. I no longer have any interest in it. Do with these as you will." He gestured to take in the remaining members of Winternight who were still alive. *"Another time, dear brother,"* Alamais said. He dipped his head toward Lofwyr, then his astral form took wing, disappearing through the ceiling of the room.

"Alamais' challenge has been dealt with," Lofwyr said. *"So your service to me is at an end. You have my leave to depart. I will see to it that you return home safely. Leave things as you see them here. My own security forces will arrive momentarily to deal with them. You have done well."* Lofwyr spread his wings wide, his gaze sweeping over the room one last time.

"Farewell," he said, flying up through the ceiling.

"A game," Silverblade repeated quietly. "Winternight, Runenthing, Goronay, even a nuclear threat, all for no more than a game."

Trouble came over and laid a hand on Talon's shoulder as he stood, staring at the ceiling.

"You okay?"

"Hmm? Oh yeah, I'm fine, for somebody who's been possessed by a dragon. I was just thinking about what might have happened if Alamais had decided not to give in. He was willing to kill everyone here, to maybe even start a war, and all of it part of some kind of chess-match with Lofwyr. Now I know why they say never deal with a dragon."

For a moment, silence held the room, until Boom cleared his throat and looked around at his teammates.

"Well, chummers," he said, "who's up for taking in the rest of what sounds to be a great concert? If Ragnarock is here, I don't want to miss it."

Epilogue

Several days later, Talon was back in Boston, waiting on a darkened street for Mr. Brackhaus. He'd received the call earlier that day and arrived at the meet site a little early. Aracos shifted from his motorcycle form back into the astral plane to keep watch, as usual. Aracos had recovered completely from his injuries sustained in the fight with Alamais, and had returned to his usual self.

The runners bid farewell to Speren Silverblade before they left Germany. He paid them the agreed upon amount from a secret account used by the Tir government. Silverblade seemed almost reluctant to bid farewell to the shadowrunners. The haughty elf actually clasped Talon's hand before he left.

"You are a skilled mage, and a capable warrior," Silverblade said. "For a *goronagee*." He smiled, a genuine smile. "I would be pleased to consider you a *sersakhan*, a friend."

"*Sielle*," Talon replied. "I am honored."

"You speak Sperethiel?" Silverblade asked, with a raised eyebrow.

Talon shrugged slightly. "Not much, but you pick up things here and there."

"I hope we have the opportunity to work together again."

"That doesn't seem likely, in our line of work."

Silverblade gave his enigmatic smile once more. "As you are fond of saying, you never know. Who can say what Fate holds in store for us. Farewell, *Tesetilaro*."

Then he slipped away into the night, presumably to find his own way back home.

"He's coming boss," Aracos said in Talon's mind. A few moments later, a nondescript black Eurocar turned the corner and prowled up the street, pulling over to the snow-covered curb. The back door opened silently, and Talon got in.

"Herr Talon," said the man sitting in the back seat.

"Mr. Brackhaus."

It was a different Mr. Brackhaus, of course. Talon had expected that. This man was lighter-haired, with craggy, Nordic features and pale eyes that Talon suspected were implants. He didn't know what had become of the Brackhaus he'd dealt with before all this started. He didn't really want to know. The man wasn't as important as the position. As long as Saeder-Krupp employed shadowrunners, "Hans Brackhaus" would be around.

"You seem well," Brackhaus observed, which Talon found interesting, since he was sure he'd never met the man before.

"Thank you."

"My employer wished me to contact you," Brackhaus went on, skipping further pleasantries. "To complete your earlier agreement."

He reached slowly into the inside pocket of his

dark suit jacket and withdrew a credstick, which he handed over to Talon. Talon took it and slotted the credstick into the portable data-reader he pulled from his own jacket pocket.

"It contains the remainder of the monies agreed upon, plus a small bonus for your good work," Brackhaus said.

Talon barely managed to keep his expression neutral as he read the numbers on the display screen. The amount was twice what was still owed to his team. A "small bonus" indeed. It would be enough money to replace all the equipment the team lost and then some, with enough left over for them to live off for a good while.

"My employer also asked me to give you this." Brackhaus produced a flat wooden box from a compartment in the back of the car's front seat and handed it over reverently. Talon rested the box on his knees for a moment. It was beautifully carved, almost certainly hand-made, from some dark-stained wood, smoothly polished. The design featured medieval images of knights and dragons. Talon wondered how old it was and made a mental note to have a friend of Boom's who dealt in antiquities take a look. He carefully lifted the hinged lid.

Inside the box was a lining of black velvet. Resting upon it was an object that gleamed in the lights that flickered past the tinted windows of the Eurocar. Talon reached inside and lifted it out with one hand.

"Wowza!" Aracos said in his mind as Talon held it to the light.

It was a necklace, made of silver, and decorated with elaborate knotwork that looked vaguely Celtic, although Talon suspected that it wasn't. From the center of the necklace dangled a smoky crystal, cut in the shape of a curving crescent, the wide base capped in silver. The crystal caught and reflected the light, revealing faint lines and symbols that covered part of its surface. Talon recognized it. It was a piece of the crystal Dr. Goronay had found, the crystal his team had been hired to recover and bring to Lofwyr.

"A small token of my employer's appreciation," Brackhaus said. "A memento, he said."

"Dragonfang," Talon murmured, almost to himself. As he spoke the word, a faint tingle ran up his arm. The necklace seemed warm to the touch, almost like a living thing, and the depths of the crystal seemed to glimmer with a darkling light. For a moment, Talon recalled the experience of being merged with Lofwyr's astral form, fighting Alamais, and of soaring high above the ground. The memories of his visions had faded somewhat in the days since they'd returned from Germany, except in his dreams, when he often recalled the sensation of flight.

"That thing has some real mojo, boss," Aracos said.

Talon contemplated the necklace for a moment. Did he really want to accept a gift from Lofwyr, the dragon who'd used him and his team as catspaws in one of his games? Shadowrunners had a saying, "Never deal with a dragon." Talon had already violated it once, and it nearly got them all killed. Was he going to ignore it again?

Still, the necklace felt so well suited to him, so *right*. And Talon wasn't exactly known for playing by the rules. He slipped the necklace around his neck, feeling the cool metal against his skin, and slid the crystal tooth under his shirt.

"Please give your employer my thanks," Talon said to Brackhaus.

"I shall. I'm sure there may be prospects of other work for you and your people in the future." The Eurocar slowed and stopped at the curb, and Talon reached for the door handle.

"You've got my number," he said, then got out of the car and closed the door behind him. The car pulled away and quickly vanished from sight among the traffic.

Talon pressed his fingers against the crystal under his shirt, feeling it tingle against his skin.

"You okay, boss?" Aracos asked him.

"Hmm? Yeah," Talon said.

"Tesetilaro," Aracos muttered in thought-speak.

"That's what Silverblade called me before he left. At first I thought it was just another elven insult I hadn't heard before, but now I'm starting to wonder. Do you know what it means?"

"Yeah," the spirit replied. *"It means 'Son of the Dragon.' It's a very old expression."*

"How do you know that?" Talon asked. "I didn't even know you spoke Sperethiel."

There was a shimmer in the air as Aracos materialized on Talon's shoulder in the form of a golden-winged falcon.

"I don't. Let's just say I know and leave it at that for now. It's one of the reasons I'm here. I suspect we'll be hearing from Lofwyr, and Alamais again sometime."

Talon didn't have anything to say to that. He took Brackhaus' credstick from his pocket and turned it over in his fingers, then flipped it up into the air and caught it as it came back down.

"C'mon," he told Aracos, "let's get going. We've got a hell of a lot of nuyen, and I for one plan to use some of it to have some fun. I'll buy you a drink."

"Trying to take advantage of me?" the spirit said with a touch of mirth.

"With your capacity? Don't count on it."

The falcon vanished as Aracos materialized in motorcycle form, engine already running.

"Just as long as I don't have to drive for the rest of the night," the spirit said, as Talon climbed aboard.

"Deal."

And the two of them roared off into the night, quickly vanishing, back into the shadows.

About the Author

Ragnarock is Steve Kenson's third novel set in the Shadowrun® universe. He is already familiar to fans of the Shadowrun® series as the author of numerous game books like *New Seattle* and *Underworld*, as well as the novels *Technobabel* and *Crossroads*, also published by Roc Books. Steve lives in New Hampshire, and readers and fans of Shadowrun® can reach him via E-mail at *talonmail@aol.com*.

ROC

SHADOWRUN

Dragon Heart Saga

❏ **#1 STRANGER SOULS**
0-451-45610-6/$5.99

❏ **#2 CLOCKWORK ASYLUM**
0-451-45620-3/$5.99

❏ **#3 BEYOND THE PALE**
0-451-45674-2/$5.99

Prices slightly higher in Canada

Payable in U.S. funds only. No cash/COD accepted. Postage & handling: U.S./CAN. $2.75 for one book, $1.00 for each additional, not to exceed $6.75; Int'l $5.00 for one book, $1.00 each additional. We accept Visa, Amex, MC ($10.00 min.), checks ($15.00 fee for returned checks) and money orders. Call 800-788-6262 or 201-933-9292, fax 201-896-8569; refer to ad # N123 (12/99)

Penguin Putnam Inc. P.O. Box 12289, Dept. B Newark, NJ 07101-5289 Please allow 4-6 weeks for delivery. Foreign and Canadian delivery 6-8 weeks.	Bill my: ❏ Visa ❏ MasterCard ❏ Amex _____ (expires) Card# _____ Signature _____

Bill to:

Name _____
Address _____ City _____
State/ZIP _____ Daytime Phone # _____

Ship to:

Name _____ Book Total $ _____
Address _____ Applicable Sales Tax $ _____
City _____ Postage & Handling $ _____
State/ZIP _____ Total Amount Due $ _____

This offer subject to change without notice.

Coming Next Month From Roc

Ashley McConnell
Stargate SG-1:
The First Amendment

Oliver Johnson
The Forging of the Shadows
Book One of the Lightbringer Trilogy

Treachery and Treason
Ed. by Laura Anne Gilman and Jennifer Heddle